I0699389

Also by the Author

The Erin O'Reilly Mysteries

Black Velvet
Irish Car Bomb
White Russian
Double Scotch
Manhattan
Black Magic
Death By Chocolate
Massacre
Flashback
First Love
High Stakes
Aquarium
The Devil You Know
Hair of the Dog

Punch Drunk
Bossa Nova
Blackout
Angel Face
Italian Stallion
White Lightning
Kamikaze
Jackhammer
Frostbite
Brain Damage
Celtic Twilight
Headshot
Vino Blanco
White Lady (coming soon)

Tequila Sunrise: A James Corcoran Story

Fathers
A Modern Christmas Story

The Clarion Chronicles
Ember of Dreams

Vino Blanco

The Erin O'Reilly Mysteries
Book Twenty-Seven

Steven Henry

Clickworks Press • Baltimore, MD

First publication: Clickworks Press, 2025
Release: CWP-EOR27-INT-P.IS-1.0

Sign up for updates, deals, and exclusive sneak peeks at clickworkspress.com/join.

Ebook ISBN: 1-943383-29-7
Paperback ISBN: 978-1-943383-30-3
Hardcover ISBN: 978-1-943383-31-0

For Peter and Carrie,
my brother-in-law and sister-out-law.

Vino Blanco

Italian for "white wine," which is wine that has been fermented without skin contact, or maceration, with the grape juice.

The resulting wine is yellowish in color and is usually a dry wine. It is more refreshing and lighter than red wine, and is often served as an aperitif, with dessert or between meals. It is also a popular cooking wine.

Chapter 1

Public speaking, according to numerous studies, was scarier than death. A surprising number of people, faced with the theoretical choice between an empty podium and the wrong end of a gun barrel, would pick the bullet. At least a bullet could only kill you once, and it was fairly quick. The agonizing experience of giving a bad speech could last an apparent eternity.

Erin O'Reilly didn't believe it. She'd been on the receiving end of more than one bullet. In her own experience, once death stopped being theoretical and started being an immediate existential threat, all other considerations became a lot less important. She'd been in more gunfights than public-speaking engagements, but she'd take her chances with an audience that wasn't likely to return fire.

This particular audience, on this pleasant April Manhattan evening, had some guns in it. About a third of the people in the room were either current or retired members of the NYPD. Most of them were carrying off-duty sidearms. Erin herself had a snub-nosed .38 revolver tucked discreetly into the unfamiliar handbag sitting on the table next to her. She would have preferred an ankle clip or a waistband holster, but her wardrobe this evening didn't permit it.

She shifted uncomfortably, tugging on the hem of her skirt under the table and hoping the emerald-green tablecloth would cover the unladylike movement. She wasn't accustomed to wearing dresses or nylons, and she hated high heels. The green dress might be flattering to her figure—it had almost knocked Morton Carlyle out of his shoes when he'd first seen her in it—but the bare shoulders made her feel practically naked, especially without her gold detective's shield or holster.

Erin leaned over and whispered into Carlyle's ear. "I can't believe I let you talk me into this."

"It was your mum's idea," the Irishman replied, keeping the warm smile plastered across his face. He seemed completely at ease. But then, it took a lot to rattle Carlyle. He wasn't even dressed unusually well tonight. He almost always wore expensive, well-tailored suits. He'd picked out a necktie and pocket square to match Erin's dress. His silver hair was immaculate, his manners flawless.

"I know," Erin muttered, trying not to glare at the nearest table. It was full of O'Reillys: her parents Mary and Sean, her brother Michael and his wife Sarah, and her little brother Tommy, who'd somehow managed to dig up a sport coat and tie for the occasion, though the tie was so haphazardly knotted it had slipped halfway down his chest. Her other brother, Sean Junior, and his wife and kids were sharing a nearby table with Ian Thompson, Ian's fiancée Cassie, and Cassie's son.

"Naught to fear, darling," Carlyle went on. "It's an engagement party, nothing more. These are our friends and family. They're here to wish us well."

"It feels like all the bad parts of a wedding, with none of the good ones," she groused. But she wasn't really unhappy. Nearly everyone she cared about in the world was packed into the

Barley Corner's main room, which had been cordoned off for the night. The former gangster bar was full of cops, cop families, and assorted oddball characters. It felt like home. Erin wasn't truly afraid of giving a speech to these people. She just wished she could be wearing her usual shirt and slacks, and standing in comfortable shoes.

A cold wet nose poked her hand. Without even flinching, she stroked Rolf's ears. The Shepherd was lying under the table, where he could keep a close eye on his partner. He could also provide floor-level security and prevent any fugitive morsels of food from escaping, should they find their way down.

"I'll warm these fine folks up for you," Carlyle said. He pushed back his chair and got to his feet, striking the rim of his wineglass with a fork. The sound was like a tiny, clear bell, cutting through the after-dinner chatter. Side conversations subsided and everyone turned toward the front of the room.

"Dear Lord, he's going to give a speech," Corky Corcoran said loudly, drawing chuckles. Corky was attending the party on his own, in spite of a couple of slowly-mending bullet wounds, because his live-in nurse was in a situation best described as "complicated." Corky had cheerfully attached himself to a tableful of cops, which had made the officers a little awkward at first, but he'd charmed his way into their friendship before they'd emptied their first bottle. Now they all thought he was a great guy, even the ones who'd heard he was a semi-reformed mobster and smuggler.

"That's right, lad," Carlyle said. "It's traditional, and you know what sticklers we Irish are when it comes to traditions. First, let me officially welcome all of you to my place of business. The Barley Corner's had its doors open for better than a hundred years, barring a few minor inconveniences such as the recent fire, the hours of closure mandated by this fine city, and the Eighteenth Amendment."

"The Corner stayed open during Prohibition and you bloody well know it," Corky replied, to more laughter.

Carlyle nodded good-naturedly. "Aye, that's so," he said. "And we're open now. I hope you're enjoying your fine chardonnay. I'm told that's French, and it's a good wine, but I'm an Irishman, so I've no idea what makes wine worth drinking. But it's a celebratory beverage, and that's what's brought us together tonight. If you'd please stand up, Erin, and let these lads and lasses see your face?"

Erin got up and stood next to him. Carlyle slid an arm around her waist and drew her a little closer. Ever the gentleman, he wasn't holding her too tightly, nor touching any inappropriate body parts.

"As I'm certain all of you know, this is Erin O'Reilly," he said. "She's become something of a celebrity these past months, what with her tireless efforts on behalf of law and order. She surely deserves many a toast to be drunk in her honor, and I'll be more than happy to match any lad here glass for glass. But that's not why we're gathered tonight.

"Some months back, I took my heart in my mouth, set my knee on the ground, and asked this colleen to do me the greatest kindness I could possibly beg of her. To my own astonishment, she's agreed to wear the ring I gave her, and we're to be wed. This gathering's to celebrate our upcoming marriage, which I hope will be long, fruitful, and filled with love, laughter, and joy."

"Huzzah!" one of the cops shouted from the back. Erin thought it was Sergeant Malcolm, her dad's old friend. He was immediately drowned out by a hearty cheer.

"Thank you," Erin said when they'd subsided a little. "And thank you all for being here tonight. It means a lot to us. Some of you know this already, but the two of us met in kind of unusual circumstances. Carlyle was actually a suspect in a murder investigation. He was innocent, of course, but it didn't really set our relationship off on the best foot. We couldn't start dating until after he'd cleared his name. And then things *really* got complicated for a while."

More laughter rippled around the room. It had definitely been a convoluted courtship.

"I just want to thank everyone who's stuck around to the end of this crazy journey," she went on. "You're the best friends we could ask for. I promise, things won't be this weird forever. When the wedding happens—and you're all invited, by the way—I guarantee we won't have any gunfire or explosions. Just cake and music and alcohol. So I hope you enjoy yourselves tonight, but those of you who go on duty in a few hours, go easy on the booze. You know what happens if you show up for your shift hammered. The rest of you, drink up!"

There was another enthusiastic round of applause. Drinks were hoisted. Corky began teaching the officers around him a song.

"That wasn't so bad," Erin murmured, smoothing her skirt and getting ready to sit back down. "I really thought—"

"Hear, hear!" a man shouted loudly from the front doorway.

Something in his tone made the people around him stop talking and laughing. Even Corky faltered into silence. The newcomer's voice was grating, jeering. The man started walking toward the middle of the room, bringing his hands together in a slow, sarcastic clap.

Erin froze. She'd seen the guy before, though they hadn't shared many words. He was in his late twenties and was good-looking in a rumpled, disheveled way. His dark hair was unkempt, his collar unbuttoned. His eyes were bloodshot, burning with a peculiar intensity. He was ignoring everyone else in the room, staring directly at Erin.

"Richie," she murmured. "Richie O'Malley."

"Hear, hear!" Richard O'Malley said again, smacking his palms together. "Let's hear it for the lady of the hour and her beautiful boyfriend! What a handsome couple they make!"

At one of the side tables, Vic Neshenko climbed to his feet and started closing in on Richie with the grim inevitability of an oncoming storm front. Vic was the biggest man in the room; six-foot three, shoulders and biceps straining his sport coat.

Carlyle held up a hand. "Richard, lad," he said. "This is a private gathering, and I'm afraid you weren't invited. I'd be delighted to speak with you in a more private venue, but this isn't the time or place."

Richie stopped. He seemed to become aware for the first time of Vic, along with Carlyle's security guys and a half-dozen cops. They'd formed a protective cordon in front of Erin and Carlyle and their faces were distinctly unfriendly.

"Relax, guys," Richie said, spreading his own hands and showing them to be empty of weapons. "I didn't come here to fight. I heard congratulations were in order, so I thought I ought to add my own. Junkyard O'Reilly and Cars Carlyle, tying the knot! What a pair! We're talking some William Shakespeare, star-crossed lovers right here. A cop and a gangster, a killer and a murderer! Aren't they something?"

"You're drunk," Vic growled, planting an enormous hand on the smaller man's shoulder. "And you're about to go out that door. You can do it on your feet, or you can do it on your face. Your choice."

Richie shook himself loose. "It's fine," he said, backing toward the door. "I'm going. My best wishes for the happy couple! They've earned it, with all the bodies they climbed over to get here. My dad and my cousin are rotting in jail right now. Red Rafferty's in a prison hospital. Plenty of other guys, good people, Irish blue-collar guys are twiddling their thumbs behind bars as we speak. And that's not the best part. Vicky Blackburn,

Mickey Connor, Gordon Pritchard, they're all dead! And they're not the only ones. So enjoy the moment! I hope it was worth it!"

Richie retreated as Vic got ready to follow through on his threat. Richie snatched a half-full glass off the nearest table and raised it in an ironic salute.

"Cheers, you backstabbers, liars, murderers and traitors!" he shouted. "Here's to your health—as long as you have it! Everybody gets what they deserve in the end!"

As Vic lunged at him, Richie darted out the door, taking the wineglass with him into the New York street.

"Let him go," Erin called. "He's just drunk."

"Public intoxication is a crime," Vic grumbled loudly.

"In that case, lad, you'd best be arresting all of us," Corky said. "Starting with me."

That broke the tension. Several guests laughed. Conversations started up again where they'd left off, and Corky resumed his musical instruction, stringing words together with incredible speed.

"There's a neat little lass and her name is Mary Mac;
Make no mistake, she's the girl I'm gonna track.
Lots of other fellas try to get her on her back,
But I'm thinking that they'll have to get up early!"

Erin took her seat and gulped down a mouthful of chardonnay, wishing it was whiskey. The white wine felt sour in her stomach. She saw her father looking at her. Retired Patrolman Sean O'Reilly's stare was serious. He retained an old street cop's instincts, as did his daughter.

Both of them sensed trouble in the air.

Chapter 2

"Who was that punk?" Sean asked quietly.

"He's nobody, Dad," Erin said. "Forget about it."

Sean grunted and rubbed his mustache. He was sitting at the bar on the opposite side of Erin from Carlyle. The three of them were sipping Guinness, the chardonnay abandoned, and watching the final acts of the engagement party.

Most of the guests had left. Corky had gotten three Patrolmen very drunk and the four of them had formed an impromptu quartet. All were attempting to sing "Dublin Pub Crawl," but only Corky was succeeding. Sean Junior, who was not on good terms with Corky, was on the opposite side of the room, chatting with Jasper Ackermann. Both men were surgeons, so Erin supposed they had plenty to talk about. Jasper's fiancée, Sarah Levine, was drawing a diagram on a napkin to demonstrate an autopsy Y-incision for Anna and Patrick O'Reilly. Their mother, looking on, was less than thrilled.

"I told you a long time ago, kiddo," Sean said. "If you're going to be a cop, you can't bring the Job home with you. Thirty-nine years of marriage and I never did."

"It's different for you, Dad," Erin said. "The Barley Corner *was* part of the Job. But that's all in the past now."

"Richie thinks differently," Sean said. "Whoever he is."

"He's Evan O'Malley's son," Carlyle said quietly.

Sean blinked. "Why isn't he in jail?" he demanded. "I thought you locked all those bastards away!"

Carlyle cleared his throat.

"I didn't mean you," Sean muttered. "Or Corcoran over there, though God knows he deserves it."

"All right, lads," Corky was saying. "Once more, with me:

"We all went into Lannigan's pub for we're a jolly crew.

We all went into Lannigan's for a final drink or two.

Lannigan's, Flannigan's, Milligan's, Gilligan's, Rafferty's, Cafferty's, Dillon's, McQuillan's,

McCleary's, O'Leary's, O'Hegarty's, Kitty McGee's, in Dublin town upon the crawl,

A hell of a time was had by all, down where the beer and whiskey flew!"

"He probably does," Carlyle admitted. "But we don't all get what we deserve, thank the good Lord for that. Richard's the one who slipped through the cracks."

"How come?" Sean asked.

Erin shrugged. "He was clean," she said. "We couldn't tie him to any of the O'Malley rackets. We thought he was going to take over the drug business, but then there was that thing with that compromised DEA agent, and we shut the gang down before Richie could get his hands on anything that mattered. As far as the law goes, he's a civilian. We can't touch him."

"But is he?" Sean asked. "A civilian, I mean?"

"So far as I know," Carlyle said. "He's never killed a man, nor done anything else of note to the underworld. He's always been a bit of an embarrassment to his da, truth be told. His chief distinction's been a lack of it. When Erin described him as nobody, she was being unkind but scarcely inaccurate."

"All Evan's muscle guys are behind bars," Erin said. She rapped the countertop with her knuckles. "And not the good kind. Anything Richie wants to do, he'll have to do himself, and I don't think he's got the balls for it."

"He had the stones to walk into a pub full of cops and threaten you to your face," Sean said. "Don't underestimate a dumb kid with nothing to lose."

"Vincenzo Moreno made that mistake once," Carlyle observed. "But young Richard's a husband and father. He may have lost his family's fortune and the power Evan accumulated, but he hasn't a wish to spend the rest of his own life in prison. The very fact he turned up in person like that is a sign of his weakness. If he was truly intending to take action against Erin or myself, he'd hardly advertise it like that and put us on our guard. In the Life, if a lad wants you dead, the first inkling you'll get is when he sets his revolver behind your ear."

"Seriously, Dad," Erin said. "It's not a big deal. We've won. The O'Malleys are finished. The Lucarellis are smashed to pieces and they're fighting one another over scraps. We even broke up Keane's little operation inside the Eightball."

"Yeah," Sean sighed. "I kind of wish you hadn't done that."

"Why? Because he was a cop? He was as dirty as they come!"

"I know that!" Sean snapped. "And I've got no time for scumbags like him. It's the look of the thing. You know how things go in the Department. If they didn't already think you were a snitch for Internal Affairs, your coworkers are pretty sure of it now."

"Not the ones who matter," Erin said, giving a fond glance to Vic's table. The big Russian was sitting with Zofia Piekarski and Lieutenant Webb, all three giving their attention to little

Mina Piekarski. The baby was lying on her back on the tabletop, wiggling her feet in the air.

"Everyone matters," Sean said. "When you're on the street and you call in a 10-13, you need every boy in blue—and every girl, too—to have your back."

"He killed my friend," Erin said quietly.

"And you had to burn his ass for it," Sean said. "I get it. But there's a price."

"You're worrying too much," she said. "On the list of guys I need to worry about in New York, Richie O'Malley is about third from the bottom."

"Who's at the top these days?" Sean asked.

Erin shrugged. "That's a good question. Most of my enemies are locked up or pushing daisies. But I'm more scared of Evan than his son, even if Evan's in jail. Kyle Finnegan and Valentino Vitelli are more dangerous than Richie, too, and they're at Riker's Island too."

"When are the trials set to begin?"

"God only knows," Erin said. "Picking the venue's going to be a nightmare. This case covers all five Boroughs, plus Jersey. There's even an international component, what with all the smuggling from Great Britain. It's going to take months just to empanel a jury, let alone try the cases. There's dozens of defendants."

"I hope none of the bastards get out on bail," Sean growled.

"No fear of that," Carlyle said. "The charges are murder and conspiracy. The only lads who might post bail are the wee harmless ones who're only looking at a handful of years. They're the small-time earners, not the hardened killers."

"If you say so," Sean said. "How about Keane and his goons?"

"Keane's in the prison infirmary at Riker's," Erin said. "So is that douchebag Detective Johns. Keane had other guys, but I'm not worried about them."

"Why not?"

"Because they hate him," Erin explained. "He coerced and blackmailed all these guys. They were scared of him, but now he's been busted, they know he's going to sell them out to save himself. They're not going to help. They're running for cover."

Sean nodded. "Glad to hear it."

*   *   *

An hour later, Erin sank onto Carlyle's couch. She kicked off her high heels and stretched out, sighing with relief.

Carlyle paused in the doorway, two whiskey glasses in his hands, and took a moment to savor the sight of her stocking-clad legs.

"Enjoy the view," she said. "Because I'm not wearing nylons and heels every day. You men think you have it rough with your dress shoes and ties? My feet are killing me."

He sat down beside her, setting the glasses on the coffee table. He took hold of her left foot and began massaging it.

Erin closed her eyes and sighed again. "Careful," she said. "I might think you were trying to get me in bed with you."

"Are you saying this would work?" he asked, gently kneading her flesh.

"Mmm," she murmured. "Yeah, probably."

He shifted to her other foot after a moment. Then, ever so gradually, his skillful fingers worked their way up her calves. Erin lay back, enjoying the twin warmth of good whiskey in her belly and her lover's hands on her skin.

An annoying, persistent buzzing sound intruded on her. She gave an irritable wave with her hand, as if it was a fly she could brush away. But the buzzing continued. It was coming from her handbag, on the floor next to Rolf. The K-9 had his chin between his paws. He gave the bag a look of mild curiosity but didn't bother to raise his head.

"Damn it," she muttered, levering herself upright and thrusting a hand into the bag, feeling for her phone.

"You're off duty tonight," Carlyle reminded her.

"Never completely," she said, fumbling the phone up to her face. Webb's name showed on the screen. "*Damn* it!" she said again, with feeling.

Carlyle leaned back, letting her swing her feet around onto the floor. She cleared her throat and thumbed the phone.

"O'Reilly," she said, trying not to sound as grumpy as she felt.

"I'm sorry to disturb you," Lieutenant Webb said. "Especially this late, on a day off. Are you available?"

"You should know, sir," she said. "You were at the party. I saw you half an hour ago!"

"And it was an excellent party," he said. "How much have you had to drink?"

She had to do a quick internal count. "Two glasses of wine," she said. "Then two pints of Guinness at the bar after. And I just had a shot of Scotch. But that's spread over a few hours. I'm good."

"Are you okay to drive?"

"Absolutely. Where are you?"

"I was taking the subway to Brooklyn," he said. "But I'm on my way back now. If you could pick me up on the way, I'd appreciate it. We're going to Riker's."

Erin felt a tingle of anticipation that had nothing to do with the alcohol in her bloodstream. "What happened?" she asked.

"Someone broke into the infirmary," he said. "They put a shiv in Detective Johns."

"What's his condition?"

"He's dead."

Chapter 3

Erin scooped up Webb outside the nearest subway entrance. She'd changed out of her dress, but since he hadn't been home yet, he was still wearing a nicer suit than Erin had ever seen on him before that evening. Without his trademark tattered trench coat and fedora, Harry Webb looked more like an overweight, balding, middle-aged corporate manager than a cop, in spite of the gold shield and revolver he now sported on his belt.

"What do we know?" she asked as she steered her black Charger north toward the prison.

"Not much," Webb said. "Someone got into the infirmary and stabbed Johns to death less than an hour ago. He was pronounced on scene."

Erin nodded. With medical equipment right there, it wouldn't have been hard to figure out he was dead.

"Neshenko's on his way," Webb added. "He'll meet us there. But not Piekarski. He's dropping her and their kid at home."

"I bet Zofia was real happy about that," Erin said.

"I heard some colorful language over the phone," Webb said. "She'll get over it. Levine's also en route. This'll probably make her night. That woman would rather stare at a corpse than knock back a martini."

"Is this our case?" Erin asked.

"That depends," Webb replied. "There's some question of jurisdiction between the Eightball, the Corrections Officers at Riker's, and our very own Internal Affairs division. Lieutenant McDowell should be there to meet us."

"Great," Erin muttered. "Just great. We'll have to get past the Cast-Iron Bitch herself if we want to get anything done."

"She actually asked for us," Webb said. "I know she has a tough reputation, but so do you and Neshenko. Let's give her the benefit of the doubt and assume we're all on the same side until proven otherwise. IAB has a major stake in this. Johns was one of theirs."

"I know," Erin said. "I'd just hoped we were done butting heads with them for a while. And I'm really not looking forward to investigating a prison murder."

"It's the same as any other homicide," Webb said. "We look for motive, means, and opportunity. We get a list of suspects and we double-check alibis. We examine them for anything suspicious: money troubles, personal disagreements with the victim, prior criminal records..."

"Prior criminal records?" she echoed. "Was that a joke, sir?"

"You're not laughing," Webb said.

"It isn't funny," Erin grumbled. Then she cracked a half-smile. "Well, maybe a little."

* * *

Erin and Webb showed their shields and turned in their guns upon entering the prison. Rolf's presence was of no real concern; the Department of Corrections had several of their own German Shepherds and Labradors patrolling Riker's Island.

The detectives found Vic waiting outside the visitor's area, in the company of a woman a few years older than Erin. She was tall and slender, five-foot ten with no assistance from her shoes, which Erin saw were sensible Patrol footwear. She wore dress blues, perfectly tailored. Her hair, black with a hint of gray at the temples, was tied back in the same ponytail Erin herself usually favored. Her nametag read "McDowell."

"Lieutenant McDowell," Webb said, offering his hand.

"Lieutenant Webb," McDowell replied, taking his hand and giving it a brief, firm shake. "I've already met Detective Neshenko. I assume this is O'Reilly?"

"Yes, sir," Erin said, saluting. Some female commanders preferred "ma'am," but those who didn't could be very touchy on the subject.

McDowell held out her hand. "Pleased to meet you in person, O'Reilly. Fiona McDowell. I've heard a great deal about you."

That sentence could mean any number of things coming from an Internal Affairs Lieutenant, so Erin decided not to say anything in reply.

"Thank you all for coming in," McDowell continued. "I know it's your night off, and I apologize for the inconvenience."

"What inconvenience?" Vic said. "There's nowhere I'd rather be on a Saturday night than hanging around Riker's with a bunch of skags, mopes, and three-time losers. This is my idea of fun."

"In that case, I'm glad we could oblige you," McDowell said without changing expression. Sarcasm apparently had no effect on her. She had a face that might be attractive if she smiled, but Erin hadn't seen her do it yet so couldn't say for sure. Her eyes were a remarkable shade of blue-green, reminding Erin of the ocean off Coney Island. She wore no wedding ring, nor any other visible jewelry.

"Officer Piekarski has family obligations," Webb said. "But the rest of us are now present. What's our move?"

"The body's in the infirmary," McDowell said, setting off down the corridor. "Let's start there."

"Can I ask a quick question, sir?" Vic asked.

"By all means," McDowell said.

"How come IAB's involved with this? It's a murder in a prison. Just because a cop's the victim doesn't necessarily mean you guys want to get your hands dirty with it."

"This isn't just any murdered officer," McDowell said. "He's one of two principals in the worst Internal Affairs scandal of the past twenty years. He was also working directly under my predecessor, who happens to be recuperating in the very same infirmary. A predecessor, needless to say, who is also implicated in multiple felonies."

"Holy shit," Vic said. "You think Keane killed him!"

"That's one of my hypotheses," McDowell said. "I've enlisted your squad's assistance to prove it, one way or the other. Lieutenant Webb, you're Incident Commander. I'm here solely in an advisory capacity. For the moment."

Escorted by a Corrections Officer named Purvis, they found their way to the infirmary. The prison hospital looked like any other modern medical facility, with the exception of the restraints built into the beds, the security cameras, and the heavy locks on the doors. The room was divided into several curtained-off alcoves. Two more COs, a pair of nurses, and a doctor were standing in a group a few feet from the last set of curtains.

"Who's in charge here?" Webb asked.

The doctor stepped forward. "I'm Dr. Birch," he said. "This is my infirmary."

"Lieutenant Webb, Major Crimes. Can you tell me what happened here?"

"I don't know first-hand," Birch said. "I wasn't present during the incident. I was operating on one of our other patients, removing some bone splinters from his knee. I heard the alarm as we were finishing the surgery."

"I'm the one who found him, sir," one of the nurses said.

"What's your name?" Webb asked.

"Appleton, sir. Freddie... I mean, Frederick Appleton." He swallowed, his Adam's apple bobbing nervously. He had red hair, freckles, and a pasty complexion. He looked about nineteen years old to Erin.

"What did you find?" Webb asked.

"Well, sir, I was making my evening rounds," the nurse said. "The curtains around the patient's bed were closed. I pulled them open and I found him like... like that. When I saw the blood and the... the thing in his throat, I hit the alarm. Then I started to administer aid, but I could tell right away it was too late."

"How did you know that?" Erin asked.

"His eyes," Appleton explained. "Fixed, open, nonresponsive. Here... take a look."

He drew open one flap of the bed-curtain, revealing what was left of Detective Johns.

Nobody said anything for a few moments. All of the cops, McDowell included, had done time on Patrol. They'd all seen plenty of blood and broken bodies. Nobody threw up or even turned pale. Vic gave the corpse a long, considering look.

"That's a lot of blood," he finally commented. "Carotid, you think?"

"Definitely," Webb agreed. "But I think it went through the spine, too. See there?"

"That must be why he's just lying there," Vic said. "Paralyzed him. You'd need some serious strength to shove that thing clean through his neck like that."

Erin leaned forward. "What's the weapon?" she asked.

"Sharpened spoon handle," Vic guessed. "Somebody jacked it from the mess hall and put a point on it. Your basic prison shiv. I'm impressed. To stick that through the vertebrae... damn."

"It probably slipped between two of the bones," Webb said. "Lucky strike."

"Or highly skilled," Erin said.

"You have cameras," Webb said to Birch. "Where's the footage?"

"They'll have it at the nearest security station, I suppose," Birch said.

"You said you were operating on another prisoner," Erin said. "Which one?"

"Inmate Keane," Birch said. "He'd been shot through the kneecap when he was arrested and the bone was badly shattered. Some of the splinters were drifting too close to the artery."

"Yeah, we know all about the knee," Vic said.

"How?" Birch asked.

"I'm the one who shot him," Vic said with a grin that made the doctor take a step back and avoid eye contact.

"There goes that theory," Erin said. "Sounds like Keane has an airtight alibi. Where is he now?"

"Third bed," Birch said. "I ordered all the patients to be curtained off, so they wouldn't have to see the blood or be disturbed more than necessary."

"Is he awake?" Erin asked.

"I don't know," the doctor said. "He was only under local anesthesia. It wasn't a major operation. I expect he's probably—"

"Is that you, Detective O'Reilly?" a familiar voice called from the third bed.

"Yeah, Lieutenant," Erin said, unable to resist putting a sarcastic twist on the man's title. "It's me."

"I thought I recognized your voice. Come here for a minute. I want to talk to you."

Erin set her jaw. She didn't want to talk to Lieutenant Andrew Keane; not now, not ever again. But he wasn't the Boogeyman. He was just an ambitious, amoral guy who'd lied, cheated, and killed his way to the top. He wasn't the first crime boss she'd taken down, and she hoped he wouldn't be the last. She walked to the curtain and pulled it open.

Keane looked oddly pitiful lying in that prison hospital bed, clad only in a thin gown. He'd lost weight and his complexion was waxy. He had a thick coat of stubble on his chin and his hair was uncombed. An IV bag hung over the bed, sending a saline drip into his arm. The other arm was cuffed to the bedrail.

Keane's mouth twisted in what he probably intended to be a smile. "You're not seeing me at my best," he said. "But you're looking good. You have a touch more makeup than usual, and you've done something with your hair. Did we interrupt a night out?"

"Forget about it," she said. "If you called me over to ask about my private life, this conversation is over."

"Ease off, O'Reilly," he said. "Is that how they taught you to do interviews? I heard you caught the Heartbreaker Killer by seducing him right there in the interrogation room. Or was that an exaggeration?"

"I said what I had to in order to get his confession," she said grimly. "But you're the one who wants to talk to me. I've got nothing to say to you."

"Not even if I can help with your case?"

"You weren't in the room when Johns died," she said.

"Neither was his killer."

Erin blinked. "Bullshit!" she blurted. "That's a prison shank in his throat. Those things aren't remote-controlled."

Keane's crooked smile widened. "I didn't say they were. And I'm not talking about the man who stabbed him. The stabber was just a tool, the same as the blade itself. You want the man who wielded the tool."

"And you know who that is?" she asked, pitching her voice lower so it couldn't be heard by the other patients.

"I might," Keane said, also speaking quietly.

"But you want something in return." It wasn't a question.

"I want something in return," he echoed.

"What? Early release? A Swiss bank account? The keys to the frigging city? I don't have time for this and I don't have the power to make a deal."

Erin turned to go.

"Wait!" Keane hissed. He reached for her. The handcuff drew him up short, the chain rattling.

She paused. "Well?"

"He wasn't the only target! I need protection!"

"You're saying the killer wanted both of you?" Erin asked.

Keane nodded. "I'm helpless in here," he said more quietly. "Get me somewhere safe. Set up a meeting with the DA. Then I'll talk. I'll give him everything he wants. I can close dozens of cases. I can throw him an entire network of dirty cops, corrupt city officials, and mobsters. You and he can both build careers on it!"

"I already have a career," she said. "But I don't want you getting stabbed in bed. That'd be too easy on you, too quick. I'll get you your damn protection. But you'd better come through."

Chapter 4

"What was that all about?" Vic asked as Erin rejoined them. The other detectives were still examining Johns' body.

"Oh, the usual," Erin said in an undertone, moving to the side of the room to avoid eavesdroppers. The others followed her. "He wants a ticket out of here and offered me whatever I wanted."

"Three wishes? Some magic beans? The Brooklyn Bridge?"

"Keane thinks he was one of the targets," she said. "He hinted he knows who gave the order."

"How convenient," McDowell said dryly.

"Do you believe him?" Webb asked.

"We'll see," Erin said. "He wants to talk to the DA."

"Coincidentally, the DA also wants to talk to him," McDowell said. "Systemic corruption and murder have a way of attracting attention. I'll set up the meet."

"In the meantime, let's work the immediate problem," Webb said. "Neshenko, I want you to get over to the security station and take a look at the tapes. There's a good chance we'll have our guy on film. Then we can go home and let DA Markham handle the cleanup. Simple."

"I wouldn't bet on it," McDowell said.

"Why's that?" Erin asked.

"We're dealing with a conspiracy," McDowell said. "There's nothing simple about those." She raised her voice. "Dr. Birch?"

"Yes?" the doctor said.

"Who else has been in this room? We'll need everybody who was here any time from a half-hour before the murder to the present."

"I'll get you a list," he said.

"No," McDowell said. "Get the people. In person, in here. Now."

"Ma'am," the flustered doctor said. "I don't have that kind of authority. You'd need the Warden—"

"Then get the Warden and politely request he do it." McDowell's voice snapped like a volley of pistol shots. Birch flinched at each word.

"I'll see what I can do," he said and fled.

"Nobody else leaves," McDowell said.

"My shift was over hours ago," one of the guards complained. "You can't keep me here. They've got us working extra overtime as it is. Last week I clocked a hundred hours. You believe that? A hundred! My wife doesn't even remember what I look like!"

Vic had paused in the doorway to listen to McDowell. He winked at the Corrections Officer. "Don't worry, buddy," he said. "I'll remind her, next time I visit her."

"Neshenko..." Webb said warningly.

"On my way to check those tapes, sir!" Vic said, snapping a brisk salute for the benefit of the Internal Affairs Lieutenant. He hurried off.

"Looks like we may be here a while," Webb said. He turned to Nurse Appleton. "Who are the other patients?"

"Let's see," Appleton said. "We've got three, not counting Keane and Johns. That's Unger, Veidt, and Aiello."

"What are they in for?"

"I have no idea," Appleton said. "I don't know their criminal records and the inmates don't talk to me."

"No," Webb sighed. "I meant, what are their medical complaints?"

"Oh. Unger cut himself on a bandsaw in the wood shop. He needed stitches on his arm. Veidt got bitten in a fight in the exercise yard. And Aiello has a stomach bug. He was puking when he came in."

"Okay," Webb said. He turned his attention to the whiny guard. "Now can you tell me what they're in for in the other sense?"

"Unger's in for armed robbery," the CO said. "Veidt is aggravated assault. Aiello's a murderer."

"Who'd he kill?" Erin asked.

"You got me," the guard said. "You probably know more about him than I do. He just got transferred a couple days ago."

"From where?" Webb asked.

"Otisville. He's in town for some sort of court thing, an appeal or some shit. Beats the hell out of me, sir. I can't follow any of that lawyer crap. All I know is, he's got three life sentences stacked on top of each other, so maybe if he wins this appeal he'll only have to serve two of them. Waste of time and money, you ask me."

"Let's talk to these guys," Webb said. He, Erin, McDowell, and Rolf walked to the first bed and pulled back the curtain.

A beefy man with an unruly mop of black hair, heavy eyebrows, and a bulbous nose glared up at the detectives. His left hand and arm were swathed in bandages.

"Somebody gonna tell me what the hell is going on?" he demanded.

"Which one is this?" Erin asked Purvis.

"Inmate Unger," the guard replied. "Albert Unger."

"How are you feeling, Mr. Unger?" Webb asked.

"My arm hurts like hell," Unger said. "Who're the babes?"

"That's *Detective* O'Reilly and *Lieutenant* McDowell to you," Webb said. "I'm Lieutenant Webb. Where were you during the past two hours?"

"Is this guy shitting me?" Unger asked. "What's it look like? I been lying right here, on account of I got my arm chewed up by a friggin' bandsaw! I lost, like, a pint of blood. This place don't have workman's comp, and they don't give a shit about safety or nothing! I oughta have my lawyer sue the crap out of them!"

"What did you see or hear?" Webb asked.

"Nothing," Unger said. "Not a thing. And I ain't no snitch. Some cop gets clipped, you think I care? That bastard had it coming, you ask me. If it wasn't today, it would've been next week in the exercise yard. Or next month in the showers."

"If you didn't see anything, how do you know who got killed?" Erin asked.

Unger gave her a sly look. "Two Lieutenants and a hotshot detective?" he said. "That ain't on account of some dickless hood getting shanked. It had to be one of them cops. Could've been either one, they're both assholes."

"His bed is less than ten feet from yours," Erin said. "You must've heard *something*."

Unger licked his lips. "Tell you what," he said. "Flash me your titties and I'll tell you everything I know."

Erin didn't bother replying. She stepped back from the bed and turned to the next set of curtains.

"C'mon!" Unger called after her. "It's a fair trade! You don't have to let me touch 'em or nothing. I ain't seen a girl in real life for almost two years!"

"He could've done it," Webb said quietly. "His left arm's hurt, but he'd only need one good hand to stab Johns."

Erin nodded. She stepped between the curtain flaps to the next bedside.

She was surprised at how old this inmate was. His face was lined and leathery, his hair going gray at the temples. He had to be at least fifty-five, probably older. His complexion was olive, his eyes very dark brown. A bedpan lay on his chest, just under his chin.

"And who would you be?" Webb asked, coming in beside Erin.

"Roy Aiello," the old guy said. "I heard your introduction when you were talking to Al, so you don't have to repeat yourself. I gotta say, it's an honor to meet the two of you. I know some guys up at Otisville, you put them there. They say you're the real deal."

Erin frowned. Aiello's name was ringing a faint bell in her memory. "Pleased to meet you, Roy," she said.

"Is it really true you got in a fistfight with Mickey Connor?" Aiello asked.

"Yeah," she said.

"And then you blew his head off?"

"I did that, too."

Aiello whistled. "And after that you capped Snake Pritchard and put Evan O'Malley and Kyle Finnegan in here. You've been busy."

"You know them?" Erin asked.

"We don't talk," Aiello said. "Finnegan's in solitary right now, did you hear?"

"I didn't know that," she said. "What'd he do?"

"Bear Bradley picked a fight with him in the cafeteria," Aiello explained. "Finnegan busted both his eardrums with a plastic fork. They had to farm Bear out to some specialist, or he'd be lying here with the rest of us."

Erin winced. "Yeah, that sounds like Finnegan," she said, trying not to imagine what it would have felt like to be Bradley. "So what's your deal? Why are you here?"

"I've got an appeal coming up," Aiello said. "Might shave fifty or sixty years off my sentence. Of course, that still leaves another hundred or so, but you gotta start somewhere."

"I've heard of you," Erin said.

Aiello smiled. He had a nice smile, if you only looked below the nose. It didn't reach his eyes. "Of course you have," he said.

"What was it they call you?" she asked. "On the street?"

"I haven't been on the street since you were in kindergarten," he said. "I've been behind bars thirty years."

"What did they get you for?"

"Murder One," Aiello said pleasantly. "Well, one, two, and three, but who's counting? Anyway, the second one was tainted evidence. My lawyer thinks I can get that conviction overturned."

"So you're saying you didn't kill him?" Webb asked.

"I don't have to say that," Aiello replied calmly. "I don't have to prove I didn't kill anybody. The world's full of people I haven't killed. The state has to prove I did kill a particular guy. That's the rules. I don't think I can get number three tossed out, though. That happened on the inside. They had witnesses and video and everything. *That* one, I definitely did, and I'm not scared to admit it."

"You're 'Icepick' Aiello!" Erin exclaimed. She'd finally made the connection. "You're the one who stabbed Vittorio Acerbo at Otisville."

"What about it?" Aiello replied. "That was an internal thing, just business. I liked him, you know. I was doing him a favor."

"How so, exactly?" Webb asked.

"He was losing his touch," Aiello said. "And he was coming loose. Some days he didn't even remember where he was. A guy like that, if he lives too long, he's no good to nobody. What were we supposed to do? Let him just mumble his way through the next ten years, crapping himself and drooling? I made it quick. He hardly felt a thing. There's this spot, right at the base of the skull, it's like flicking a light switch."

"You killed him so Vinnie the Oil Man could take over the Lucarellis," Erin said. "That didn't work out so great for Vinnie in the end."

"No, it didn't," Aiello said, smiling again. "But you weren't the one who got Vinnie. That was Alfie Madonna. He's in here too, you know. He's doing okay. He's got himself a rep now. Nobody messes with him."

"Good to know," Erin said dryly. She'd known Alfie Madonna, had watched the kid murder Vincenzo Moreno in the middle of a courtroom. That was how he'd made his precious reputation. "So why'd you kill Detective Johns?"

"Who says I did?" Aiello retorted.

"I do," she said. "He wouldn't be the first guy you've stabbed. But I don't need to guess. We'll have the security tape in a minute and it'll show us exactly what happened."

"Oh, in that case, you don't need me to say nothing," Aiello said. "But it's nice of you to stop by. You got a message for Alfie? I can see he gets it."

"Forget about it," she said. "How are you feeling?"

"Better," he said. "I guess I just ate something that didn't agree with me. I don't know if you knew, but the food in here is really, really bad. I can't wait for my hearing, so I can go back to Otisville and get something decent to eat."

The third hospital cot was occupied by Quentin Veidt. He sported an impressive amount of gauze around his ear but was otherwise a handsome, cheerful-looking man of about thirty. He had a thick, wavy head of blond hair and a lopsided smile that reminded Erin a little of a young Harrison Ford.

"Mr. Veidt?" Erin said.

"Quentin, please," he said. "Sorry about the face. Don't worry, I never liked that ear anyway. It wasn't my good side."

"The guard told us you got bitten," Erin said.

"Yeah." Veidt laughed good-naturedly. "It surprised me, too. I wasn't looking for trouble, but it's got a way of finding me. That's why I'm here, after all. Say, ma'am, can I ask you something?"

"What?"

"What're you doing on August Twenty-fifth, 2018?"

"I have no idea," she said. "I don't plan my life years in advance. And that's a very specific date. Why do you ask?"

"Because that's when I'm getting out," he said. "Assuming good behavior. And if you're not doing anything, I would like to take you out for a steak dinner. Afterward, we can go for a walk at Battery Park in the moonlight. We can talk and get to know one another. After that, who knows?"

"You just met me," she said. "Why would you ever think I'd be interested?"

"You've got a thing for bad boys with good hearts," Veidt said. "I have that *Time* article about you in my cell, and the tabloid thing too. The piece written by that Carver paparazzo."

"Then you know I'm engaged," she said. "To a very dangerous man."

"Can't blame a guy for trying," Veidt said, unabashed. "I'd hate to think of you going to waste. Tell you what. If things aren't working out for you and him, pencil me in and look me up. Don't worry, I'm not going anywhere in the meantime."

"I'll keep it in mind," Erin said levelly. "Now, what did you see here?"

"Nothing, sorry. My curtains were closed. I wish I could help you, I really do. I'm not a bad guy, I swear. I just made one stupid mistake. Is that cop really dead?"

"Yeah," Erin said.

"Geez," Veidt said. "And I was right here when it happened. It could've been me."

"Did you hear anyone talking to him? Any sort of a struggle?"

He shook his head. "The first I knew anything was wrong, Nurse Appleton started yelling for help. Whoever got that guy, he was a real pro. Like a cat, or maybe a ninja. Because that poor guy never even screamed. I'm guessing he didn't see it coming. Maybe he was asleep or drugged. I was close to dozing off myself. Good luck on getting any sleep now. Hello, nightmares."

"Thanks for your help, Quentin," she said.

"My pleasure," he said. "Could I ask for one favor, please?"

Erin braced herself for another crude sexual request. "What do you want?"

"Could you drop by my cell and sign my copy of *Time* before you go?"

She opened her mouth, realizing a moment too late that she had no idea what she was going to say. *Erin O'Reilly*, she thought. *Convict centerfold and celebrity.*

Chapter 5

"What'd I miss?" were the first words out of Vic's mouth as he barged back into the infirmary.

"A couple sleazy guys made passes at me," Erin said. They were on the opposite side of the room, but Unger might have been able to overhear her anyway. She didn't really care whether he did or not.

"And our local celebrity had to deal with an autograph-seeker," Webb added. "What'd you find on the video?"

"It didn't take you long," McDowell observed.

"I watched every second of tape," Vic retorted.

"I find that difficult to believe," McDowell said, glancing at her watch.

"That's because you're Internal Affairs," he said. "You have a suspicious mind, but lack the discernment of a genuine detective."

McDowell's eyes narrowed. "Careful, Detective," she said.

"Sorry," Vic said. "I should've used smaller words to make sure you understood."

"Knock it off, Neshenko," Webb snapped, ignoring the chuckles and smirks of the prison guards. "Explain."

"I watched every second of the tape," he repeated. "All zero seconds."

"Where's the tape?" Erin asked.

"That's the real question," Vic said. "It's there, but all we've got is black from about half an hour before the stabbing. The friggin' camera was turned off and nobody noticed."

All eyes went to the Corrections Officers. Purvis shrugged.

"Beats me," he said. "I just keep an eye on the inmates. I don't do tech stuff."

"Who's in charge of the cameras?" Webb demanded.

"I dunno. Facilities, maybe?"

"Not much use, are you?" Vic said, glaring at Purvis, who responded with another shrug.

McDowell had walked over to the camera and was staring thoughtfully up at it. "O'Reilly," she said. "Would you mind bringing a chair over here?"

Erin fetched a chair from the nurse's station and rolled it across the room. She held it while McDowell climbed up and examined the camera.

"This has been doctored," the IAB Lieutenant announced. "Someone cut the power cable."

"With a sharpened spoon handle, I expect," Webb said. "Neshenko, did you see who cut the power?"

"Yes, sir, I know exactly who cut the power," Vic said. "That's why I didn't tell you who it was immediately. I prefer to keep you guessing, sir."

Webb gave him a slow, unamused stare.

"Of course not," Vic said. "I would've led with that. But I can tell you all the patients were in their beds, except Keane who wasn't even in the room. You can see the rest of them on the tape."

Erin frowned. "I really thought it was Aiello," she said quietly.

"Why?" McDowell asked.

"Because he's done it before," she said. "He's called 'Icepick' Aiello for a reason. And he offed Old Man Acerbo."

"Lots of guys in here have stabbed people," Vic said. "It's kind of a thing in maximum-security. Don't you watch any prison movies?"

"He's a Lucarelli associate," Erin continued.

"What difference does that make?" McDowell asked.

"Keane was working with Valentino Vitelli and the Lucarellis," Erin explained. "It makes sense one of his guys might be done in by one of their hitmen."

"What's the motive?" Webb asked.

Erin cocked her head toward the hallway. "Outside, maybe?" she suggested. "We've said too much in here already."

"Good call," he said.

They trooped out, Vic closing the door behind them.

"Keane's going to flip on the Lucarellis," Erin said.

"Are you sure of that?" McDowell asked.

"As sure as I can be," Erin said. "Keane's a survivor. And he just offered to serve up everyone he knows in exchange for protection and a deal with the DA. If he wasn't going to flip before, he sure as hell is now that he thinks they're trying to kill him. He's got nothing to lose."

"Do you think the Lucarellis know that?" Webb asked.

"They know Keane," she replied.

"But they didn't kill Keane," Vic said. "They killed his buddy."

"They might be sending him a message," Webb said. "If so, it backfired."

"And I'm telling you, Aiello didn't cut the camera cable," Vic said. "You can see him on the feed right before it goes dark. He's just lying there in bed."

"So he had an accomplice," Erin said.

"Who?" McDowell asked. "Where?"

"Another prisoner?" Erin suggested.

"Or a guard," Vic said darkly. "I didn't see anyone on the feed. They must've come in flat against the wall. That camera isn't placed too well. I think there's a blind spot on the left."

"No footage," Webb sighed. "And no witnesses who want to talk. I can't say that surprises me. Snitches don't do well in prison. That leaves forensic evidence. CSU should be here soon."

"And in the meantime, we have a crime scene open to contamination," McDowell said.

"It's being watched by the guards," Webb said.

"One of whom may be an accomplice," McDowell reminded him. "I'm going back in there."

She immediately pushed through the door into the infirmary, scattering startled COs and nurses.

"You know, she isn't that bad," Vic said thoughtfully. "With a nickname like the Cast-Iron Bitch, I was expecting something a little more hardcore."

"Don't let her fool you," Webb said. "That woman has a reputation. Didn't you hear what she did in the One-Oh-Five?"

"Refresh my memory," Vic said.

"She cleaned out the entire Detective division," Webb said. "Gambling violations. The lucky ones got fired. Two ended up serving prison terms. One of those was her ex-partner."

"Oh," Vic said. "Gambling? Really? People still care about that?"

"My understanding is, some loan sharks were involved."

"When was this?" Erin asked.

"Seven or eight years ago."

"Weren't you still with the LAPD then?"

"I was. But I did some research on our new Internal Affairs Lieutenant. It pays to be informed, don't you think? My point is, Lieutenant McDowell is as tough as they come."

"But fair, right?" Vic said. "The usual thing is, 'tough but fair.'"

"She's tough," Webb repeated. "I'd recommend not giving her a reason to come after you. Because she was willing to nail an old friend of hers to the wall the minute he stepped out of line, and I get the feeling she doesn't particularly like you."

"Copy that, sir," Vic said.

*   *   *

Sarah Levine arrived at the same time as the CSU team. To Levine's annoyance, she had to wait while the evidence techs photographed the scene from every possible angle. She had a brief discussion with the CSU Lieutenant about the blade in the victim's throat. They agreed that Levine should examine the injury before removing the weapon. Levine then spent the next several minutes staring intently at the dead man, taking a few notes and saying nothing. Only after that did she take any notice of the detectives.

"How does it look, Dr. Levine?" Webb asked.

"Definitely homicide," Levine said. "It is extremely unlikely the victim would have been able to deliver a stab with sufficient force to his own neck, and in such an outlying instance, the nerve damage would have caused the hand to remain on or near the implement."

"Glad we cleared that up," Vic said. "Has anyone ever heard of a guy killing himself by stabbing himself in the friggin' *spine?* There's gotta be twenty easier ways to go."

"Lack of defensive wounds, combined with the victim's prone posture, denotes absence of a struggle," Levine continued. "In all likelihood, he was asleep when stabbed."

"His eyes are open," Vic pointed out.

"That is likely a reflex," Levine said. "In nearly all cases of stabbings to the throat or upper body, the victim attempts to defend themselves by raising their hands. While one of this victim's hands is restrained, the other is free. However, that hand is lying at his side."

"Makes sense," Webb said. "It was after lights out in the prison. He probably was asleep."

Something was troubling Erin. "Dr. Birch?" she called.

"What?" Birch replied sharply. He wasn't happy at being held prisoner in his own infirmary, particularly so late in the evening. He was doing some paperwork at the nurse's station to pass the time and being as grumpy as possible.

"Wasn't it kind of late to schedule a surgery? Why were you operating on Keane after bed check?"

"It wasn't scheduled," Birch answered. "Which you would know, had you bothered to read the charts. The bone splinters were causing significant pain and were impinging on the popliteal artery. If a splinter had migrated into the artery, it could have either pierced or occluded it."

"What would that have done?" Erin asked.

"In layman's terms, an occlusion could have starved the lower tissues for blood. This could have led to gangrene and necessitated an above-the-knee amputation."

"Awesome," Vic said.

"Horrifying," Webb corrected. "What's awesome about it?"

"Then I could've said I'd blown a guy's leg off with a handgun," Vic said happily. "Not many guys get to say that. It'd up my street cred."

"So the operation was spur of the moment?" Erin asked.

"It was an urgent procedure," Birch said. "If we'd waited until morning, he could have lost the leg or suffered life-threatening complications."

"What are you thinking?" Webb asked.

McDowell was already nodding. "Good insight, O'Reilly," she said.

"Okay, stop with the mind-reading, please," Vic said. "It's creepy enough having Internal Affairs looking over my shoulder, let alone into my head."

"Do you have something to hide?" McDowell asked.

Vic rolled his eyes and didn't bother to answer.

"I was thinking Keane should have been here when Johns was stabbed," Erin said. "The killer—"

"Or killers," Webb interjected.

"Or killers," Erin agreed. "They must have planned this for a specific window of time, so the camera could be disabled. They didn't know Keane would be in the operating room. I think if he'd been here, he would've been killed too. Keane was telling the truth. He's also a target."

Webb nodded. "That makes sense. Dr. Levine? Dr. Levine!"

Levine had stopped listening to the detectives some time ago and had returned her attention to the body. At the repetition of her name, she blinked.

"Yes?" she said without turning away from her task.

"What else can you tell us about the stabbing?"

"The blow was administered from the victim's left," Levine said. "Angle suggests the attacker was probably leaning across the victim. I see no secondary injuries. There is a single penetrating wound, transiting the carotid and piercing the C3 vertebra. This is the bone which features in the so-called 'hangman's fracture' and contains the spinal nerve which controls the diaphragm. The victim was instantaneously paralyzed and lost respiratory function. Death would have inevitably followed within minutes from asphyxiation, but the victim in this instance likely exsanguinated prior to asphyxiation. Preliminary cause of death is lack of oxygenated blood flowing to the brain."

"That's a lousy way to go," Vic commented. "Even for a rat like Johns. Think about it; just lying there, knowing you're bleeding out, maybe even looking your killer in the eye and you can't do a damn thing. You can't even move."

"He probably didn't feel much pain," Webb said. "On account of the nerve damage."

"But he was paralyzed," Vic said with a shudder. "Totally helpless. Give me pain any day, but not that."

"The weapon is an improvised stabbing implement," Levine went on. "It appears to be the handle of a kitchen utensil, most likely a spoon. When I examine the point, I may be able to determine how it was sharpened. I hypothesize the killer is right-handed, as this blow required both strength and precision and came from the attacker's right side into the victim's left."

"That narrows it down to ninety percent of the population," Vic said. "I guess it's a start."

"Was it a skillful attack?" Erin asked.

"Skill and luck are essentially indistinguishable by result," Levine said. "A trained sniper might kill a target with a precise shot to the brainstem, while an untrained amateur might fire a bullet at random and strike exactly the same spot."

"Point taken," Webb said. "In your opinion, was this done by a trained knife-fighter?"

"In my opinion, this victim was killed by an attacker who is very familiar with stabbing weapons," Levine said. "It is also probably not the first victim of this killer."

"Why do you say that?" McDowell asked.

"Such a deep penetration, in the absence of hesitation marks or additional stabs, suggests an experienced and determined assailant," Levine explained. "The attacker used exactly the correct amount of force to ensure a swift and silent demise."

"We have a guy who fits that description," Erin said softly, glancing at Aiello's berth.

"He was cuffed to his bed," Webb said.

"That wouldn't stop a guy like him," Erin said.

"Especially since this was an inside job," McDowell said. "At least one guard was in on it. Guards carry cuff keys."

"Isn't that just like Internal Affairs," Vic muttered. "Blame it on the guards."

"You're running this investigation, of course," McDowell said to Webb. "But I would strongly recommend detaining and questioning every CO who was in or around the infirmary at the time the camera was disabled. I'd further recommend examining their financial records and backgrounds for possible red flags."

"I'm aware of how to screen suspects, thank you," Webb said dryly. "But your point is well taken. Looks like we'll be hauling everyone into interrogation rooms. That includes Inmate Aiello and all Corrections Officers with access."

"Hold it," Purvis said. He'd been standing close enough to catch some of their words. "You don't mean we're under arrest, do you?"

"Of course not," Vic said.

"In that case, I'm going home," Purvis said.

"In that case," Vic said, "you're under arrest."

"For what?"

"Accomplice to first-degree murder," Webb said.

"I know you guys get the perps after they've already been busted," Vic said. "So you may not be as familiar with this part of the process as we are. Listen up. You have the right to remain silent..."

Chapter 6

"I don't approve of this," said the fat, pompous man in the flashy necktie.

"I agree completely, Warden," McDowell said.

Her words caught Warden Vaughn off guard. He spluttered and blustered for a few moments, which was what guys like him did when they didn't know what to say. He'd stormed into his office clad in a suit he'd obviously thrown on in a hurry. He was unshaven, disheveled, and irritable, all of which made sense given the circumstances. The detectives had been waiting for him. Vic had thought they should go ahead and interrogate the guards without bothering to wait for the Warden, but McDowell and Webb had insisted on it.

Erin shared a sidelong glance with Vic. They were in the odd position of being on the same side as their Internal Affairs watchdog. They were actually glad McDowell was there. This was uncharted territory for them.

"You've detained three of my guards," Vaughn finally said. "With no probable cause."

"It pays to be precise in these situations, sir," McDowell said. Her tones were clipped, cold, and professional. Her diction was perfect. "Our probable cause is the deliberate sabotage of the infirmary security camera. Hallway cameras show nobody entering or leaving the infirmary either immediately prior to or following the stabbing. Existing footage proves none of the patients were out of bed before the camera was disabled. Therefore, the camera's power cable was severed by one of the other persons within. These include guards Lawton Thorpe, Bernard Purvis, and Orlando Accardi, together with nurse Frederick Appleton. Nurse Nicholas Gray and Dr. Alexander Birch were performing an emergency operation on Inmate Andrew Keane and are therefore not suspects. They are free to go."

"This is my prison and my jurisdiction," Vaughn said. "You had no right to arrest my guards!"

"Technically, we only arrested Purvis," Vic said. "The other two were smart enough to come voluntarily."

"Not helping, Neshenko," Webb said quietly.

"You should have come to me first," Vaughn insisted.

"I apologize for the oversight, sir," Webb said. "I'm unfamiliar with proper etiquette at Riker's Island. The responsibility is mine. I did inform you immediately upon detaining your personnel. I further apologize for any scheduling inconvenience."

"It's a good thing I was already on my way here," Vaughn grumbled. "Do you have any idea what time it is? I should be home, in bed, asleep."

"It's real inconvenient how murderers like to kill people in the middle of the night," Vic agreed with mock sympathy. "But I guess you got called in when they found the dead guy in your prison hospital. Responsibility kinda sucks that way. That's why I'm glad I'm not in charge of anything."

"I demand to be present for any questioning of my personnel," Vaughn said, ignoring Vic.

"Absolutely, sir," Webb said promptly.

Vaughn, looking startled, shot Webb a suspicious glance. "What are you playing at, Lieutenant?"

"I'm not playing, sir," Webb replied. "I'm attempting to solve a homicide. I appreciate any help you can provide, and I'm grateful to you for offering to assist with the interviews."

Erin hid a smile. Webb was so tired and grouchy most of the time, it was easy to forget how smooth and slick he could be when the situation called for it. She thought she saw just a hint of a smile crinkle the corner of McDowell's mouth, but it was gone before she was sure of it.

"Well, okay then," Vaughn huffed.

"I'm betting Accardi is our guy," Vic said.

"Why?" Vaughn asked.

"It's an Italian name."

"You're stereotyping," Vaughn said.

"No I'm not," Vic said.

The Warden put his hands on his hips. "Yes, you are! Italian-Americans are very fine men and women. Some of my best friends—"

"I'm not saying they aren't, sir," Vic interrupted. "I know some Italian cops, great guys. Bobby Firelli can watch my back anytime. I'm not the one stereotyping anybody. We think the Mafia had Johns killed, and they like to work with Italians and Sicilians. *They're* the ones doing the stereotyping, Warden. If they were equal-opportunity assholes, I would be too."

"I hate to admit it, but he has a point," Webb said.

"Do you regularly screen your COs' financial records?" McDowell asked.

"We do everything we can to ensure the integrity of our officers," Vaughn said. "Without violating the law or their privacy."

"I'm going to ask that question again, sir," McDowell said. "You may have noticed it is a yes/no question. If you answer with any word other than one of those two, I will assume it is equivalent to 'no.'"

"You can't talk to me like that!" Vaughn spluttered. "Who do you think you are?"

"Lieutenant Fiona McDowell, NYPD Internal Affairs, Precinct Eight," McDowell rapped out. "My department is dedicated to preserving the integrity of law enforcement in this city, and I intend to fulfill that duty to the best of my ability. Pussyfooting around your delicate feelings is a very low priority by comparison."

"Lieutenant McDowell has a very interesting definition of 'advisory capacity,'" Vic whispered very quietly in Erin's ear. "I think I'm getting a little crush on her."

"We keep our eyes open for any irregularities which are brought to our attention," Vaughn said stiffly.

McDowell nodded. "That's a 'no,' then," she said. "Duly noted."

"We'll interview Accardi first," Webb said. "Then we'll move on to the other guards. We'll save Nurse Appleton for last. Can you assure me, Warden, that Inmate Keane is perfectly safe?"

"He's as safe as we can make him here," Vaughn said.

"How comforting," Vic muttered. "How many prisoners were killed here last year?"

"I'm not prepared to discuss that data," Vaughn said.

Vic snorted. "Isn't there a committee talking about closing Riker's?" he asked. "I think I saw something about that in the paper. Yeah, Erin, before you ask, I don't just read the Sports section."

"Nothing has been decided yet," Vaughn said, even more stiffly than before.

"I am aware of at least seven lawsuits filed against this facility," McDowell said. "All of them allege complicity of guards in prisoner violence. The US Attorney for the Southern District of New York released a report in 2014 alleging systematic abuse of prisoners, and a second report regarding mistreatment of juvenile prisoners. These filings are a matter of public record. I am making no specific accusations against the leadership of this prison at this time. I am simply stating that this facility's culture condones violence and brutality at all levels."

"Your job is to police the NYPD," Vaughn said. "If you think it's hard minding a bunch of trained, disciplined officers, you should try riding herd on a miniature city packed full of violent thugs. The overcrowding isn't my fault. The lack of funding isn't my fault. The inadequate sanitation isn't my fault."

"Wow," Vic said. "It sounds rough all right. With so little control over everything, it's amazing anybody gives you any respect at all. What exactly do they pay you for, if you don't run this place?"

"Keane is being watched?" Webb pressed, trying to steer the conversation back onto its original ground. "By reliable people?"

"I have a solid officer guarding the infirmary," Vaughn said, glaring at Vic. "He'll have round-the-clock surveillance, just as if he was on suicide watch. That's the best I can do, and will take more manpower than I can really spare. I did mention the overcrowding. My COs have been on mandatory overtime for months now."

"And we appreciate their sacrifice on behalf of New York City," Webb said. "Now, if we're ready, let's go see what the guards have to say for themselves."

*   *   *

"That's the problem dealing with law-enforcement professionals," Vic said gloomily, half an hour later. "They know how the system works."

"And they know better than to talk to cops," Erin agreed.

"Which one's guilty?" Vic asked McDowell. "From your extensive experience dragging shady cops into the light?"

"I'm not sure," McDowell said. "We need more information."

"We could hardly have less," Vic said. "All any of them said was 'lawyer.' Only guilty guys are supposed to ask for lawyers."

"That's not true and you know it," Webb sighed. "Unfortunately, so do they."

"The main problem is, everyone's guilty," McDowell said.

"I don't think they're all in on it," Erin said.

"That's not what I meant," McDowell said. "Here's a fundamental tenet of Internal Affairs for you. Everyone is guilty of *something*. When you get called on the carpet, the first thing that comes to mind is what you did wrong. You could be having an affair, or cheating on your income taxes. Every single person has something they don't want known."

"That's not just Internal Affairs," Erin replied. "It's every cop, everywhere. That's why everyone lies to us."

"Even if we don't give a shit about the *Playboys* they had under their bed when they were thirteen," Vic said.

"And if there's a pattern of misconduct at Riker's..." Erin began.

"Precisely," McDowell said. "These guards have to assume we're in contact with the committee deciding whether to keep the prison open. And assuming they're all guilty of some sort of malfeasance, which they are, they have no interest whatever in cooperating with us."

"Including the Warden?" Vic asked. Vaughn had left upon conclusion of the short-lived interviews, saying he was going home to bed.

"He has an interest in *appearing* to cooperate with us," McDowell clarified. "But his goals and ours are very different."

"We want to figure out who killed Johns," Erin said. "He wants to make sure he and the prison come out of this looking as good as possible."

"That's going to be difficult, given a man was murdered here," Webb said.

"You'd think he'd want to solve this thing and get it all over with," Vic said.

"You really don't think like a bureaucrat," Webb said.

"Thank you for saying so," Vic replied. "What now?"

"If you want to put in some overtime, you can come to the Eightball with me," Webb said. "We'll have an all-night party. Beer, pizza, loud music…"

"Really?" Vic asked.

"Of course not. We'll be digging into these guys' backgrounds and bank records, looking for connections to the Mafia and financial irregularities. It'll be tedious and miserable, but you'll have pretty good coffee, vending machine snacks, and the dubious pleasure of my company."

"Good enough for me," Erin said. "I'm in."

"I better call Zofia," Vic said. "Otherwise she'll think I'm out banging hookers two at a time."

"Is that typical behavior for you?" McDowell asked.

"Nah," Vic said. "I never do fewer than three at once. Otherwise there's just too much of me to go round."

Erin shot Vic a look, silently willing him not to antagonize Internal Affairs. "And I'll call my fiancé," she said. "He'll still be up. Hell, the Barley Corner doesn't even close until two."

"I thought you'd shut the doors after the engagement party," Vic said.

"No, we only had the place booked until ten. That still leaves four good drinking hours."

"You know why they put Prohibition into effect, don't you?"

"Because the Irish were spending too much time in the bars and not enough in the factories and sweatshops."

Vic grinned. "Our girl knows her history."

"This girl knows her alcohol."

Carlyle answered his phone right away. Erin was still getting used to the fact that he wasn't changing burner phones every month anymore. She actually had his name on her Contacts list with a permanent cell number she could speed-dial, like a normal human being.

"All well, darling?" he asked.

"I'm all right," she said. "What do you hear about the Lucarellis these days?"

"You do know I'm no longer actively engaged in the Life, don't you?" he replied.

"Yeah. You were more useful when you were disreputable, you know that?"

"But these days I'm likelier to stay out of prison and avoid being murdered. Shall I talk to Corky?"

"I thought he was out of the Life, too," she said.

"So he says," Carlyle said slowly. "But be that as it may, a great many of his mates aren't. He still hears things."

"Okay. Find out if anything's moving on the street. It's looking like a Lucarelli lifer stabbed one of our dirty detectives, and I want to know why."

"I'll see what I can do. Are you coming home?"

"Not yet. I'm going to get some work done at the Eightball."

"Shall I wait up for you?"

"Only if you want to. I don't know how long I'll be."

"Then I'll look forward to our next meeting, whenever it is."

"I'm sorry for running out on you," she said. "I'd rather have stayed. Things were just getting interesting."

"Hold that thought, darling."

"Oh, I will. You can count on it."

Chapter 7

"I used to think being a detective would be exciting," Vic said two hours later. He stared morosely at his computer screen and took a sip from a bottle of Mountain Dew. "Now it's just paperwork, computer crap, and boring conversations with assholes."

"That reminds me of something Winston Churchill said," Webb said.

"Winston Churchill was a detective?" Vic asked.

"No. But he ran the British Navy for a while and he definitely understood government work. He said, 'Don't talk to me about naval tradition. It's all rum, sodomy, and the lash.'"

Vic snorted. "We could use a little more rum and sodomy in this office."

"If you want those, you'd better go talk to Sergeant Brown in Vice," Erin said. "He can hook you up. He's probably got access to the lash, too, if that's your thing."

"What've we got on our suspects?" Webb asked.

"Veidt is pretty much clean," Erin said. "He doesn't have a record aside from the assault charge. According to the report, he got in a bar brawl in Soho. Apparently there was a girl involved and Veidt cracked the other guy's skull with a bottle. He felt terrible about it. He's actually the guy who called 911 afterward. The responding officers say he was crying when they got there."

"I bet he saw all those movies where a guy busts a beer bottle over another guy's head and it hardly does a thing," Vic said. "It just shatters. You know what really happens when you smack someone with a bottle? Those things are hard."

"The bottle isn't always the thing that breaks," Webb agreed. "He doesn't exactly sound like a hitman. No Mob connections?"

"Not that we know of," Erin said. "He's an interior decorator."

"The Mafia isn't into that," Vic said. "They may go to the mattresses, but not the sofas."

"What about Unger and Aiello?" Webb asked.

"Unger's more promising," Erin said. "He's got a rap sheet a mile long. He's a stickup man. He's been in and out of prison since he was sixteen and he has underworld contacts. He's been hitting armored cars."

"Who's he work with?" Vic asked.

"He's a solo act," Erin said.

"Really?" Vic was impressed. "One guy knocking over a bread truck all by himself is asking for trouble. Those armored car boys run in pairs, they're armed, they wear body armor, and a lot of them are ex-military. If I was gonna do it, I'd want four guys, minimum. That's how they do it in *Heat* and *The Town*."

"And the movies are an excellent how-to guide for aspiring criminals," Webb deadpanned.

"Hey," Vic said. "The North Hollywood shootout was directly based on the bank robbery in *Heat*."

"You do remember I was with the LAPD when that happened, right?" Webb said. "I'm well aware of North

Hollywood. I'm also aware that those robbers were both shot and killed. It was a terrible heist."

"Unger's never been shot," Erin said. "And as far as we know, he's never shot anyone either. He's good or he's lucky."

"Not that lucky," Vic observed. "Seeing how he's sitting in Riker's as we speak."

"That's true," Erin said. "His last job, one of our Patrol units came up behind him while he was in the middle of hitting a truck. Our guys caught him up to the elbow in the cookie jar."

Webb frowned. "I assume he used guns in his robberies?"

"AR-15 rifle," Erin said. "They got a handgun off him, too. Unger's a former Army guy."

"No knives?"

She shook her head.

"And he's never shot or stabbed anyone that we know of?" Webb pressed.

"Nope," Erin said. "But he does know how."

"Let's talk about 'Icepick' Aiello," Webb said.

"He's a career wiseguy," Erin said. "A made man in the Lucarellis. He was telling the truth back at the prison. He's killed three people we know of, including Vittorio Acerbo."

"His former boss," Vic said.

"That's right," Erin said. "Vinnie the Oil Man ordered the hit as part of his takeover of the Family."

"Yeah, I remember," Vic said. "We were scooping up dead Italians all over town for a couple days there."

"The Oil Man isn't ordering anything these days," Webb said.

"It's hard to give orders when your throat got cut clean through to the backbone," Vic said. "And pretty much all his *capos* are dead or in prison."

"Who's calling the shots for the Lucarellis now?" Webb asked.

"Kingston Schultz," Erin said.

"That Jamaican lawyer?" Vic said in disgust. "I friggin' hate lawyers!"

"But mob bosses are fine?"

"Nah, I hate them too. But at least they're honest. They don't pretend to follow the law."

"Schultz isn't Italian," Webb said. "Let alone Sicilian. The Mafia would never put him in charge."

"Not directly," Erin said. "But he's the guy behind Vinnie's murder. Whatever the Lucarellis have cooking, he'll be one of the guys in the kitchen."

"'You see, you start out with a little bit of oil,'" Vic quoted. "'Then you fry some garlic. Then you throw in some tomatoes, tomato paste, you fry it; you make sure it doesn't stick. You get it to a boil; you shove in all your sausage and your meatballs...'"

"Good Lord," Erin said. "Just how many times have you seen *The Godfather*?"

"Almost enough to cook Italian," Vic said.

"You think Schultz may have something useful to say?" Webb asked, disregarding Vic's cooking advice.

"I'm pretty sure he'll know something," Erin said. "Whether he'll tell me about it is another question."

"What about the O'Malley brat?" Vic asked.

"Richie?" Erin said. "What about him?"

"You think he's involved?"

"What's his beef with Keane and Johns?" Erin asked.

"Beats me," Vic said. "I mostly just want the little punk to be guilty of something. He's out to get you."

"Can you explain to me how attacking a couple of my enemies counts as getting me?" Erin replied. "Forget Richie. I'll brace Schultz in the morning."

"Why not now?" Vic asked.

"He's a lawyer," Erin said. "He keeps regular hours. I think he sleeps at night."

"In a coffin," Vic said darkly. "Filled with desecrated dirt. You know what the difference is between a lawyer and a vampire?"

"What?"

"One's a bloodsucking, unholy monster. The other is a vampire."

*　　*　　*

Erin walked away from her computer a little after two in the morning. She was exhausted. Her temple throbbed, a memento of the bullet that had nearly killed her a few months ago. Her vision was blurring a little. Her hands trembled from a mixture of fatigue and caffeine.

"We used to work nights," she said to Rolf as she dragged herself down the stairs. "What's the matter with me?"

Rolf wagged his tail and pranced beside her. He didn't see any problem. Now that his partner had finally gotten up from her desk, he was certain they were going somewhere. Maybe there'd still be bad guys to chase. The night wasn't over yet.

She was halfway across the garage and was reaching for her keys when she heard footsteps behind her.

"O'Reilly! Wait up a minute."

Erin spun and had a hand on her Glock before she recognized the voice. Lieutenant McDowell had her hands in plain view and empty. The other woman was a few yards away and had stopped short when she saw Erin go for her gun.

"Sorry," Erin said, letting go of the pistol's grip and straightening. "Old habits."

"Street instincts," McDowell said. "You want to hang onto those. But maybe take the paranoia down a notch."

"Can this wait till tomorrow?" Erin asked.

"I'd rather it didn't," McDowell said. "Where are you headed?"

"Home."

"Can you spare a few minutes on the way? I'll buy you a cup of coffee."

"I've got coffee coming out my ears. It's been a long shift."

The left side of McDowell's face tightened slightly in what Erin thought might be a hint of a smile. "I don't care what you drink, O'Reilly," she said. "But it'd be in your best interest to talk to me."

"Is that an order, sir?"

The half-smile lingered on McDowell's face. "I'm not your commanding officer," she replied. "I'm operating in an—"

"Advisory capacity," Erin finished for her. "I know. But I'm not sure that means the same thing to you it does to me."

"The sooner we talk, the sooner you get to sleep," McDowell said.

Erin suppressed a sigh. "You have a place in mind?"

They stopped at a 24-hour café halfway between the Eightball and the Barley Corner. Erin ordered a cup of decaf, no sugar. McDowell took her coffee black. They sat at a table by the window. The place was deserted except for a tired-looking waitress, a scruffy-faced kid behind the counter, and a ragged man in the corner holding a deep, pointless conversation with himself.

"Okay," Erin said, trying not to sound as testy as she felt. "Here we are. What can I help you with?"

"I've only been at the Eightball a couple of days," McDowell said. "I'm trying to get the lay of the land. It might surprise you to learn, your precinct has a certain reputation downtown."

Erin suppressed a snort. "You don't say."

"Then again, it might not surprise you," McDowell said. "I've perused all your personnel files, of course. It certainly made for interesting reading. Did you know Lieutenant Webb shot and killed a man immediately before transferring from the LAPD?"

Erin shrugged. "That's between him, the LAPD, and the guy he shot."

"Detective Neshenko was more or less thrown out of ESU," McDowell continued. "Since then, he's been involved in numerous shooting incidents and has killed at least four men. He's wounded several others, impregnated a Street Narcotics cop, and received several writeups for insubordination and excessive force."

McDowell hadn't asked a question, so Erin saw no need to respond.

"The other two members of your Major Crimes unit, Kira Jones and Zofia Piekarski, are also interesting," McDowell said. "Piekarski is the aforementioned impregnated officer, and as for Jones…"

"I don't want to talk about her," Erin said through suddenly tight lips.

"You know all about Jones," McDowell said. "And then there's you, Detective O'Reilly. Smart, reckless, competent, insubordinate, lucky, dangerous. Nobody seems to know quite what to make of you. I'd imagine you know what some of your former colleagues at the One-Sixteen have to say."

"Would these colleagues be Homicide detectives, by any chance?" Erin asked.

"Upon Lieutenant Keane's arrest, and my appointment to his former post, I gained access to his files," McDowell said. "These include an official complaint filed against you by one Detective Spinelli, in which he alleged you compromised an investigation and risked irreparable damage to a valuable work of art. He demanded that you be suspended, or preferably terminated. In spite of this, you were transferred to Major Crimes at Keane's specific request. This was, in fact, a promotion. Why would he do that?"

"You'd have to ask him," Erin said.

"I'm asking you."

"No," Erin said flatly. "What you're doing is fishing."

"Oh?" McDowell's expression of polite surprise was so fake, Erin didn't think the other woman was even making an effort to be convincing. "What am I fishing for?"

"The same shit Internal Affairs always wants," Erin said bitterly. "Ammunition you can use on real cops."

"Are they true? Spinelli's allegations?"

"I disobeyed orders," Erin said. "And I got results. I caught the guys behind the art heist and I recovered the painting. What was I supposed to do? They killed a cop. Spinelli and Lyons were screwing up the investigation."

"Nobody's arguing with the outcome," McDowell said. "Come to that, Precinct Eight's Major Crimes unit has produced remarkable results. Your closure rate is exceptional. You've brought down a large number of dangerous criminals and dismantled several organized crime rackets. That's not what concerns me. What I'm looking at right now is a pattern of recruitment within the precinct."

"You think Keane's poisoned the Eightball," Erin said, suddenly understanding. "You think he brought me in *because* of the complaint, so he could use it as leverage on me."

"You're not the only one," McDowell said grimly. "Like I said, Neshenko, Webb, and Piekarski all have compromising incidents on their records."

"Everybody in the Department who's worth a damn has compromising incidents!" Erin snapped. "That's what you IAB folks never understand. We can't do the Job without stepping out of line sometimes. The only way not to violate the Patrol Guide is to call in sick every day and never do a damn thing!"

"You seem convinced I'm the enemy, O'Reilly," McDowell said. "And I can understand why you'd think that. The more I look into Keane's little playground, the more I realize how much he brought the Eightball under his thumb. Do you know what they call me?"

"Yes, sir."

"What?"

Erin looked her in the eye. "The Cast-Iron Bitch."

"Do you know why?"

"Because you'll bust anybody," Erin said. "No matter what they mean to you."

"That's right," McDowell said, meeting her stare without flinching. "I'm the one who cleans house. I'll start by using a broom and a dustpan, but if I find out the rot's gotten into the walls, I'm ready and willing to torch the whole joint. I'll burn the Eightball right down to its foundations if I have to, but I'm going to make sure the place is clean."

"Will you collect on the insurance afterwards?" Erin asked.

McDowell didn't react for a moment. Then her mouth cracked into a genuine smile. "I see how you were able to operate inside the O'Malleys as long as you did," she said. "Have you ever considered coming to work for IAB?"

"You're not the first one to offer. I'll tell you what I told him; no."

"Why not?"

"Do you have much use for K-9s in Internal Affairs?"

McDowell glanced under the table. Rolf gave her a cool stare.

"I see your point," she said. "You do understand my concern, though. About you and Keane."

"I don't owe that son of a bitch a goddamn thing," Erin said. "He lied to me and used me, and then he tried to kill me. Is *that* in your file?"

"It is," McDowell said. "Thank you for your candor, Detective. What's your opinion of the rest of your unit? Are they solid?"

"If you want me to rat on my squad, you don't know a thing about me," Erin said. "They're all good police; the best. And if you want to come after them, you'll have to go through me. We clear?"

"Your loyalty is admirable," McDowell said. "I hope it's well placed. Because you know what they say about one bad apple?"

"What?" Erin said wearily. She was in no mood to play games.

McDowell stood up. "It spoils the whole barrel. You'd better get some rest now, Detective. I'll see you tomorrow."

Chapter 8

"Detective O'Reilly. What a very pleasant surprise."

Kingston Schultz might be a Mob lawyer, a dangerous man with even more dangerous clients. He might come from a family whose Mafia connections went all the way back to Prohibition-era rum runners. He might have enough skeletons in his closet to fill a graveyard. But nobody would ever accuse him of being impolite.

"Good to see you, King," Erin said, shaking the hand he came around his desk to offer. His office looked like countless other Manhattan law firms: spotlessly clean, well-placed in a skyscraper near Central Park, tastefully decorated. You'd never guess his clientele tended toward violent criminals.

Vic grunted and kept his hands in his pockets. He scowled at Schultz, who pretended not to notice.

"Would you like a cup of coffee?" Schultz asked.

"That'd be great, thanks," Erin said. When a Jamaican offered a fresh cup of coffee, you'd be a fool to refuse.

Schultz walked to the coffee pot and poured. "Cream, no sugar, if I remember correctly," he said.

"That's right."

Rolf stuck close to Erin's side, watching her. Vic restlessly prowled the back of the room. The big Russian didn't ask for coffee and Schultz didn't offer him any.

"A piece of black cake, perhaps?" Schultz suggested, handing Erin the steaming cup. "My wife has been coaching Aayla on her baking. She is a somewhat traditional woman and fears our daughter will not be able to attract a suitable husband without culinary skills. I told her that Aayla is a well-qualified legal secretary, a bright and lovely young woman, but apparently she must also bake. I am not complaining, of course."

Schultz patted his stomach and smiled. He had a brilliant white smile, showing off flawless dental work. "Now I am pampered by both women in my life," he said.

"Just the coffee, thanks," Erin said. A heavenly scent wafted into her nostrils. She took a sip. It tasted as good as it smelled.

"I understand congratulations are in order," he said. "My heartfelt good wishes to you and to your fiancé."

"You're very well-informed," Vic said, glaring. He was already well into his bad-cop routine.

Schultz chuckled. "Hardly," he said. "After all, Miss O'Reilly, you have officially announced your engagement. It is not as if you were attempting a secret elopement. How is Mr. Carlyle?"

"He's fine," Erin said. "And your family?"

"We are well, thank you. Aayla will be acquiring her law degree next year, God willing. My wife and I are in good health. We have many blessings, for which we are grateful."

"I'm glad to hear it," Erin said. "How about Alfie Madonna?"

She was watching Schultz as she said the name. He didn't flinch, didn't even blink. "Alfredo is as well as can be expected," he said. "I look in on him when I can. He is adjusting well to life on the inside. He has garnered a great deal of respect for one so young."

Vic's snort was so loud, Erin half expected it to stir the blinds on the window behind Schultz's desk. "I guess murdering a Mafia boss will do that for you," he said. "In a courtroom, too! Either everybody'll be your friend, or they'll shank you in the showers."

"Thankfully, Alfredo has not been stabbed," Schultz said coolly. "In fact, he has been a model inmate. I will pass on your concerns for his well-being. He will be glad to be remembered by you."

Vic snorted again. "Don't make too much of it," he said. "Plenty of murderers remember us once they end up behind bars. That's because we're the ones who put them there."

"Detective O'Reilly," Schultz said, turning his attention back to her. The smile was still on his face and still looked mostly genuine, but she was conscious of something hardening at the back of his eyes. "Pleased though I am to see you, I doubt very much that this is a social call. If it were, I venture to guess you would have left your colleague at home."

Translation, Erin thought. *Vic's being an asshole, so let's quit dicking around and get to the point.*

"I'm afraid we're here on business," she said. "How well do you know Icepick Aiello?"

"If you are referring to Roy Aiello," Schultz said, "I was acquainted with him a great many years ago. I had none of the gray hairs currently decorating my scalp, nor was my daughter yet born. I cannot imagine any of my anecdotes of our youthful antics would be of any possible interest to the New York Police Department. For one thing, the statute of limitations on any hypothetical illegal activities in which Mr. Aiello may have engaged has long since expired."

"That's true enough," Erin agreed. "Except for murder."

"Besides," Schultz continued. "Mr. Aiello has been a guest of the state for the past thirty years. His activities during that time are doubtless well documented."

"Yeah," Erin said. "For instance, night before last, he was admitted to the Riker's Island infirmary. Then he stabbed a cop to death."

Schultz raised an eyebrow. "Really?" he said. "From the sound of it, security at the Island must be quite lax. Why would he do such a thing?"

"That's a good question," Erin said. "He's a lifer, serving consecutive sentences for multiple murders. He knows he's never getting out of prison. He's already killed one man at Otisville, but you know that."

"I did hear that he was responsible for shortening Vittorio Acerbo's sentence," Schultz said.

"Andrew Keane could hurt the Lucarellis," she said bluntly. "He could do damage to Valentino Vitelli's interests."

"Then Lieutenant Keane will need to be quite careful," Schultz said. "He will want to ensure his interests are being served, regardless of who he wishes to harm."

"Interesting," Erin said.

"What is so interesting?" Schultz asked politely.

"I told you a cop was dead," she said. "Then I started talking about Keane. A lot of guys would've assumed Keane was the dead one. But you knew he wasn't."

"As your colleague previously commented," Schultz replied. "I am quite well-informed on certain subjects. But sadly, I cannot assist you on the matter of Mr. Aiello's most recent alleged infraction. I do wish you the very best of luck in your inquiries. Is there any other matter upon which I can be of assistance?"

"No," Erin said. "Thank you for your time."

"For you, Miss O'Reilly, I will always have time," Schultz said.

*   *   *

"Do you think this elevator is bugged?" Vic asked as they rode toward the lobby.

"I doubt it," Erin said. "He's a Mob lawyer, not the damn NSA."

"Then what the hell?" Vic snapped.

"What do you mean?" Erin asked.

"He knows more than he's letting on."

"Of course he does!" she shot back. "That's obvious."

"Then what's not obvious to me is why you waltzed out of there without leaning on that son of a bitch."

"He's a defense attorney," Erin said.

"I know. That's one of the reasons I hate him."

"And he's a professional criminal."

"That's the other reason."

"He knows how police interviews go. He wasn't going to give anything more away."

"And?"

"And what?"

"You said 'more,'" Vic said. "That means he gave something away."

"Yeah," she said. The elevator came to a halt. They trooped out into the lobby.

"So spill," he said.

"He knows Keane was the main target. He also knows Aiello missed. He has ears in the prison. He probably knows who put Aiello up to it and why."

"What good does that do us?" Vic asked. "If he isn't going to tell us, what does it matter what he knows?"

"I'm not sure yet," she said. "But he all but confirmed Aiello is our guy. And he's been communicating with him."

"How do you figure that?"

Erin smiled. "Because Schultz is handling Aiello's appeal. He's the reason Icepick is back in town in the first place."

"He neglected to mention that," Vic said. "You checked the case file before we came?"

"Of course I did. I'm a detective. Didn't you?"

"I'm just a lazy, no-good Detective Third Grade," Vic said. "I leave that fancy thinking to you Second Graders. How'd you know Schultz would be involved with that?"

"Like you said," she replied. "I'm a fancy-thinking Detective Second Grade. And it occurred to me that Aiello being transferred to Riker's probably wasn't a coincidence. If the appeal was part of the plan to take Keane and Johns out, then it made sense his legal team would be in on it."

Vic stopped, his hand on the front door. "Then let's go back up there and arrest that bastard right now," he said.

"For what?"

"Conspiracy to commit murder, for starters."

Erin shook her head. "We can't possibly prove that yet. It's circumstantial at best. We need hard evidence, along with a motive and a concrete connection. If we go to the DA and tell him we want to arrest a defense attorney because his client knifed someone, what do you think he's going to say?"

"He'll throw us out of his office," Vic sighed. "After giving us a lecture about the importance of the goddamn legal system and how we can't interfere with it. Plus he'll probably say something about it setting a bad precedent if cops start busting defense lawyers."

"See?" Erin said. "You might make Detective Second Grade someday, if you can just stay out of trouble long enough."

"Maybe," Vic said. "I figure it'll happen about six months after I retire... or die. So we know the Mob is offing bad cops. Should you be worried?"

"Me? Why?"

"Oh, I dunno. Maybe because you threw a bunch of these jerks in jail after pretending to be a mobster."

She shook her head. "No way. They know I was just doing my job."

Vic grinned. "Just business, nothing personal?"

"Something like that."

"What do we do now?"

"We find out what's going on in the Lucarellis."

"Simple enough. Let's just get on the phone with them. Oh, wait. They don't talk to cops."

"I know one who will. I need to make a call."

*　*　*

"Mumble, mumble, grunt," said a muffled voice.

"Is that any way to answer the phone?" Erin said. "This is Erin O'Reilly."

The man on the other end of the line cleared his throat. "Sorry," he said. "Firelli here."

"No, I'm the one who's sorry," Erin said. "You're still working nights, aren't you."

"Just a sec." There was a brief pause, in which Erin heard Firelli quietly say, "It's fine, Sandy. It's just work. Go back to sleep." Then there were some faint background noises, ending in the click of a door latch.

"Okay," Firelli said, louder and more awake. "I had to step out of the bedroom. What's up?"

"I'm sorry," Erin repeated, wincing. She'd momentarily forgotten his schedule. Street Narcotics Officer Roberto Firelli customarily worked nights. In order to maintain some semblance of family life, his wife had fitted her own schedule to match his. Sandra Firelli handled the nighttime shift at a suicide hotline. It would be hard to say which of them had the more emotionally taxing job, but in spite of that—or maybe because of it—they were a rock-solid couple.

"An apology and five bucks will get you a hot dog," Firelli said.

"Look, I can call back later. You just got off the clock."

"Forget about it. I'm awake now. Talk to me, O'Reilly."

"I need to set up a meeting with Dario the Hatchet."

"How soon?" Firelli sounded alert now. Dario D'Agostino was an old friend from the old neighborhood, that rarest of breeds; a retired gangster. Dario had known Firelli as Bobby the Blade back when the cop had been just another street hood. In fact, Dario knew pretty much everybody in the Little Italy underworld. These days he ran a small family movie theater and stayed out of trouble, but he still heard things.

"As soon as you can make it happen," Erin said.

"What's the situation?"

"You heard what went down at the Eightball?"

"Yeah. Piekarski told us. I still can't believe a couple IAB guys were dirty. I mean, we all knew Internal Affairs were a bunch of assholes, but seriously!"

"A Lucarelli associate stabbed one of them to death in the Riker's infirmary."

"Shit." Firelli said it in a quiet, contemplative tone, like a man who'd found a minor error on his tax forms. "Who's the perp?"

"Icepick Aiello. He's been inside a long time, but Dario will know him."

"I bet he will. What do you need to know?"

"I need info on whatever the Lucarellis are up to. I need to know who's in charge, who they're mad at, and why they'd want to whack a couple cops who used to work with them."

"Copy that," Firelli said. "Let me drop him a line. I'll get right back to you."

"Thanks. I really appreciate this."

"Damn right you do. You owe me one. You know how this works."

"The world runs on favors," Erin said, smiling. It was one of Carlyle's favorite sayings. "How about that time I saved your wife's life?"

"As I remember it, I saved her life. You were just along for the ride." Firelli paused. "Thanks, though. I haven't forgotten it."

"Great," Vic said as she hung up. He'd been sitting in the passenger seat of Erin's Charger while she talked, working a toothpick from one side of his mouth to the other and back again. "What's this old fart gonna know? How long's he been out of the game?"

"You never really leave," Erin said. "Once you're in the Life, it's part of you."

"How do you square that with your sugar daddy?"

"Carlyle's different."

"How, exactly?"

She glared at him. "He's reformed."

"You never really leave," Vic said. "I heard that from someone who really understands this stuff. Y'know, I could really go for some caffeine right now."

"You could've gotten a cup from Schultz ten minutes ago!"

"That was Mob coffee. I don't drink Mob coffee."

Erin rolled her eyes. "Okay, fine. We'll go to a Starbucks."

A few minutes later, Erin was holding a cup filled with her usual: cream, no sugar. She was staring at Vic's drink with undisguised disdain.

"What?" he finally demanded.

"Mocha latte," she said. "Extra cream and sugar, whipped cream on top."

"So?"

"Chocolate shavings on the whipped cream."

"You working your way toward a point?"

"You understand if that was beer instead of coffee, it could legally be classified as non-alcoholic, right?"

"Geez. Just because I don't take it black, you think you can bust my balls."

"I'll admit it's a coffee-adjacent beverage," she said.

"I don't like the taste of coffee, if you must know," he added.

"I've seen you drink it."

"Only when I didn't have a choice."

Erin's phone buzzed. "I don't understand you," she said as she fished it out. "O'Reilly."

"You're lucky Dario's one of those old guys who doesn't know how to sleep," Firelli said. "Go on over to his theater. He'll be there in half an hour. So will I."

Chapter 9

"You didn't need to come yourself," Erin said.

Firelli shook Erin's hand and clapped her on the shoulder. "Yeah, I did," he said. "You know how these old-school *mafiosi* are. It's all about the personal touch. Dario likes you, sure, but I'm the guy he knows. Besides, you're not Italian."

"I can't believe that still matters," she said.

"Neshenko," Firelli said.

"Firelli," Vic replied.

"Did O'Reilly tell you to be on your best behavior?"

"She doesn't even bother anymore," Vic said. "She just assumes I'll be an ass."

"Well, don't be," Firelli said. "You know why they call him Dario the Hatchet?"

Vic snorted. "You dismember one guy and all of a sudden you've got a nickname and people think you're hot shit. That's the Mob for you."

"It was two guys," Firelli said. "With a fire axe. He acts like a sweet old man, but he's as street-tough as they come. And he doesn't need to talk to you. He's doing this as a favor to me. I've vouched for you. So be nice."

"Fine," Vic said. "Zofia told me about this guy. She says he's okay, so I'll be a gentleman. Hey, check out the marquee. He's showing *Serpico*. I love that movie!"

"Maybe if you hang around you can catch an early matinee," Erin said.

"You wanna hear my Pacino impression?" Vic asked.

"No," Erin and Firelli said in unison.

"All my life I wanted to be a cop, you know," Vic said, ignoring them and diving into character. "It's like I can remember nothing else. I remember this one time—"

"Some of us know the difference between being a cop and playing a cop," Firelli said, holding the door for Erin.

"Lay off him," Erin said. "He's having fun. He's worse if he's grumpy."

A young woman of Italian extraction was in the lobby. She gave them a bright smile and winked at Firelli.

"Hey, Bobby," she said. "Am I gonna need to tell your wife you brought your girlfriend around?"

"You know you're my only girlfriend, Cece," Firelli replied with a grin.

"Shave off that mustache, I might give you a smooch," she said.

"Sandy likes the 'stache," Firelli said. "She says it makes me look distinguished."

"It makes you look like a salesman," Cecelia D'Agostino said. "And not the good kind. The kind you wouldn't buy a used car from."

"And we were getting along so well," Firelli said. "Where's your *nonno*?"

"Grandpa's in his office. Want me to walk you up?"

"I remember the way."

Cecelia blew him a kiss and turned away in a swirl of skirts.

"Not bad," Vic said judiciously. "If I was single, I wouldn't mind hitting that. You tapping her?"

"No," Firelli said. "For two excellent reasons."

"Those being?" Erin asked.

Firelli held up a finger. "I love my wife and would never cheat on her with anybody, especially a girl twelve years younger than me. Christ, I remember her when she was in grade school!" A second finger joined the first. "And her grandfather is Dario the Hatchet. I like being able to count to ten on my fingers."

They went through a small, dark door, up a narrow flight of stairs to Dario's office. The door stood open. Firelli rapped on it with his knuckles.

"Is that you, *figlio?*" an old man asked.

"Yeah, it's Bobby," Firelli said. "I've got Erin O'Reilly and Vic Neshenko, plus Erin's dog."

"Oh yeah, I remember the charming Miss O'Reilly and her dog. Come on in, all of you. I'll pour you something to drink."

They filed into the cozy little room. There was barely room for all of them. Rolf snorted at the stuffy old-building smell. Dario D'Agostino was on his feet to greet them, leaning on his cane with one hand. His hair was snowy white, but his eyes were dark and very keen.

"Bobby, c'mere," he said. "It's always good to see you, kid."

Firelli embraced the old man with genuine affection, receiving a kiss on the cheek. Then Dario turned to Erin.

"And I'd never forget that face, Miss O'Reilly. Congratulations! Come over here and get a kiss from a man who's not too old to remember what it's like to kiss a pretty girl."

Erin good-naturedly approached and got a chaste peck on her cheek.

"You I haven't met," Dario went on, glancing at Vic. "But I've heard of you. Toothpick Vic. Vic the Russian. Good to meet you."

"You gonna kiss me, too?" Vic asked.

"Do you want me to?" Dario asked, eyes twinkling.

"I'm good, thanks," Vic said.

"It's a little early for this," Dario went on, looking at his desk. "But I got my hands on this great *vino blanco*. From France. Loire Valley. 1999 vintage. The best year in the past fifty, that's what they tell me. You gotta try it and tell me what you think."

"We're on duty," Erin said apologetically.

"Nonsense," Dario said. "You tell me you're gonna take a breathalyzer in the next hour? A glass, half a glass even, won't make no difference. Here, for my sake. You're gonna hurt my feelings, you say no."

"I don't need convincing," Firelli said. "I'm not on the clock. I'm just along for the ride."

Dario popped the cork out of the bottle, poured, and handed out glasses. Erin, a dedicated whiskey drinker, sipped politely. She thought the white wine was a little weak compared to her usual drink, but not bad. Vic tossed back the entire contents of his glass at one go. Firelli took a moment to inhale the bouquet. He swirled the wine around the glass and sampled it. Then he licked his lips and nodded.

"That's good stuff," he said.

Dario smiled. "I'm glad you like it," he said. "You gotta take the rest of the bottle with you, take it home to that beautiful wife. You wanna stay happy, Bobby, you gotta take care of the woman in your life. Happy wife, happy life."

"Amen to that," Firelli said.

"Now then," Dario said. "Let's talk business. What is it you wanna know?"

"Let's start with the Lucarellis," Erin said. "Who's calling the shots these days?"

Dario was still smiling. "Who do you think?"

"Kingston Schultz," she said.

He chuckled dryly. "The lawyer? That's a crazy thought."

"Why?" she challenged. "Because he's a lawyer?"

"Because he's Jamaican. Back when I was in the Life, we never would've let him get so near the top."

"Because you Mafia guys are a bunch of racist pricks," Vic said.

Erin and Firelli both winced. *This is you being* nice?! Erin thought.

Dario's chuckle turned into a full-throated laugh. "You're a straight shooter, kiddo," he said. "I like you. You're right, you know. Do you like movies?"

"I love them," Vic said. "Especially the ones where the bad guys get what's coming to them."

"Crime movies?"

"The best kind."

"Then maybe you know the scene I'm thinking of. *True Romance*. Christopher Walken's talking to Dennis Hopper. Walken's looking for Hopper's son. He knows Hopper knows where he is, and Hopper knows Walken's gonna make him talk. So Hopper deliberately gets Walken mad."

"That's a great scene," Vic said. "Hopper tells Walken his ancestors were Africans. It pisses Walken off so much, he blows Hopper away right there. And he doesn't get the info he's looking for."

"Right," Dario said. "That scene works because it's true. Insult a Sicilian's blood and he'll spill yours all over the floor. King Schultz, he couldn't never get made, let alone climb to the top of the heap."

"If he's not in charge, who is?" Erin asked.

"Slow down, Miss O'Reilly," he said. "I never said King wasn't calling the shots."

"Yeah, you did," Vic said.

"This friggin' guy," Dario said, cocking an eyebrow at Vic. "Did you bring him along on account of his muscles? I like him, I do, and we was getting on great, but he's got a big slab of beefsteak between his ears."

Vic growled. Erin put herself between him and Dario, just to be on the safe side.

"I said it was a crazy thought," Dario said. "That don't make it wrong."

"But you did say the Family would never let him near the top," Erin said.

Dario nodded. "So what's that tell you?"

"It tells me he's running things, but he's doing it behind the scenes," Erin said. "Discreetly."

"Good girl," Dario said.

"And it tells me not everybody's happy about it," she went on.

"Top marks," the old gangster said, smiling. "You got yourself a good street education. You got a dangerous brain. Evan O'Malley should've seen you coming, but I guess it says something about you that he didn't. I gotta respect you for that."

"Thanks," she said. "Speaking of mobs that are falling apart, how are the Lucarellis doing?"

"It's a mess," Dario said. "You got three factions. There's the old guard, the guys who were loyal to Old Man Acerbo. There ain't many of them left. Acerbo, Material Mattie Madonna, Wonderboy Crea, all those guys went down when Vinnie the Oil Man took over. There's a few mopes still kicking around; mostly earners, not *capos* or soldiers. The Oil Man left them alone because they wasn't dangerous and they brought in good money. There ain't one of them with the balls to take over, but they're getting restless. Then you got Vinnie's people, but ever since the Oil Man got clipped and Valentino Vitelli got busted, they got no boss. So they're running around like a bunch of chickens who don't got no heads. And then there's King Schultz. And here's the real crazy thing."

Dario paused to take a sip of his drink. "My doc says a glass of wine's good for my heart," he said. "I didn't take care of myself when I was a kid, because I always figured I'd get whacked before I got old so it didn't matter none. I guess the joke's on me. Now I've lived so long, I gotta start thinking about the future when all I really wanna do is think about the past."

"King Schultz?" Erin prompted gently.

"I was getting to that," Dario said. "You young folks, always in such a hurry. Here's the real crazy thing, like I was saying. The other two sides of this little triangle, they got soldiers and earners but they got no boss. Schultz, he's a boss if I ever saw one, but he's got no people!"

"What do you mean?" Firelli asked.

"Nobody," Dario said, making a sweeping gesture with his hand. "He don't employ no one at all, except the people working in his law office, and they're a hundred percent legit. He's a boss, all right, but he's like no boss nobody ever heard of. He don't give orders, neither."

"No, he doesn't," Erin said quietly. "Just suggestions."

"This makes no friggin' sense," Vic said.

"No payroll, no soldiers," Firelli said. "That's a strange way to run a criminal organization."

"Makes it hard to take him down," Dario said. "Your way, at least."

"Is anyone trying?" Erin asked. "To do it *your* way?"

Dario pointed a long, bony finger at her. "Now that's the question," he said. "You want to know if there's a civil war."

"We haven't been finding extra bodies on the street," Firelli said. "Little Italy's been pretty quiet lately."

"On the surface, maybe," Dario said. "But if you put your ear to the ground, you'll hear the rumbles, and it ain't the subway. I happen to know three guys dropped off the map last week. You might find them, sooner or later, but only if you know where to dig. And there's gonna be more."

"Is that why Roy Aiello killed Detective Johns?" Erin asked.

"Icepick killed him because that's what he does," Dario said with a shrug. "You got him for three murders, plus that fourth one he just did. But word is he did five times that many, maybe more. Guys like him, they make me wonder why you people shut down the electric chair. If he was a mad dog, you'd shoot him on the street."

"We're not like you guys," Vic said. "We can't just blow jerks away if we don't like them."

"Aiello's a weapon," Erin said, understanding what Dario was getting at. "Someone pointed him at Johns and Keane. Is it because of what Keane knows?"

"Maybe," Dario said. "What does he know? Is it enough to get him out of jail?"

"I don't know."

"I think you better ask him. But there's just four good reasons to kill a man: money, power, women, and revenge. The Bloodhound isn't into women, from what I hear. And I expect you grabbed his money when you took him in. That leaves power and revenge."

"The only power he has now is what he knows," Erin said. "And the only way he can use it is by bargaining with the DA."

"If he tells what he knows, it'll make him a rat," Dario said. "And that means they'll kill him for revenge. So maybe it don't matter which reason is which. It comes to the same thing in the end. But you find out who he's got dirt on, that's the guy who wants him dead the worst."

"Do you have any idea who that might be?" Erin asked.

The old man shook his head. "I never even knew Keane was dirty. He kept that one close to his chest, I gotta say. Clever kid, real sharp. Too bad we won't never get to see what he could've become. He could've done some real damage out there, made a name for himself."

"You're talking like he's already dead," Erin said.

Dario's smile was a thin, wavery line on his weathered old face. "That's because he is."

*   *   *

"You have a really funny idea of being on your best behavior," Firelli said, once they were outside the theater again. The detectives were considering their next move. Rolf was sniffing at the doorway, deciding whether to cock a leg and mark over the spot left by another dog.

"I was!" Vic said indignantly. "I didn't threaten him, I didn't hit him, and I didn't pull a gun. I was practically an angel!"

"You're just lucky he hung around a lot of street hoods when he was younger," Firelli said. "He likes guys who don't bullshit him. But you really don't want to piss him off."

"You think I should be scared of him? He's, like, a hundred years old. And he said himself he's got a bad ticker. If I got in a fight with him, the only thing I'd worry about is killing him by accident!"

"There's more than one way a mobster can be dangerous," Erin said. "You could break Carlyle in half, but if he wanted to kill you there's a better than even chance you'd wind up dead. Besides, Dario's a good source. We don't want to alienate him."

"He didn't tell us a goddamn thing we could use! This whole thing was a waste of time!"

"We know there's a power struggle going on in the Lucarellis," Erin said. "And we know Schultz is pulling strings. I think we need to go back to Riker's Island."

"And talk to Keane?" Vic said sourly. "Yippee. Can't I just get some pliers and yank out some of my own teeth instead?"

"Keane's one of the people we need to see," Erin said. "But I think it's time I looked in on another inmate, too. I'd like to see how Alfie Madonna's doing."

"What's he got to do with this?" Vic asked.

"I don't know," she said. "Maybe nothing. But he knows Schultz better than most. I think he'll know something."

"Anything else you need me for?" Firelli asked. "Because I'd love to pitch in, but what I'd love even more is to plant my face in a nice, comfy pillow for the next eight hours."

"Go home to your wife," Erin said. "You've done plenty. Thanks."

"Forget about it," Firelli said, predictably.

Chapter 10

"A cop visiting a prison is like a coffin-maker hanging around a cemetery," Vic said.

"How's that?" Erin asked. She slid her Glock and snub-nosed .38 across the counter to the Corrections Officer.

"You know some of the guys wouldn't be in there without you," he explained, handing over his Sig-Sauer. "But there isn't really any point in coming to look. I mean, it's not like they're going anywhere. We already did our job."

He reached around to the back of his belt and pulled out another gun that Erin supposed was technically a pistol.

"Holy shit," Erin said. "Where were you keeping that thing?"

"You remember my Delta Elite," he said, grinning and giving the CO the massive handgun. "It's my backup."

"What about your ankle gun?"

He stooped and unbuckled his ankle clip, producing a little .32 semi-auto. "This is my backup-backup."

"Do you have a third hand I don't know about? Or did we declare war on Canada? Why would you ever need to carry three guns?"

"Ever since those IAB dicks tried to kill Zofia and Mina, I've been carrying extra," Vic said. "I want to be ready. And technically I have four, if you count my M4."

"I guess I should be grateful you're not hauling your assault rifle everywhere," she said. "That hand cannon of yours ought to be plenty big. Not that it's good for hitting anything."

"It's accurate to a hundred meters," he said as the CO buzzed them through the security doors into the prison. "You just need practice. I think maybe it's a little big for your hand, but I'm telling you, it's a good gun."

"It makes a handy club," Erin allowed. "If you run out of bullets, you can bludgeon the bad guys into submission."

Another CO fell in step with them. "Where can I take you, Detectives?" he asked.

"Who're we hitting first?" Vic asked. "The Madonna brat or the dipshit in the infirmary?"

"We'll save Keane for later," Erin said. "We need to talk to inmate Madonna. Alfredo."

"He's in GenPop," the CO said. "This way. Be careful. We have some dangerous inmates here. We do surprise searches and inspections, but someone always manages to hide a shiv somewhere."

"I wouldn't worry," Erin said, glancing down at Rolf, who was right beside her.

"They ought to make you check your dog at the gate," Vic said. "That mutt's at least as dangerous as your Glock."

Rolf looked smug.

The CO led them down several hallways, through a couple more security gates. They found themselves in a plain, long room furnished with what looked like picnic tables molded from some sort of synthetic material. A pair of metal-railed staircases led up to open galleries on either side of the room. A bored-looking guard lounged in the corner. Four inmates sat at the nearest table, playing cards.

"Madonna!" the CO called. "Get your ass over here!"

The smallest and youngest of the four got to his feet. He did it slowly, leisurely, making sure everyone knew he was standing up because he wanted to. He was skinny, dark-haired, and unimpressive. But he moved with a swagger and Erin could see, from the way the other prisoners looked at him, that he was respected. She barely recognized Alfie Madonna.

"What do you want, Barker?" the kid asked.

"You got visitors," the CO said. "Step this way."

Alfie started to say something. Then he saw Erin and the words ran away from his lips. He lost his careless smirk. His eyes widened.

"Holy shit," one of the other inmates said. "That's Junkyard O'Reilly."

"Come on, Madonna," Barker said. "We haven't got all day."

"Of course you do," Alfie said, recovering. "And so do I. It's not like either one of us is going anywhere, right?"

"At least I get to clock out at the end of shift, scumbag," Barker growled. "And I go home to my wife. You get to jerk off with your bunkmate. Now get moving."

Alfie puckered his lips and blew Barker a silent air kiss. Erin was surprised. Directly taunting a prison guard was risky at best, dangerous at worst. Alfie Madonna had done a lot of growing up since the last time she'd seen him. He'd been wearing a suit then, spattered with Vincenzo Moreno's blood. Now he wore prison overalls. But it wasn't just that. He was older, tougher, more sure of himself.

"We need a place we can talk," Erin said to Barker. "Just us."

"We're pretty crowded," Barker said doubtfully. "But we could try upstairs. There's a place guys meet with their lawyers."

"Perfect," Erin said.

They walked along a row of cells, nearly all occupied by rough-looking prisoners. Tattoos and scars were very much in evidence.

"You really shouldn't be in here," Barker said to Erin.

"How come?" she asked.

"Some of these guys haven't seen a live woman in months."

"I told you, don't worry about it."

"You really shouldn't," Alfie interjected. "You haven't seen what this lady can do. She's badass. Saved my life a couple times."

"Waste of effort," Barker muttered. "Okay, you want the door on the end. I'll stay outside."

"Ill met by moonlight, proud Titania," a man said just to Erin's left.

Every muscle in her body went tense. She clamped a lid on her street reflexes, which were screaming at her to lash out and take the bastard down hard. She forced herself to hold perfectly still for a couple of seconds. Then, without turning, she said, "How's life on the inside, Kyle?"

Kyle Finnegan was standing at his cell door, less than three feet from her. His hair was uncombed as always, his eyes wandering vacantly. The dent in his head where a Detroit Teamster had tuned him up with a tire iron was obvious. He somehow managed to make the prison coveralls look unkempt.

"Back up, buddy," Vic said, putting himself between the Irish mobster and the rest of the group. "I haven't beaten the crap out of any mopes today, so I'm ready to dance if you are."

"Whoa," Barker said. "Don't worry about him. He's locked in. For protection."

"Yeah?" Vic was unconvinced. "Whose?"

"Everyone else's," Erin said, finally giving Finnegan the full benefit of her stare. "This is one of the most dangerous guys in here. He ought to be in Solitary, where he can't do any damage."

"I know my price, I am worth no worse a place," Finnegan said.

"He just got out of there," Barker said. "This morning. And this guy's friggin' nuts. Hell with Solitary, he oughta be in a psych ward."

"You're not wrong about that," Erin said. She was very glad of the steel door separating her from Finnegan. She'd faced down bigger and tougher guys, but none stranger. He was the sort of man who, if she sicced Rolf on him, would bite the dog.

"Alfredo Madonna," Finnegan said, looking past the detectives in Alfie's general direction. "Quite a time we're having in here, wouldn't you agree?

"The patient dies while the physician sleeps;
The orphan pines while the oppressor feeds;
Justice is feasting while the widow weeps;
Advice is sporting while infection breeds;
Thou grant'st no time for charitable deeds;
Wrath, envy, treason, rape, and murder's rage,
Thy heinous hours wait on them as their pages."

"I'm glad this punk's locked up where I can see him," Vic said. "Does anyone have any idea what he's saying?"

Alfie shrugged. "Beats the hell out of me," he said. "Did you want to talk to me or what?"

"Yeah," Erin said. "Come on."

Barker ushered them into the meeting room. It was bare and unadorned; just a table with benches bolted to either side of it. Alfie slid onto one of the seats, sitting sideways and resting one arm on the table in an overly-casual slouch. Erin sat opposite him. Rolf settled on his haunches beside the table. Vic remained standing near the door, arms crossed.

"Okay," Alfie said. "Here I am. I know you made that promise to my dad to look after me, but we both know that ain't why you're here. And you know me better than to think I'm gonna rat on nobody. It's making me look bad, you coming in here like this. It don't matter what we talk about, somebody's gonna think I'm squealing. And you know that, because you're smart. So what gives?"

"You heard what happened in the infirmary?" Erin asked.

"I heard some stuff," Alfie said cautiously.

"How well do you know Icepick Aiello?"

"Met him a couple times." He shifted uncomfortably. "Listen, you know who I am and you know who he is. I can't be saying nothing about him."

"Of course not," Erin said. "He's one of yours. I know you, Alfie. You have your code. It's what got you where you are."

"Damn right," Alfie said, missing her double meaning.

"You killed Vinnie the Oil Man," she said.

"Says who?"

"Alfie," Erin said patiently. "Everyone in this room knows you did. Everyone in the *world* knows it. Vic and I watched you do it. You pled guilty. Not that you had much choice, since other witnesses included two US Marshals, a bailiff, a judge, a stenographer, and a Channel Six news crew. Not to mention Vinnie's own bodyguards, one of whom you put in the hospital."

"Judge Barberis was in Vinnie's pocket," Alfie said. "He wasn't no innocent bystander and you can't trust what he says."

"Whether you did it isn't the point," she said. "I want to talk about why and how you did the job."

"He killed my dad."

"Your dad didn't want this for you," she shot back. "He wanted you safe. He didn't want you to die behind bars."

"I'm not gonna die here," Alfie retorted. "In here, I got respect. I never got that on the street. In here, I'm *somebody*."

"Yeah," Vic said. "You're inmate number Who the Fuck Cares. How many years did you get?"

"Twenty to life," Alfie replied. "But I figure I'll be out in ten. Hell, I'll be younger then than you are now!"

"And you'll have a nice little nest egg waiting for you," Erin said.

"What're you talking about?" Alfie demanded.

"Your dad left you a big pile of real estate, didn't he?" she asked.

"What if he did?"

"King Schultz is looking after it for you."

"Well, yeah," Alfie said. "He's the family lawyer. What's wrong with that?"

"Alfie," she said quietly. "Whose idea was it to take out Vinnie?"

"Mine!"

"I know you wanted him dead. Who came up with the plan?"

Alfie's eyes shifted. "I can't tell you that," he said. "That's conspiracy shit. I give you any names, you take them down for helping, and I ain't gonna do that. I told you!"

"You ain't no rat," Erin said, nodding. "Okay. But here's the thing. I do know you, Alfie. You're a tough kid. You loved your dad and you respect the code he taught you. You've got guts to spare. You knew you wouldn't get out of that courtroom, but you whacked Vinnie anyway. You're old-school, kiddo, and your dad might be sad you ended up here, but he'd be proud of you, too."

Alfie nodded. He swallowed a lump in his throat and, to Erin's gratification, she saw tears well up in his eyes. She felt a little dirty manipulating him this way, but that was a detective's job. Figure your subject out, find out what made him tick, worm your way into his confidence, make him think you understood him because you were his friend. Then betray and destroy him.

"But you're not a planner, kiddo," she went on. "You're a soldier, a man of action. You talked things over with somebody you trusted. He suggested some ideas. Vinnie was a careful man. You'd never get close to him on the street. But in a courtroom, where everyone knew you couldn't carry a gun or a knife, he just might be cocky enough to let his guard down a little. It was a good plan except for one thing: getting away with it."

"I didn't care about that," Alfie said stubbornly. "I was ready to do my time. I could've got him on the street and you'd have still known it was me. It was always gonna end this way."

"The guy who came up with the plan *wanted* you in prison," she said gently. "That wasn't a side effect. It was part of the goal."

"Why?" Alfie replied. "Suppose, for a second, I did have a friend. Why would he want me in here?"

"Why don't you ask yourself that?"

She watched him think things over. Being a detective was oddly like being a therapist, or maybe a priest. All three occupations wanted to get their clients to talk about themselves, to confess their inner secrets. All three even believed it was for the subject's own ultimate good. One of the most important things, as she'd learned from her talks with the Department's psychiatrist, was to get the subject to say it. You couldn't put words in the poor bastard's mouth. But you could drop hints.

Erin's dad was retired. He was back upstate, having left after the party, and might well be out on the lake this very moment, rod and reel in hand. She wondered what he'd think of her own little fishing expedition.

"No way," Alfie decided aloud. "He'd never do that to me. Not to ace me out of Dad's property. Dad trusted him, and so do I."

So it was Schultz, she thought. It wasn't a confession that would hold up in court, but it was the confirmation she'd been looking for. "You know what happens in the Life," she reminded him. "Every man's looking out for himself."

"It don't matter," he insisted. "Vinnie's people was gonna kill me. Taking him out was the only way I was gonna make it in here. And you wanted him taken care of, too. Don't pretend you wasn't happy it went down that way."

"Vinnie was a son of a bitch," she said. The words came out way too easily. They were too close to the truth. "He was a vicious bastard and he had it coming. The world's a better place without him."

"Besides," Alfie said. "My friend never told me to do nothing. It was just, like, ideas."

"Suggestions?"

"Yeah. I wanted to do it!"

"Is that what he does?" she asked. "Gives you a little nudge toward what you already want to do?"

"I guess," Alfie said. "What do you care? He was just speaking, y'know, hypothetically. That ain't illegal. Are we done here?"

"Yeah," Erin sighed. "I suppose so. Do you need anything?"

"I'm good," he said. "King gets me cash for the commissary. Nobody screws with me. I mean, I'm the guy who did the Oil Man, and I didn't even have a real weapon when it went down. They're all scared of me. I'm fine."

"Keep your eyes open," she said, standing up.

"Why?" he challenged. "I ain't gonna be your spy. I ain't feeding you tips on these guys."

"You think I care about any of that?" she retorted. "Everyone in Riker's is already a prisoner! I've got plenty to deal with on the outside. But a war's brewing in the Lucarellis. Your family's split into three factions, and some of all three are in here with you. That reputation may not keep you as safe as you think. I'm looking out for *you*."

"Thanks, I guess," Alfie said reluctantly. He stood and moved to the door.

Vic opened it. "Hey, Barker," he said. "We're done in here."

"Good," the CO said. He'd been watching a trio of inmates who were walking his way. He turned to Alfie. "Let's get him back with his douchebag friends and—"

"Knife!" Vic shouted suddenly. He was looking past Barker at the three inmates, who were now only a few feet away.

Barker was an experienced Corrections Officer. Every good CO knew the possibility of taking a stab from an improvised blade. He moved fast, spinning to face the oncoming convicts, hands coming up into a defensive stance.

The first guy was already too close. Erin, her view blocked by the door and Alfie's body, didn't see exactly what happened. Barker grunted, an oddly strained sound as the breath was driven out of him. Then his legs buckled and he started to fall.

And everyone was moving.

Erin reflexively reached for a gun that wasn't there. At the same time, she flung out her other hand in a gesture for Alfie to stay back. Alfie ducked behind the table, eyes wide. He suddenly looked much younger and very frightened. Rolf, picking up on Erin's energy, went stiff-legged and bristling, ready for action.

Outside, the inmate who'd stabbed Barker yanked his weapon free. But retrieving the improvised knife cost him a critical half-second. Vic took one step forward, grabbed the man by the crotch with one hand and the collar with the other, and heaved him over the railing. The inmate gave a startled yelp which cut off abruptly as he slammed into the floor ten feet below.

Erin got to the door as the other two men rushed Vic. They were armed with nothing more than a sharpened toothbrush handle and a box cutter, but anything sharp could be deadly, and Vic and Erin were unarmed.

Rolf, however, had a whole mouthful of weapons.

"*Fass!*" Erin shouted, rushing toward the fight.

Vic was bigger than either of his attackers and he'd just tossed their buddy like a sack of potatoes. But there were two of them and the numeric advantage gave them confidence. They lunged at him, stabbing and slashing.

Vic stopped the right-hand guy in his tracks with the heel of his hand, slamming it into the man's nose. Vic's hand was big enough to palm the inmate's face. He held on, digging his fingers into the sides of the skull and squeezing. The poor bastard gave a muffled scream.

His buddy came in from Vic's left, the box cutter drawing a bright line of blood on Vic's forearm. The inmate's triumphant grin was wiped off his face a second later and he went down under almost a hundred pounds of energized K-9. Rolf got his target's arm in his teeth, clenched his jaw, and began vigorously whipping his head from side to side, snarling happily.

Erin made it out the door just as Vic forced his opponent to his knees, bending the man backward, using his face as leverage. Blood was streaming between Vic's fingers from the guy's ruined nose.

"Clear!" Vic growled.

"Watch it!" Erin shouted back. Vic's attention was focused on the target in his hand. He hadn't looked farther down the gallery, where four more goons were in the process of charging. The vicious efficiency with which Vic and Rolf had taken the first three down had made them hesitate, or they already would have been on the cops. But they were coming. All carried some sort of improvised weapon.

Erin stepped over Barker's twitching body, stooping to snatch the nightstick from the wounded CO's belt. Behind her, Vic slammed his opponent's head against the doorframe and let go, leaving the man stunned and bleeding. Rolf was still latched onto his quarry. Erin left him to it, knowing that was one fewer opponent at her back. She shifted her grip on Barker's baton and braced herself.

"We don't want you," the front inmate said. He waved his homemade knife, gesturing for her to move.

"Tough shit," she replied. "Here I am."

"Get her!" one of the guys at the back shouted. Then they rushed her.

In the movies, the hero could fight off a whole crowd of attackers because they came at him one at a time, like gentlemen, and were knocked down one at a time, like idiots. That wasn't how it went in a real melee. If you were fighting four guys at once, you could count on one or two good swings before you got swarmed under. So you'd better make those first swings count.

Erin hadn't done much nightstick work since her Patrol days, but her muscles remembered how. She jabbed the end of the stick into the leader's stomach. He doubled over and she jerked the weapon back, bringing it around in a swing at the second guy's head. Her aim was a little off and she clipped his shoulder instead of his ear. The blow still knocked him sideways, but it didn't put him down.

The third man sidestepped around his winded buddy and stabbed at Erin. She twisted away from him, which brought her directly in line with the last guy just in time to catch his fist against her right bicep. It wouldn't have been a serious hit, but he'd driven a long nail through a wooden dowel to make a makeshift push-dagger. The dowel was gripped in his fist, the nail protruding between the middle and ring fingers.

A hot spike of pain drove into Erin's arm. She hissed and flinched. Then the man she'd hit on the shoulder came in on her flank and stabbed her in the side, under her arm. Metal grated against bone. She stumbled away from the sudden pain, flailing with the nightstick.

By sheer luck, she brought the baton straight down between the man's eyes. The shock traveled clean up to her shoulder and she dropped the stick, hand stinging, but her victim went limp and collapsed in a heap.

Erin's heel caught on something soft and yielding. She went over backward, hitting the concrete floor flat on her back. She saw Vic come over her and heard a meaty thud as he did something awful to one of her attackers. Then someone else stabbed at Vic and he cursed, sounding more angry than hurt.

"Rolf!" she gasped. *"Pust! Hier! Fass!"*

The three commands ordered the dog to release his current target, come to her, and attack whoever looked like an enemy. Rolf immediately opened his jaws, leaving his first victim cradling a lacerated arm. The K-9 didn't fully understand what was going on, but he could hear the pain in Erin's voice and it sent him into a fury. He sprang to his partner's aid, mouth gaping, ears flattened, the fur on his neck standing on end. His snarl was terrifying, primal.

One man had somehow gotten around Vic and was bending over Erin. He drew back his arm to drive his shiv into her and was suddenly gone, knocked clean off his feet by the force of Rolf's charge.

There was the briefest lull, less than two seconds. Erin felt hot blood soaking into her blouse and trickling down her arm. Then an alarm began hooting and a man started screaming. The screaming was close, loud, and absolutely gut-wrenching. It also sounded funny, as if the man couldn't use his mouth properly.

Erin tightened her abdominal muscles and sat up, rolling onto one knee and taking in the situation. The gallery was carpeted with bodies. In addition to Barker, she counted five downed men. Two lay perfectly still. The other three were writhing in pain, clutching various injuries. Vic was standing over one of these, glaring down at him. The big Russian was bloodied to the elbows, chest rising and falling, fists tightly clenched. Rolf was nowhere in sight.

Erin grabbed the railing and pulled herself the rest of the way up. She followed the sound of the screaming and saw a crumpled shape at the bottom of the stairs. The dog had tackled him and knocked him all the way down to the lower level. Rolf was on top of the body, gripping the huddled form with his jaws. As she watched, he gave his victim a good shake.

The alarm continued its insistent blare. All over the prison wing, inmates were dropping to their bellies and spreading their arms, doing their best to show they weren't a threat. The thunder of booted feet rumbled toward the scene of the fight. Corrections Officers shouted at the prisoners to get down and stay there.

"You good, Erin?" Vic asked.

"I'm fine," she said, wondering if it was true. Her side was really hurting. But the blood seemed to be coming out in a slow trickle, not an arterial pulse. She could breathe and she didn't think she was about to keel over. "You?"

"I'm okay," he said. "Holy shit. Your dog's got that son of a bitch by the *face!*"

It was true. Rolf had missed his usual hold. Instead of grabbing the man's arm, he'd gotten his jaws on either side of his target's face and was holding on with his usual implacable determination. That explained the muffled quality of the man's screams. He was screaming into Rolf's wide-open mouth.

"Jesus," Erin murmured. "Rolf! *Pust!*"

Rolf released the man and pranced away, tail wagging. He glanced up at Erin, tongue hanging out, waiting to be told what a very good boy he'd been. The man he'd bitten had no fight left in him. Blood was all over his head. He clapped his hands to his face and curled into a miserable, bleeding ball.

"Vic," Erin said.

"What?"

She pointed at his arm.

He looked down and saw a shiv protruding from the muscle of his forearm. It stuck out grotesquely at a right angle from the flesh.

"Oh," he said and reached for it.

"Don't!" she said.

"Right," he muttered. "Leave it in. Let the doc take it out. Geez, this isn't my first knife fight."

The Riker's Island riot squad poured into the room, brandishing clubs and shields. Just like usual, the backup was arriving a little late to the party.

Erin became aware of a rhythmic sound nearby. She turned to see what it was.

Kyle Finnegan was standing at the door of his cell, looking at her. He was clapping slowly, methodically. The applause seemed half sarcastic, half sincere.

"Then will he strip his sleeve and show his scars," Finnegan said. "And say, 'These wounds I had on Crispin's Day.'"

The color seemed to drain out of the world. Erin's vision was going fuzzy around the edges. She swayed. Sitting down seemed like a good idea, so that was what she did. Men were running up the stairs, yelling and asking questions. None of that seemed very important. She ignored them.

A cold, wet nose wormed its way up under her left arm. Rolf's face thrust itself into her field of view. His big, brown eyes were soft and worried. He whined quietly.

"Good boy," she told him dully. "*Sei brav*, Rolf. *Sei brav.*"

Chapter 11

"First time I've ever been shanked in a prison," Vic said. "I can check that off my bucket list."

"Glad I could be a part of it," Erin said. She sucked in her breath in a sharp hiss as Dr. Birch's needle looped another stitch into the laceration in her side. "What else is on the list?"

"Oh, the usual," Vic said. "Disarm a nuclear bomb. Walk on the moon. Have a threesome with Scarlett Johanssen and Katheryn Winnick."

"I'm going to tell Zofia about that last one."

Vic grinned and flexed his arm experimentally, examining the fresh bandage. "Don't. She'd probably want to join in. It'd spoil the fantasy."

"All done, ma'am," Birch said, stepping back. Erin pulled the hem of her blouse down and took a couple of deep breaths.

"Thanks, Doc," she said.

"Don't mention it," he said dryly. "It's the least I could do for the detectives who suspected me of being an accomplice to murder."

"Hey now," Vic said. "We know you weren't in the room. You were operating on Keane in here."

"If you can call this an operating theater," Birch said. "We don't have the budget for the equipment we really need. You'd think the city didn't care whether inmates died."

"Yeah," Vic said with heavy sarcasm. "And we wouldn't want to think that, would we."

"You're one to talk," Birch said. "Thanks to you, my infirmary's as overcrowded as the rest of this facility."

"Next time I'll just let them stab us all to death." Vic wasn't easing up on the sarcasm.

Birch either missed his tone or chose not to hear it. "I have one cervical fracture and concussion," he said. "He's lucky to be alive and not paralyzed. One massive facial laceration who'll need plastic surgery, together with a slight skull fracture. Another concussion. A broken arm, with corresponding lacerations from canine teeth. A dislocated shoulder. A broken nose *and* a broken wrist. That's not even mentioning assorted bruises and contusions for everybody."

"That's what they get for screwing with the NYPD," Vic said. "If they didn't want to get their asses kicked, they should've brought more guys."

Birch sighed. "You ought to be an inmate, not a policeman. You're a thug with a badge."

"If you didn't have that thug with a badge, you'd have another body in your morgue right now," Erin snapped. "We saved Alfie Madonna's life. You should be glad nobody got killed."

"I'll be glad when you're off this island," Birch replied. "And I hope you take your murderous nonsense with you. Why didn't you go to one of the city hospitals to get your injuries tended?"

"I didn't want to bleed all over the upholstery in Erin's car," Vic said.

"We still need to talk to your patient," Erin said. "We figured it'd be more efficient to get patched up here, since we were in the neighborhood anyway."

"And I don't like dirty animals in my surgery," Birch added, glaring at Rolf.

"Sorry," Erin said. "But we couldn't help it. Vic was bleeding. I couldn't make him wait outside. We've tried to get him to bathe regularly, but he just won't listen."

"Hey!" Vic said. "He was talking about the dog!"

They left the prison's operating room and walked down the short hallway to the infirmary. The ward, as Birch had complained, was packed. In addition to the casualties from their melee, half a dozen other prisoners were crammed in. Guards were doing their best to keep everyone under control, but it wasn't easy.

Erin collared a passing nurse. "Where's Keane?" she demanded.

"They moved him," he replied. "For protection."

"Good call," she said. "Where've they stashed him?"

"Linen closet thataway," he said, pointing a thumb. "We made room by shifting some sheets and blankets. Look for the door with a guard outside."

"Thanks," she said.

They turned for the door and nearly ran into Lieutenant Webb. Their commanding officer was standing in the middle of the doorway, staring at the carnage.

"Hello, sir," Erin said.

"Good Lord," Webb said. "What in the name of God happened here?"

"I told you on the phone," she said. "We got in a fight."

"This isn't a fight," he said, waving a hand at the beds filled with groaning, bleeding men. "This is a small war! Why didn't you wait for me before you got into this mess?"

"Are you saying you wanted to be included in a prison knife fight, sir?" Vic asked.

"I'm saying I didn't want there to *be* a knife fight! What are you doing next?"

"Talking to Keane," Erin said. "Without knives, I promise."

"Is he here?"

"No."

"Then why are you?"

"We were just leaving," she said, getting up and moving past him out of the infirmary. "Follow me, sir."

"Who were those guys who jumped you?" Webb asked.

"We don't know yet," Erin said. "I'm guessing Lucarelli muscle."

"Why did they want you?"

"They didn't. They were after Alfie Madonna."

Webb took off his hat and rubbed his scalp. "Why?"

"Internal power struggle, I think," she said.

"But the Madonna kid doesn't have any power," Webb said. "Even if he wasn't in prison. He's just a punk kid who got lucky and knocked off a mob boss."

"He's got respect in here," Vic said. "He's a certified tough guy."

"So what?" Webb retorted. "He's still a nobody. His street rep may have kept him alive, but it doesn't make a rival send half a dozen guys to kill him. Who's he working for? Nobody! He acted as a lone wolf, unless I'm very much mistaken."

"I don't think that's entirely true, sir," Erin said.

"By all means, O'Reilly, enlighten me."

"This goes back to Kingston Schultz," she said.

"You keep circling back on him," Webb said. "Explain."

"He was behind Alfie's plan to kill the Oil Man," she said. "If anyone else knows that, they'd figure Alfie was associated with Schultz."

"Schultz doesn't have many foot soldiers," Vic said.

"He doesn't have *any*," Erin corrected. "Someone trying to hit him, or send him a message, might try to do it by taking Alfie out."

"Or Schultz might do it himself," Vic added. "If the Madonna brat can finger him for the Oil Man's murder, Schultz might figure he's a loose end that needs to be snipped off."

"We'll probably know more once we ID the attackers," Erin said.

Webb nodded. "Good work protecting the kid," he said. "And I suppose it's a good thing you were there."

"We're gonna be sore in the morning," Vic said. "But it was one hell of a good fight. You know what they say about knife fights?"

"What do they say, Neshenko?" Webb asked in flat, uninterested tones.

"It's easy to tell who won," Vic said. "The loser dies at the scene. The winner dies at the hospital."

"I'll keep that in mind," Webb said. "Do you think Keane had anything to do with this attack?"

"I don't see how he could have," Erin said. "He's been under direct observation since the last incident. But we can ask him."

"Because I'm sure he'll tell us the truth, the whole truth, and nothing but the truth," Vic said, rolling his eyes.

The Corrections Officer outside the linen closet was pretty spooked. Word of the fight had gotten around. He double-checked the detectives' identification and insisted on calling the Warden before letting them through. Webb commended his caution. Vic rolled his eyes.

"This guy isn't a friggin' VIP," he muttered. "He's a *criminal*, for God's sake."

"Those categories aren't mutually exclusive," Webb said mildly.

Erin psyched herself up. She didn't want to talk to Keane. She'd never been comfortable with him, even before she'd known he was a bad guy. But that was the Job. She took a few deep breaths and squeezed the recorder hidden in her underwire. On the off chance Keane did say anything worth hearing, she didn't mean to miss it.

The prison hospital staff had rigged up a makeshift ward in the closet. Keane's bed was equipped with a saline drip and a heart monitor. He was still cuffed to the bed. When the door opened to admit the Major Crimes squad, he favored them with a sardonic smile, though the tightness around his eyes showed he was in significant pain.

"We don't seem to have any vacancies in here," he said. "But you might want to find a quiet place to lie down. Some of you look a little the worse for wear."

"Look who's talking," Vic said. "I should've shot you in *both* kneecaps. You're a shit-stain on the Department, you goddamn crooked piece of crap."

Keane smiled grimly. "And yet here you are, needing my help."

"I don't need jack shit from you, asshole," Vic growled.

"Neshenko," Webb said quietly. "Why don't you wait outside?"

"I'm fine here," Vic said.

"I'm sorry for the misunderstanding," Webb said. "My mistake. I shouldn't have phrased an order like a question. Outside. Now."

"I guess you don't need your chief legbreaker," Keane said once Vic had reluctantly departed. "After all, mine is already broken."

"As Detective Neshenko pointed out, you do have two legs," Webb said. "One of which is not currently broken."

"Did you just threaten me?" Keane asked.

"I made an anatomical observation," Webb said. "If you inferred a threat, that's probably a sign of your guilty conscience."

"Guilty? So now you're trying to trick me into some sort of admission without my lawyer present?"

"We're not your biggest problem right now," Erin said. "You should be thinking about the Lucarelli thugs running around Riker's knifing people."

"Is that what's happening?" Keane asked. "Who else has been knifed so far, besides poor Detective Johns?"

"Nobody," Erin said.

"I don't believe you," Keane said.

"I don't care."

"There was an attack on another inmate," Webb said. "You probably haven't heard of him. He's just a small-time gangster."

"Another Lucarelli associate?" Keane asked.

"Yes, now that you mention it," Webb said. "Good guess."

"And you protected him?"

"Yeah," Erin said. "We did."

"How touching," Keane said. A spasm of pain crossed his face. "My meds are wearing off and you're in a hurry. Let's forget the small talk and cut to the chase. What do you need from me, and what do I get?"

"You get your life," Erin said. "If we can stop this war, we may be able to keep you from getting stabbed to death right here in this godforsaken closet."

"Tempting," Keane said. "But I think I'll hold out for a better offer." His voice was growing more strained. Sweat began to bead on his brow.

"Like what?" Erin demanded. "You killed a cop. You murdered my friend, you slick bastard. If you think I'm going to bend over backwards for you..."

"What O'Reilly means is, we're going to get the answers we need, one way or another," Webb said. "We can get them while you're still breathing, or we can take our time once you're in the morgue."

Keane glanced back and forth between them. "Isn't one of you supposed to play good cop?" he asked. His words came out almost breathless, between quiet gasps.

"We *are* the good cops," Webb said. "I sent the bad cop out of the room, remember? Would you rather try your luck with him?"

Keane's smile tightened into a grimace. His hands curled into fists and a vein stood out on his forehead. A thin sheen of sweat coated his face. He seemed to have forgotten they were there.

"I'll get the nurse," Erin said into Webb's ear.

"Wait," Webb said, and the coldness in his voice made Erin take half a step back from him.

"Sir?" she said. It was one thing to talk about torturing information out of a suspect, but to actually withhold medical attention was crossing a line. Erin hated Keane, but she didn't want his pain-twisted face following her into her nightmares.

"O'Reilly," Webb said loudly. "You are not to leave this room until I say so. He's made his bed. Now he's lying in it. Don't tell me you're feeling sorry for this sack of shit."

Keane writhed on the mattress. He gave a hiss of pain and struggled against the handcuff on his wrist.

"Sir, this isn't right," Erin said. She was confused. She'd never thought Webb was such a hardass. Maybe Kira Jones' death had hit him harder than he'd let on.

"I'm ordering you to stand fast," Webb said, staring hard at her.

"Please," Keane whispered. His heart monitor showed his pulse skyrocketing. He was breathing fast and shallowly.

Erin stood it for a few more seconds. Then she shook her head.

"No, sir," she said and yanked the door open.

"O'Reilly, don't help this man!" Webb snapped. "You're disobeying a direct order."

"Write me up," she called over her shoulder as she ran past a startled Vic toward the infirmary.

She was back in less than two minutes with a nurse and a cocktail of powerful pharmaceuticals. The nurse injected Keane and a few seconds later his muscles relaxed as the drugs hit him. His breathing slowed and he slumped back against his pillow.

"That should take care of him for a while," the nurse said. "I'll check back in an hour, okay?"

"Thanks," Erin said.

"I never thought you were such a bleeding heart," Webb said, his voice showing nothing but disgust. "I'm going for a cup of coffee, if they have any in this shithole. You do what you want, since it's plain you won't do as you're told."

He stomped out, slamming the door behind him.

Erin walked over to Keane's bedside and looked down at him. "I hope you're happy," she sighed. "You're an Internal Affairs cop, all right. Even now, you're still getting me in trouble."

"Thank you," Keane said quietly. He reached up as far as the handcuff allowed. To Erin's own surprise, she found herself taking his hand. His fingers were slick with sweat.

"You're a human being," she said. "I wouldn't let even a dog suffer like that."

"Of course not," he said with a faint smile. "You like dogs better than people."

His words surprised a light chuckle out of her. "That's true," she admitted. "A cat, then."

"Can I ask you one more favor?" he said.

"What?" she asked warily.

"I'd really like a notebook. And a pen or pencil. Can you do that? They don't have a television in here, or anything to read. I'm a little foggy right now, but I need something to fill the time. While I'm waiting for the Mafia assassins, that is."

Erin reached into her own hip pocket and drew out the little notebook she always carried. It was redundant in these days of Smartphones and online data storage, but she'd had one since her Patrol days. She tore out the used pages and handed the book to him, along with her ballpoint pen. She made sure to pull off the clip from the pen, knowing there were guys who could use that to pick a handcuff lock. The pen was a cheap disposable Bic. She supposed it could be used as a weapon, but even by prison standards it would be a pretty weak one.

"Thank you," Keane said again. "You do know they're going to come for me again, don't you?"

"Yeah," she said. "We have a guard on your door."

The familiar half-sneering, mocking smile appeared on his face. "That donut-pusher couldn't keep out a Jewish grandmother," he said. "I don't suppose you'd give me a gun?"

"Not a chance. They don't even let me carry one in here."

He nodded. His eyes were clouded from the drugs, but he was studying her with apparent curiosity. "You really are incorruptible," he said.

"Maybe nobody's met my price yet," she said, shifting uncomfortably.

"I don't think so," he said. "I think you're not for sale at any price. Not even for personal, emotional rewards. You have every reason to hate me."

"I *do* hate you," she said.

"But you helped me."

"Yeah. I'll probably regret it tomorrow."

"Who's my replacement?"

"What do you mean?"

"At Precinct Eight. Who did they bring in?"

Erin wondered what his angle was, but she couldn't see how it could hurt to tell him. He could find out through other channels regardless.

"Fiona McDowell," she said.

His smile crept back onto his face. "My sympathies," he said. "I hope you've been dotting your I's and crossing your T's."

"I'll be fine," she said. "So, who tried to kill you?"

"You want to know who killed Johns."

"Yeah, for starters."

"I didn't see it happen. I wasn't even in the room. You're asking me to speculate."

"Yeah."

"It won't hold up in court. It won't even get you a warrant."

"I don't care. It'll point me in the right direction."

"How do you know I won't just aim you at someone I want dead or in prison?"

"Because I won't lock up some poor schmuck on the strength of your word alone," she said. "I know what that's worth. But I'm a detective, and sometimes that means getting tips from liars and criminals."

"It gives you pleasure to stand there, being better than I am," Keane said. "Lording it over me."

"It gives me no pleasure whatsoever being anywhere near you," she shot back. "Damn it, you could've been one of us!"

"And just who do you mean by 'us?'"

"The good guys."

"You truly believe that. But you're the one who got in bed with a mobster and terrorist."

"Carlyle's a better man on his worst day than you are on your best," she snapped. "He's a good man who did some bad shit. You're a rotten son of a bitch clean through."

"It's simpler for you to believe that," he said. "I'm just a man trying to make it in the world."

"Bullshit. You made selfish choices every step of the way. Vic shot you, but he's not the reason you're lying on a prison cot. You want the answer to that, look in the damn mirror."

He nodded. "I suppose I deserve that. But don't I deserve a second chance, too? Like your Irishman."

"It's never too late to do the right thing," she said. "But don't think it'll wipe out all the bad you've done."

"Valentino Vitelli is in here," Keane said. "In another wing. He has plenty of reasons to kill me. So do Schultz and Santino."

"Who's Santino?"

"So you already know about Schultz."

Erin didn't bother arguing about that. "Santino?" she pressed.

"Giovanni Santino," Keane said. "The street calls him Foggy."

"Why?"

"Do you really care about his nickname?"

She decided she didn't. "Why would he want you dead?" she asked instead.

"He's the biggest fish the Oil Man didn't fillet," Keane said. "But he stayed loyal to Old Man Acerbo. His nephew's in here. Squeaky Santino. Maybe you've heard of him? I think you may have been the one who arranged his residency in this institution."

"It rings a bell," she said, but couldn't immediately place him. "I've arrested a lot of punks."

"Present company included," Keane said. "I'm pretty tired right now. The rest of those drugs are kicking in. Thank you again. I owe you."

"I'll keep that in mind."

"If I think of anything else, I'll let you know," he said.

"You do that," she said. "Rolf, *fuss.*"

The Shepherd took up his usual place at her hip as she walked to the door.

"O'Reilly?" Keane called softly.

She paused. "What?"

"I was wrong about you."

"How so?"

"I brought you in because I thought you were controllable. You're not. I don't think you know just how rare that is. Have you ever heard that the best thing is the respect of your friends, and the second best is the respect of your enemies?"

"I hadn't heard that, no," she said.

"You've earned mine," he said. "For what that's worth."

Erin didn't have the slightest idea what to say to that, so she left without saying anything.

Chapter 12

"You okay?" Vic asked.

"Where's Webb?" Erin demanded.

"He went that way," Vic said, aiming his thumb down the hall. "Looking for coffee, or so he said. What's up?"

"I'm going to rip him a new asshole."

"Now this I've gotta see. You sure you want to do that?"

"You didn't see what he did." She was walking with swift, angry strides. Vic was nine inches taller, but he had to jog to keep up.

"I'm serious, Erin," he said. "I'm the insubordinate one, so I know what I'm talking about. If you go off on him, you could get suspended. Hell, you could even get sacked."

She didn't reply.

Vic grabbed her shoulder, forcing her to stop. "Listen!" he said. "Maybe Webb screwed up, but bosses hate when you rub their noses in it. I know you're hurting right now. I know that jerkoff back there killed Kira and you don't want to play nice with him. But that's the Job!"

"Vic," she said slowly. "Get your hand off me right now."

He straightened his fingers and held up his palm. "Okay," he said. "I just don't want things to get any worse today."

"If I start punching him, you have my permission to pull me off," she said. "After I get two good hits."

They found Webb in the nearest guard breakroom. The Lieutenant was gingerly sipping coffee from a paper cup and talking with one of the COs. He glanced up at them and raised his eyebrows.

"How'd it go?" he asked.

"How do you think it went?" she snapped. "I can't believe you did that!"

"Did it work?"

She blinked, angry words piling up in her throat. "Work? *That's* what you're worried about?"

"Of course," Webb said. "Did he buy your compassionate act?"

"It wasn't an act!" she shouted, crossing the room and barely resisting the urge to smack the cup out of his hand. "I wasn't going to stand there and watch him suffer! What sort of bitch do you think I am?!"

"I know exactly who you are, Erin," he said quietly.

The use of her first name, something he hardly ever did, cut through her rage. "Huh?" was all she could think of to say.

"I knew perfectly well you weren't going to obey that order," he said. "But Keane had to hear me give it, and he had to believe it. Take two deep breaths and think for a few seconds. What's the best way to break a suspect?"

"Good cop, bad cop," she said. "But—"

"Keane knows us," Webb interrupted. "He knows what he did to our squad. He killed Kira Jones, he tried to kill you. His henchman shot at Vic's baby, for God's sake! How would he ever believe one of us was on his side?"

The penny dropped. Erin wasn't much of a blusher, but she felt her face tingle. "You set me up," she said. "You *wanted* me to disobey. That's why you made such a point of insisting it was an order, and making sure he heard you say it. That way I could be the angel of mercy. He'd see me risking my career just to ease his damn pain. You son of a bitch!"

"I'll give you a pass on that one, Detective," Webb said. He was smiling slightly now. "You've earned it. But you really are walking the line on insubordination."

"Okay," she said. "You're a real son of a bitch... *sir*."

"That's better."

"Did you have to do it that way?"

His smile widened. "We might've been able to work something else," he said. "But sometimes I need to remind you that I really am good at this criminal-psychology business."

"We're supposed to play mind games with the bad guys," she said sulkily. "Not with each other."

"Wait a second," Vic said. He was grinning. "Webb played you? In an interrogation? This is fantastic! I wish I'd seen that!"

"I'm sorry if I hurt your feelings," Webb said.

"Forget about it," Erin said. "I'd rather be manipulated than find out you're a complete bastard."

"Oh, I'm a bastard when I have to be," Webb said. "Nice guys don't make Lieutenant. Something you'd be well advised to remember if you plan on getting promoted. I assume you were wearing a wire?"

"Yeah. I got every word on tape."

"Anything useful?"

"Yeah," she said. "Keane thinks it was either Schultz, Vitelli, or Giovanni Santino."

"Good," Webb said. "Vitelli's right here at Riker's, so we know he's not going anywhere. And we've already got our eye on Schultz. That leaves this Santino mope... hold on."

"What?" Erin and Vic asked in unison.

"I was getting IDs on the guys who jumped you in the cell block," Webb said. "Would you believe one of them is Michael Santino?"

"I'd believe it," Erin said. She snapped her fingers. "Squeaky! I remember him now!"

"Which one of us kicked his ass?" Vic asked.

"Remember that drug den we busted a while back?" she asked. "The pizzeria?"

"Yeah," Vic said. "That was where Firelli got shot. I'm not gonna forget that in a hurry."

"Squeaky was one of the guys we arrested there," she said. "He's a Lucarelli. And he's Giovanni's nephew. Did you recognize any of the guys who attacked us?"

"I was looking at their hands, not their faces," Vic said. "Knives have a way of getting my attention, especially when they're pointed at me."

"He's in the infirmary, whichever one he is," Webb said. "I think we'd better talk to him next."

"Assuming he's conscious," Vic said.

*   *   *

Michael Santino was awake, but clearly wishing he wasn't. His face was sheet white, his muscles rigid. His nose was bandaged and both eyes were blackened and swollen nearly shut. His right wrist was encased in a cast. Though the chaos of the crowded infirmary surrounded him, he seemed unaware of it. He was absorbed in his struggle with the pain of his injuries.

"We can't do an interview here," Webb said. "Too many distractions, not enough privacy."

Vic collared the nearest guard. "Hey, buddy," he said. "What happens to jerks who get in fights? You throw them in Solitary, right?"

"Absolutely," the CO said. "And they lose good time, even if they don't get fresh charges."

"That's what I thought," Vic said. He turned to an overworked, harried-looking nurse. "Can this punk walk?"

"There's nothing wrong with his legs," the man replied. "But he really should be medicated."

"A little peace and quiet would be good for him," Webb said. "Can you prioritize getting him some meds, so we can move him?"

A short while later, after Webb had a conversation with the Warden, the detectives were escorting a distinctly shaky Santino to the solitary-confinement cells in the company of a Corrections Officer. Santino was cruising on pain pills and feeling a bit better.

"You're going to do some hard time," Webb said to him. "I can't help you with that. You attacked a guard and two NYPD detectives. You're damned lucky the guard's going to pull through."

"I didn't stab him," Santino said.

"Who did?" Webb asked.

Santino didn't answer.

"I know, I know," Webb said. "No snitching. But here's the problem. You're an accomplice to the attack, so you're going to be held responsible. Like I said, I can't help that. But I can see that your stay in Solitary is a little more comfortable. I can get you books, maybe even TV."

"Look, it wasn't nothing personal," Santino said. "Your people just got in the way. We didn't want nothing to do with them."

"I don't blame you," Vic said. "But you did try to stab me. That's why I broke your nose and your arm."

"You wasn't supposed to be there! He said—"

"Who said?" Webb asked.

Santino's mouth closed with an audible click of teeth.

They reached the Solitary Confinement cells. The CO opened the nearest one. The door was heavy and metal, with a tiny window in it. The window was equipped with a sliding metal shutter. The cell held a simple cot, a stainless-steel toilet, and nothing else. The room smelled like disinfectant and despair. Rolf snuffled curiously at it and snorted.

"Not a lot of room in here," Webb said. "But I guess you'll get used to it."

"I oughta be in the hospital, man," Santino said. "That big bastard beat the shit out of me!"

"I'm dripping with sympathy, Squeaky," Vic said. "If you hadn't tried to shank me, I might just have to give you a great big hug. And I haven't forgotten what you did to Firelli, either."

"Firelli?" Squeaky replied. "Who's that?"

"The cop you and your asshole friends shot last year, numbnuts!" Vic snapped. "The reason you're in here in the first place!"

"I didn't shoot him! I was just in the wrong place at the wrong time!"

"Tell me something," Vic said. "Just out of curiosity. Has anything you've done, at any time in your life, been *your* fault? Or is it always somebody else? Have you actually *done* anything? Or maybe you're just a total waste of space."

"Squeaky's not so bad," Erin said, slipping into her all-too-familiar good cop role. "He's telling the truth about Firelli. Buggy Mileno was the triggerman on that one."

"Yeah!" Squeaky said. Apparently agreeing with cops didn't violate his code of silence, as long as he didn't volunteer anything and it made him look better.

"Let's get you settled here," Erin said. "Rolf, *sitz Bleib.*" She led Squeaky into the cell and sat him down on the bed. She sat next to him. There wasn't a lot of room, but the side-by-side position built rapport.

"I'm sorry about all of it," Santino said. "It wasn't supposed to go down like this."

"I know it wasn't your idea," she said. "All I'm trying to do is keep everyone alive, you included. If this Lucarelli business turns into a full-fledged war, bodies are going to be dropping on all sides. You'll be safe for a few days, but once they dump you back into GenPop you'll be looking over your shoulder all the time. I'm hoping we can stop that from happening."

"Oh yeah?" he said. "How are you gonna do that?"

"Did you ever notice the bosses aren't the ones on the front lines?" she replied, avoiding the question. "They're sitting safe in their offices, or their special cells, with their walls and bodyguards keeping them safe. You foot soldiers are the ones doing the bleeding and dying. Does that seem fair to you?"

Squeaky shrugged and winced at the pain in his wrist. "It is what it is," he said.

"You don't have to be a soldier," she said. "Your uncle's in the Life. Why doesn't Foggy help you out, give you a little boost?"

"What's he got to do with anything?" Squeaky demanded, startling Erin with the anger in his voice.

"He got you into the Lucarellis," she said. This was a guess, but she would've gladly wagered a week's pay on it.

"That was a long time ago," he said.

"So you and he aren't on good terms now?"

Squeaky shrugged again.

"How'd he get the name Foggy?" she asked.

He hesitated.

"Come on," she said. "That's ancient history, right? Way outside the statute of limitations?"

"I guess," Squeaky said. "I was just a kid. The way I heard it, he jacked this tanker truck. It was way back in the Seventies, gas was real expensive, and he was gonna sell it to this gas station. But it turned out, it wasn't a gasoline truck. This idiot who tipped Dad off didn't check. It was carrying that liquid carbon dioxide shit. And the cops got after him, and he wiped out and the truck split open. And all that shit came pouring out, and it made this huge cloud of, like, fog. The cops couldn't see him, so that's how he got away. And he always told it like he'd done it on purpose, so everybody started calling him Foggy."

Erin laughed. "That's a good story," she said. And it was even better that she had Squeaky talking. The biggest hurdle in interrogation was to get the ball rolling. Once you had the conversation going, anything might come out.

"Yeah," Squeaky said. "I wish I could've seen it."

"How about you? There's got to be a story behind a name like Squeaky."

"Not really. I had these new sneakers, back when I was about thirteen. Foggy told me to take a package to some of the guys. They were in this fancy hotel, it had these marble floors, and my shoes squeaked when I walked across them. They called me Squeaky and it stuck. You know how it goes. You don't get to choose your nickname. How about you?"

"Me?"

"I know who you are. Junkyard O'Reilly. But I don't know why they call you that."

"It's because of Rolf. My K-9. I did a couple of rough things, and word got around I was as mean as a junkyard dog. At least, I think that's what it was. It might be because I ran into a junkyard dog once, while I was working a case. He tried to rip my face off."

"And you shot him?" Squeaky guessed.

"Hell no," Erin said. "I told him to sit his ass down, and that's what he did. Then we got on fine."

"What happened to the dog?"

"They were going to put him down," she said. "But I saved him. I hope he's with someone who's taking good care of him."

"So you're not as badass as people say you are?" Squeaky asked. He grinned, as if they were sharing some big secret.

"Oh no, I'm exactly that badass," Erin said. "But you're right, we don't get to choose our names. What about Buggy? Where'd that come from?"

Squeaky chuckled. "Oh, that's because he's bug-nuts crazy."

"I believe it," she said. "Was he the one Vic chucked over the railing?"

"Yeah. Your boy's one strong son of a bitch."

"He lifts a lot of weights."

"Good thing. Buggy would've shanked his ass and then we'd all be in even more shit than we are."

"What'd Alfie do to piss you guys off, anyway?" she asked. "Seven guys going after him. That's a lot of trouble to go to for one little kid."

Squeaky shrugged. "I don't call the shots. Do you know why you do all the shit you do?"

Erin smiled. "No way. You wouldn't believe some of the crap that comes down from the Commissioner's office."

"Shit rolls downhill," Squeaky agreed. "Is it true you blew Mickey Connor away?"

"Yeah."

"Damn. That guy was hardcore."

"You're telling me. I've got the scars to prove it."

He nodded. "Look, if we'd known it was you, we never would've tried nothing. Buggy said it'd just be Barker, and Barker's an asshole. Some of the guards, they're okay, but he's a real jerk. I didn't know Buggy was gonna stick him, of course. I thought we'd just shove him out of the way."

"Of course," Erin said. He was probably bullshitting her, but it cost nothing to agree with him.

"When you came out of that room, I just about shit myself," Squeaky said. "I would've backed off, but your big buddy was right there, and you know what happened. Shit, my face hurts. You think my nose is gonna grow back right?"

"Did they set it in the infirmary?" she asked.

"Yeah. Hurt like a bitch."

"Then you should be okay. So it was Buggy's call, going after Alfie?"

"Yeah, but he was just following orders, too."

"From Foggy?"

"Shit no. Foggy *likes* Alfie."

"Really? Why?"

"Alfie whacked the Oil Man," Squeaky said. "Foggy hated Vinnie, on account of what Vinnie did to the old man."

"Foggy was loyal to Acerbo," Erin said, understanding. "But you aren't."

"What for? He had his time. He didn't know when to step down. He should've made room for us younger guys. Vinnie understood. You gotta change with the times. Acerbo was too old-fashioned."

"Then it was Valentino Vitelli," Erin said.

"Maybe." Squeaky's eyes shifted. "If it was, I wouldn't wanna be the guy that said so. But it'd make sense, right?"

"Vitelli was Vinnie's right-hand man," she said. "Was he the one who said Alfie would be alone?"

"No." Now Squeaky looked uncertain. "It was some other guy. Buggy talked to him. A guy who knows what's going down at Riker's. He's usually right. I dunno what went wrong this time."

"Do you know who this guy is?"

"Nah, nobody tells me nothing. Look, if I knew, I'd tell you. That bastard screwed us, and we got the shit kicked out of us. I don't owe him nothing. But he could be anybody."

Erin could see that was all she was going to get. She stood up. "Thanks, Squeaky," she said. "I'll see what I can do for you."

"And if anybody asks, I didn't say nothing," Squeaky said.

"Not a word," she said.

Chapter 13

"This is like one of those old Agatha Christie stories," Webb said.

"Come again?" Vic said.

"Locked rooms," Webb explained. "All the suspects are stuck on a deserted island. Then they start getting picked off one by one."

"Yeah," Vic said. "Except instead of a bunch of English upper-class twits, we're in a prison full of violent psychos. Lucky us."

"Lucky us," Webb repeated. He leaned against the concrete wall and patted his breast pocket. "Damn."

Erin knew what he'd been looking for. But like other New York state facilities, smoking was prohibited at Riker's Island. Webb had handed over his cigarettes along with his sidearm when he'd entered, though he'd apparently forgotten.

"I just realized something," Vic said. "This case is stupid."

"Is that so," Webb said.

"Yeah. We're investigating the murder of a crooked cop. That's a crooked cop who tried to kill my kid, in case you've forgotten."

"None of us are likely to forget that," Webb said.

"This asshole was killed in prison by another asshole, also in prison, who's never ever getting out. Am I right?"

"Your restatement of the facts is accurate," Webb said. "It's your point I haven't yet grasped."

"Let's suppose we convict this Icepick punk for the killing," Vic went on. "And maybe we can figure out who passed him the order. So what? Unless we have him on tape saying it, we'll never prove it. So the big guy walks and the little guy gets another life sentence tacked on. Big freaking deal. Aiello's what, fifty?"

"Fifty-four," Webb said.

"Right. He'll live another twenty years, tops. Even if he wins that bullshit appeal his lawyer filed, he's still serving two life terms. What're we gonna do? Lock up his rotting corpse after he kicks off?"

"Thank you for the reminder about his lawyer," Webb said. He looked at Erin. "It really sounds like Schultz might be behind this."

"I think so, too," she said.

"You're not listening," Vic said. "My point is, *who cares?*"

"You're going to need to explain that," Webb said. His voice was deceptively soft and calm, but Erin saw the way his jaw tightened.

"Schultz never goes to jail over this," Vic said. "So the whole business is just one of those thought-experiment things. And the only victim was a shit stain on the Department. Nobody's gonna miss him. And we were gonna lock him up for the rest of his damn life, too. The killer saved New York's taxpayers about twenty grand a year. So what the hell are we doing here, getting shanked by punks when we could be out acting like real police?"

"Are you finished, Detective?" Webb asked.

Vic took a breath and considered. "Yeah," he said.

"How do you feel about this, O'Reilly?" Webb asked.

"It doesn't matter how I feel, sir," she said. "It's the Job. A guy got killed, so we need to find out who did it and build the case. Then we hand it off to the DA and get another case."

"Excellent answer," Webb said. "You asked who cares, Neshenko. *I do.*"

"Bullshit, sir," Vic said. "You don't care about anything."

Webb pushed off from the wall and advanced on Vic. He had to look up into the big Russian's face, but Vic backed away as the Lieutenant approached. Webb's eyes were cold and hard.

"I'm going to say this once," he said. "So listen up. I have two failed marriages and two ex-wives. I have two daughters in LA that I hardly ever see. I live in a crappy Brooklyn apartment and drive a broken-down station wagon. I have bad lungs and a worse heart, because I drink like a fish and smoke like a chimney. You don't want to know my life insurance premiums. My life is a goddamn dumpster fire. Do you understand?"

"Well, yeah," Vic said, shifting uncomfortably. "I don't get what—"

"What I have is the Job," Webb interrupted. "I'm a cop. I once turned down an offer from a gorgeous adult-film actress to take two hundred grand and run away with her, because this cheap gold shield is who I am. Detective Johns disgraced his shield. So did Lieutenant Keane. I'm not going to follow their example. I care because a man was murdered in my city, on my watch. I don't care whether he was a good citizen or not, because that doesn't matter to me and it shouldn't matter to you. If that's not enough for you, then you'd better hand over that shield and walk away, because the minute you start ignoring crimes just because the victims happen to be bad guys, you're not a cop anymore. You're just a thug with a pension. I happen to think you're better than that, even if you don't.

"Besides," he added. "You violent idiots are pretty much my only family these days, so I don't want to watch you turn into cynical burnouts. I see enough of that in my bathroom mirror."

There was a short pause. "Wow," Vic said.

"That was actually a pretty good speech, sir," Erin said.

"I don't give a damn," Webb said. "Are you ready to get back to work now, or did you need a longer hissy fit?"

"No, sir," Vic said. "I'm good. What's next?"

"Back to the Eightball, I think," Webb said. "We need to do some research on the Lucarellis, particularly how things are divided between Giovanni Santino, Valentino Vitelli, and Kingston Schultz. I think we could use a little fresh air after all this, anyway. Have you noticed all prisons smell pretty much the same?"

"Yeah," Vic said. "And they're nasty. Sir, did you really turn down a porn star and two hundred grand?"

"Yes," Webb said.

Vic whistled. "I should've moved to LA," he said. "Nobody's ever made me an offer like that."

*   *   *

Sitting at her computer in Major Crimes made Erin feel like a white-collar corporate drone. This usually left her bored and irritated. But today, with the fresh stitches over her ribs still throbbing, she could see the better points of a quiet desk job. However, she could also see the fresh bullet holes in the brickwork from the recent shootout with Keane and Johns, so she supposed peace and quiet were relative things.

Her computer informed her that she had a meeting with Lieutenant McDowell in less than ten minutes. So she didn't even get started on the Lucarelli research. Instead, she went to the bathroom to clean up. Dirt and blood were smeared on her face and hands. She'd scraped some skin off her cheek at some point during the fight and couldn't even remember how it had happened. Her clothes were filthy and her hair was a tangled mess. She did what she could with hurried soap, water, and a hairbrush. Rolf was a lost cause. What he needed was a bath, and even if she'd had time, she lacked the facilities in the second-floor restroom.

The meeting was in the small conference room on the third floor, adjoining the Internal Affairs office. Erin felt a pang as she and Rolf passed Kira's desk. The computer and files had been removed, but the KIRA JONES nameplate still sat on the front of the desk. A big pile of flowers and cards covered the desktop. Kira would have appreciated the gesture, Erin thought, but she might not have cared for the lilies and white roses. She remembered the other woman's blue-and-red hair, black leather, and motorcycle. She had no idea what Kira's favorite flower had been. Probably something urban and hard to kill, like a dandelion. She cleared her throat and blinked several times, making sure she wasn't about to start crying in front of the Cast-Iron Bitch.

McDowell was waiting for her, clad in dress blues. Her face was utterly unreadable. "Come in, Detective," she said. "Take a seat."

"*Sitz,*" Erin told Rolf, who sat next to her chair. "*Bleib.*"

"I apologize for the short notice," McDowell said. "Thank you for coming."

"I only just got back," Erin said. "Things got a little out of hand at the prison."

"Is that blood on your blouse?"

"Like I said, things got out of hand."

"Whose blood?"

"Some of mine, some of theirs."

"Who did you get in a fight with?"

"Some inmates tried to attack the prisoner we were interviewing. Vic, Rolf, and I stopped them. Nobody got killed, but we put seven guys in the hospital."

"Seven?" McDowell was politely impressed. "How did that stack up?"

"Rolf got two of them," she said. "I nailed another one or two. Vic handled the rest. He's really good at close quarters."

"And how badly are you hurt?"

"A few stitches," Erin said. "I'm fine."

"How is the investigation proceeding?"

"We're zeroing in on a few suspects."

"I trust you'll keep me in the loop?"

"I assume Lieutenant Webb is communicating with you," Erin said. "He'll be collating our information. And you can come down to Major Crimes anytime to look at the murder board."

"I'll do that," McDowell said. "But it's not why I called you here."

Erin waited. It was best, in her experience, not to volunteer information to Internal Affairs. *Take your time,* she thought. *It's not like I have a homicide investigation to conduct or anything.*

"As I mentioned in our last conversation," McDowell said, "I'm aware of the circumstances of your transfer from the One-Sixteen in Queens. Since that transfer was recommended by Lieutenant Keane, I've been doing some further research into it."

I'll bet you have, Erin thought. She said nothing.

"Detective Spinelli has some very uncomplimentary things to say about you. However, even a quick perusal of Spinelli's record suggests that I not attach too much weight to his words. Your former commanding officer, Lieutenant Murphy, disagrees with his assessment. However, the fact remains that you were suspended from duty for interfering with a major investigation. And rather than being punished, you were promoted."

Spinelli couldn't find his own asshole with both hands and a flashlight, Erin thought. She studied the wall a little above and to the left of McDowell's shoulder. She concentrated on maintaining her poker face.

McDowell opened a manila folder that lay in front of her. "As you may be aware," she said, "only about twenty-seven percent of police officers ever fire their weapons in the line of duty. Less than one percent of officers fatally shoot even one person during their entire career. In the past two years, you've been involved in a frankly incredible number of incidents. You are personally confirmed to have killed four men and one woman, and to have wounded several others."

All of whom were trying to kill me and coming pretty damn close to succeeding, Erin thought. But McDowell hadn't asked a question, so Erin didn't see any reason to say anything.

"One of these victims, Michael "Mickey" Connor, was unarmed at the time of his shooting," McDowell said.

That was too much. "Did you *see* Mickey Connor?" Erin said. She started calmly, but as the words poured out of her, she got louder. "That man was twice my size! I mean that literally. He weighed over three hundred pounds. He used to be a heavyweight boxer. He put Rolf and me in the hospital and almost killed both of us! He was wearing a bulletproof vest and he was hopped up on God knows how much coke! I shot him three times, and you'd better believe that was the minimum necessary force! If I'd had time I would've emptied my gun!"

"Has it occurred to you that you and your squad have a tendency to resolve situations with lethal force?"

"It's never our first choice."

"And yet Detective Neshenko has shot at least as many people as you have." McDowell leaned forward. "You are not a unit of ESU door-kickers. You are detectives. Your job is to investigate and solve crimes. But you persist in placing yourselves in harm's way. Your results are, as I've said, exemplary. But do you know why the city of New York employs the Emergency Services Unit to serve high-risk warrants?"

"They have the weapons and the training to handle those situations," Erin said mechanically. "But Vic has the same training. He came from ESU in the first place!"

"That's half an answer," McDowell said. "The other half is the application of overwhelming force. A desperate felon will usually surrender when he sees half a dozen guys in full tactical gear pointing assault rifles at him. If he sees a couple of plainclothes cops, he may figure he has a chance. My concern, Detective O'Reilly, is that you may be creating the very situations we hope to avoid."

"I call for backup whenever I can," Erin said, aware of the sulkiness in her voice. "I'm not the Lone Ranger."

"Your squad is an experiment," McDowell said. "It's a small offshoot of the Major Crimes Division of the NYPD. The idea was to have a small, nimble unit that could operate more or less independently. The inclusion of an officer with specialized tactical training was deliberate, as was your recruitment."

"You wanted my K-9," Erin said.

"Precisely. Unfortunately, it appears that while you have been extremely effective, you have also been involved in proportionally more officer-involved shootings than any ESU squad in the area. This has raised concerns which have been taken to the highest level."

"The Commissioner's worried about liability," Erin translated, trying and failing not to sound cynical. "We wouldn't want anybody suing the city after we have to shoot a homicidal perp or two."

"The Commissioner is considering disbanding your unit," McDowell said coldly. "I'm conducting an analysis of your methods and procedures. The PC will likely accept my recommendations regarding your future."

"Disbanding?" Erin echoed incredulously. "Does he have any idea what we've done? We stopped a terrorist from blowing up his goddamn office! We probably saved his life, not to mention a few hundred civilians, cops, and city employees!"

"Are you suggesting that the ends justify the means?" McDowell asked.

"No! I'm just..." Erin didn't know how to finish the sentence. It hung in the air between them. *And you're just telling me this now,* she thought. *When it's convenient for you. After working with us and watching us for a couple of days. But I bet you still expect me to trust you, even knowing you're reporting on us.*

"There were already questions, before this unfortunate business with Lieutenant Keane," McDowell said. "However, Keane's involvement with the squad may by itself jeopardize your continued operations."

Erin's mouth had gone very dry. "What'll happen if we do get shut down?" she managed to ask.

"You will be transferred to other postings," McDowell said. "In all likelihood your unit will be split up between several Areas of Service, to avoid any appearance of impropriety. Lieutenant Webb is nearly due for retirement in any case. He might be encouraged to go ahead and hang up his shield. Where Neshenko and Piekarski go is, of course, none of your concern. As for yourself, I did mention the possibility of an opening in Internal Affairs."

"Are you going to start using K-9s in IAB?" Erin replied.

Rolf was staring up at her with his deep brown eyes, patiently waiting for the humans to finish talking so they could get back to doing what they'd been put on Earth to do: chase bad guys.

"No," McDowell admitted. "However, I'm aware of several underlying medical conditions with your K-9. It may be time to put him out to pasture as well."

"You can't do that!"

Erin hadn't meant to say it. It was the wrong thing to say on every possible level and she knew it. The phrase was cliché, it was whiny, and it wasn't true. McDowell could most definitely do it, and Erin could see in the other woman's eyes that she would if she felt she had to. But the words popped out before she could swallow them.

"Can't?" McDowell asked. One eyebrow moved fractionally.

"You shouldn't," Erin corrected. "It would be a mistake."

"Because of your past results?"

"We took down two major crime families, simultaneously! We stopped a terrorist plot. We broke up a human-trafficking ring. We put dozens of perps behind bars. We do exactly what a Major Crimes unit is supposed to do. You're right, some people have gotten hurt. And not just the crooks. I've been to too many Departmental funerals. I saw the flowers on the way in. But this isn't about the past. It's about the future. Do you think we got all the bad guys? Do you think there's nothing left for us to do? Because this isn't over."

"You're referring to your current investigation, I take it?"

"The Lucarellis are still out there," Erin insisted. "What's left of them. They're disorganized, but that's just making them vicious and panicky."

"I know," McDowell said. "I was at Riker's Island too."

"Is this why you're here?" Erin demanded. "To look over our shoulders on this job and see if we've still got it? Is this some kind of test?"

"I'll be forwarding my recommendation to the PC at the end of the month," McDowell said.

"That's less than two weeks away!"

"Correct."

Plenty of time to jump to conclusions, Erin thought sourly. "What's going to make up your mind?" she asked.

"You."

"Me?!"

"All of you," McDowell clarified. "I need to see how you conduct yourselves. I need you to convince me that you are capable of the standard of professional conduct required of NYPD detectives."

I look like an extra in a bad zombie movie, she thought. *We don't have standards in Major Crimes, we have* exceptions. "We are," she said firmly. "Absolutely."

"Good." McDowell's eyes softened ever so slightly. "I do have everyone's best interests very much in mind, Detective. I'm not your enemy."

You're doing a good job faking it, Erin thought. "I know," she said.

"As long as you do good police work, you don't have anything to worry about."

And if you believe that, I've heard there's a bridge in Brooklyn for sale, nice and cheap, Erin thought. "Copy that," she said. "Are we done here, Lieutenant?"

"Yes. I'll continue to look in on your investigation in my capacity as advisor. Dismissed."

Erin stood up. "*Fuss,*" she told Rolf, who fell in step next to her.

"Oh, and Detective?"

Erin cursed silently. She'd half-expected a parting shot, but the anticipation didn't make it more pleasant. "Yes, sir?" she said.

"I understand you met with Andrew Keane at the hospital."

How the hell had that gotten to her so quickly? "That's correct," Erin said cautiously.

"What did he tell you?"

"Nothing definite," Erin said. "He gave me one lead: Giovanni Santino. We're looking into him. I'll have the full conversation in my report." *Which I haven't filed, because you haven't given me time to write it*, she thought but didn't add.

"And what about his own misconduct? Did you discuss that?"

"In general terms. I didn't get anything of substance. But I think his bargaining position has shifted a little."

"How so?"

"When we arrested him, he was concerned about getting out of prison," Erin said. "Right now, he's mostly just worried about staying alive."

"I see. And are you?"

"I'm always worried about staying alive," Erin said. "I got stabbed earlier today."

"I was talking about Keane. Do you think his concerns are justified?"

"I got stabbed," Erin repeated. "That prison's a deathtrap. If I was an inmate, even if I hadn't done a damn thing to piss anyone off, I'd still be worried about getting killed. Keane has enemies in there with him. So yeah, if you're asking whether he's in danger, the answer is yes."

"Are the authorities taking precautions?"

"They have a guard on him and he's being kept separate from the other infirmary patients. It's about the best they can do."

McDowell nodded. "I hope they keep him safe," she said. "His testimony is essential for cleaning up the Eightball. Thank you, Detective. That will be all."

Chapter 14

Erin went straight to Vic's desk. He looked up and opened his mouth to make some sort of smart remark. She stopped him with a quick, emphatic shake of her head. He saw the look in her eyes and gripped the arms of his swivel chair.

"What do you need?" he asked.

"I'm taking Rolf for a quick walk," she said, keeping eye contact. "Want to tag along?"

"Sure," he said, pushing back his chair. "I could use a little air that doesn't smell like shit."

That was the great thing about Vic. He wasn't as dumb as he acted, he was remarkably softhearted under his thuggish façade, and he was as tough as they came; but most importantly, when the shit went down, he didn't waste time on petty bullshit. He took action. And he always, *always* had her back.

"We'll be back in a few minutes," Erin said to Webb.

He waved his hand absently, engrossed in his computer. Vic, Erin, and Rolf headed downstairs, past Sergeant Malcolm at the front desk, and out onto the Manhattan streets.

"Trouble?" Vic asked as soon as they were outside and out of earshot of any other cops.

"Yeah," she said.

"Where did you go?"

"Upstairs. I got roped into a meeting with Lieutenant McDowell."

"Oh, Jesus." Vic slapped a hand to his face. "That's just what we need. What'd that bitch want?"

"She wants to shut us down."

"What the hell are you talking about?"

"The squad. The Major Crimes unit. She's here under orders from the PC himself. We have until the end of the month to convince her to keep us. Otherwise, that's it. We're done."

Vic was almost too confused to be angry, but Erin could see the anger starting to build in him. "That doesn't make a damn bit of sense," he said. "We've done more for this friggin' city than any other five squads put together! What've we gotta do? Build a time machine and hunt down Jack the Ripper? Arrest Judas for selling out Jesus Christ Himself?"

"Vic, stop it," she said, putting a hand on his arm. "You're right. I agree with you. But that isn't the point."

"Then what the hell is? I don't believe this shit! We've both got scars from the work we've done. We've been shot, we've been stabbed, we've been beat up. Shit, I'm bleeding through my stitches right now from getting shanked! I won't be eligible for the Departmental blood drive! I've lost too many pints in the line of duty!"

"Stop it!" she snapped again. "Focus and listen!"

His nostrils flared. Erin was reminded of a bull, stamping and pawing the ground as it eyed a matador. He actually snorted. But he nodded slowly.

"Okay," he said. "I'm listening."

"We're in danger," she said. "Just like in a firefight. And when the bad guys are laying down fire, do you stand up and run at them like a moron, or do you take cover and think?"

"I return their friggin' fire, is what I do."

"But you don't deliberately give them a target."

"Right," he muttered.

"What I need from you is to be your very best self," she said. "No insubordination. No jokes at the Department's expense. Watch your language. No picking fights, not even with assholes who deserve a beating. Unless you want a transfer."

"That depends," he growled. "Where would they send me?"

"Where do you think?"

He considered the possibilities and didn't like any of them. "Traffic duty, probably," he sighed. "Or back to Patrol. Maybe ESU would take me again, but I doubt it. I've been in too many critical incidents. I'd probably flunk the psych evaluation. Fine. I'll play ball. But what did we do wrong?"

"We're tainted by association."

"Association? With what?"

"Keane."

Vic's thin surface layer of calm shattered. "That fucking guy? I blew his goddamn kneecap off! I hate his greasy, slimy, Internal Affairs guts! If that bitch thinks any of us were on his payroll, she's out of her damn mind! If it'll convince her, I'm more than happy to walk right back into Rikers, tear the IV tube out of Keane's arm, and shove it up his tight bureaucratic ass so hard it comes out his nose!"

"That won't help," she said. "That'll just tell her you're an out-of-control lunatic who's looking for excuses to hurt people. In addition to being Felony Assault, so she'd take your shield and throw you in jail."

"Then what in the name of Saint Michelangelo are we supposed to do?"

"Don't you mean Saint Michael?" Erin said, momentarily baffled. "The patron saint of police?"

"What'd I say?"

"Michelangelo. The Sistine Chapel guy."

"I was thinking of the Ninja Turtle. The one with the orange mask and the nunchucks."

"I'll take your word for it."

"You grew up in the Eighties, too."

"Yeah, but I was a girl. I may have been a tomboy, but I didn't have Ninja Turtles. That was my brothers."

"Whatever. Stop dodging the question."

"We show McDowell what we're made of," Erin said. "We solve this thing, and we do it without anybody else getting killed. We act like good police."

"That ought to be easy. I *am* good police."

"I know that," she said, giving him an affectionate smile. "But McDowell doesn't. All she sees is that image you throw at the world. She knows we're good at our job, but that's not enough. She needs to know we're solid. Look, I'm marrying a former mob boss and you were going out with a hooker who worked for the Russian Mafia. It doesn't look good."

"That was a long time ago," he said sullenly. "And I didn't know she was a hooker. Or that she was working for the *vory*. It was a misunderstanding."

She grabbed his shoulders and gave him a shake. "Get it through your head!" she snapped. "That doesn't matter! Nobody cares about the truth! If Carlyle only taught me one thing, it's that. Perception is what matters. And for the next two weeks, the perception has to be that we're the spitting image of police perfection. Do you understand?"

"Okay, okay," he said. "Sheesh. But I can't even remember where I left my Patrol Guide. I think I was using it as a doorstop in the bathroom. It's probably got mildew."

"Just try," Erin said. "This is important. You're looking at reassignment. If I get shoved into the wrong slot, they'll take away my K-9. I could lose Rolf!"

"You're right," he said, more seriously. Then his eyes glinted with sudden mischief. "I know! We could have McDowell whacked. You know a couple guys, right?"

She smacked his shoulder. "I'm serious, Vic. That's exactly the sort of joke we can't tell."

"Sorry," he said. "That was out of line. But just so we're clear. We also need to close the case, right?"

"Of course."

"I wanted to make sure. I don't know if I've got my priorities straight. What if it comes down to a choice between looking good and catching the bad guys?"

Erin smiled grimly. "We do the Job. If self-preservation was our top priority, we wouldn't be carrying guns and shields in the first place."

"Damn right," Vic said. "Does Lieutenant Webb know about any of this?"

"I don't know. He's pretty sharp. He might figure it out on his own. But if he doesn't, I don't think we should tell him. It'll just make him more stressed."

"Good point. He's cruising for a heart attack as it is. I'd hate to be the guy who kills him by giving him bad news. Was there anything else?"

"No. Rolf's taken care of his business. Want to head back?"

Rolf had cocked his leg three times while they'd been talking. The first one had been because he'd needed to. The second and third were because he was walking his beat. He wanted everyone to know he was on duty.

"Sure," Vic said. "Maybe we can bust some Mafia goons and go home early."

"Arrest reports," she reminded him. "Have you ever gone home early after making a major collar?"

"They don't even pay us overtime when that happens," he sighed.

*   *   *

"Are you done with your short, unapproved vacation?" Webb asked when they walked back into Major Crimes.

"Would you rather Rolf piss on the floor?" Erin replied.

"It'd smell the same as the holding cells," Webb said. "What were you doing upstairs?"

"Liaising," she said. "With our friend in IAB."

"I don't have any friends in IAB," Vic said. "Not anymore."

"It's good you're keeping McDowell in the loop," Webb said. "Do you know what the Lucarellis have been up to lately?"

"Crime?" Vic guessed.

"I was hoping for a little more specificity," Webb said.

"Slaying each other while squabbling over the remnants of their once-proud empire?" Vic tried.

Webb and Erin both stared at him.

"I didn't even know you knew some of those words," Webb said.

"I watched a History Channel documentary on the Roman Empire last week," Vic said.

"I didn't think that sounded like you," Erin said.

"He's right, though," Webb said. "A pair of *capos* just dropped. One of them literally. Aniello Migliore, AKA The Russian, took a nosedive from his living room window last night."

"Suicide?" Vic asked.

"Suicides usually open the window first," Webb said dryly.

"The Russian?" Vic continued. "That's an Italian name. Why was he called that?"

"I have no idea," Webb said. "But he was apparently one of the highest-ranking guys left in the Family."

"Who was the other *capo*?" Erin asked.

"Joseph DiNapoli," Webb said.

"What happened to him?" she asked.

"Run over by a garbage truck," Webb said.

"Yeesh," Vic said. "That's a lousy way to go. I'm guessing it wasn't an accident?"

"Unlikely," Webb said. "The truck was identified as belonging to a company operated by a Lucarelli front."

"Did we catch either of those?" Erin asked.

Webb shook his head. "Apparently the Feebies had an open investigation on DiNapoli," he said. "So he's gone Federal. And the Organized Crime Task Force snapped up Migliore."

"I'm sure that won't cause any interagency confusion or turf protection," Vic said with heavy sarcasm.

"You're telling me," Webb said. "But I find it remarkable that with those two deaths, the entire senior leadership of the Lucarellis is now either deceased or incarcerated."

"What about Foggy Santino?" Erin asked.

"I've been looking into him," Webb said. "He's a midlevel boss, low-ranking enough that he wasn't targeted in the Oil Man's purge. The fact that he's just about the tallest guy left standing should tell you how bad things have gotten."

"We don't need to do anything to these jerks," Vic said. "They're doing a great job killing one another off. Give it another week and we can scoop up the bodies and arrest the only mope who isn't dead. That was a joke!" he added quickly.

"The two *capos* who died," Erin said. "Were they loyal to Valentino Vitelli?"

"I think so," Webb said. "Vitelli was the Oil Man's second-in-command, and Vinnie left them in place after his coup. What are you thinking?"

"I'm thinking it's possible Santino bided his time until Vitelli got thrown in jail," she said. "Then he got his revenge for

Vinnie and Vitelli killing his old boss by knocking off their underlings."

"You think he was behind the attack on Johns in the infirmary?" Webb asked.

"Could be," Erin said. "But I still think that might have been Kingston Schultz."

"That's the trouble with a three-way fight," Vic said. "Anyone might hit anyone else."

"Where's Santino now?" Erin asked.

"Little Italy," Webb said. "He owns a bar called Misty's."

"Maybe we should go talk to him," she said.

"Yeah," Vic agreed. "Before someone whacks him. But I think we ought to get someone who knows the territory. I need to line up a sitter."

"A which?" Webb said.

Erin was a little ahead of her commanding officer this time. "A babysitter," she explained. "Piekarski used to work Little Italy, remember? I bet she'd love to come with us."

Webb shook his head. "I don't like having a couple in the field together," he said.

"You never had a problem with them before," Erin said.

"They didn't have a kid then," he said. "What if this goes bad?"

"So only us childless detectives are expendable?" she replied.

"Of course," Webb said with a poker face. "Fewer survivor benefits."

Chapter 15

"So a Russian, a Polack, and an Irish girl walk into a bar..." Vic said.

Erin gave him a look. "We're about to talk to a Mob boss and *that's* what you come up with?"

"Just trying to lighten the mood," he said. "This guy's son tried to stab me. I'm trying to get in a good mood so I don't shove his head through a wall."

"I'm in favor of you not doing that," Erin said. "What's the punchline?"

"I don't have one. I was hoping one of you did. Now you're leaving me hanging."

"Okay," Piekarski said. "Let's hear 'em. Vic, give me your worst Polish joke, then I'll give Erin my worst Irish joke and she can hit you with a bad Russian one."

"That seems fair," Erin said.

"When do we hear an Italian one?" Vic asked.

"Once we're not in Mafia territory," Piekarski said. "Firelli's the only one who's allowed to tell Italian jokes here in Little Italy."

"You want it, here it comes," Vic said. "Why was Jesus born in Bethlehem?"

"That's a Polish joke?" Erin asked.

"Wait for it," he replied.

"I give up," Piekarski said. "Why?"

"He would've been born in Poland, but they couldn't find three wise men and a virgin."

Piekarski smacked him, but she smiled. "Okay, Erin. That reminds me of another. How do we know Jesus was Irish?"

"He turned water into wine?" Erin guessed.

"No. His mom thought he was God, and he thought she was a virgin."

"Good one," Vic said. "You're up, Erin. Hit me with your best Russian shot."

"Okay," Erin said. "Why do Russian cops go around in groups of three?"

"I don't know," Vic said.

"So one knows how to read, one knows how to write. The third likes to hang around intelligent people."

"I wouldn't know what that's like," Vic said, grinning. "You two had better do the talking."

It took Erin's eyes a moment to adjust to the dim light in Misty's. The room was low-ceilinged and narrow, with scarcely room for a row of tables on the opposite wall from the bar. Though it was the middle of the workday, she was unsurprised to see a handful of tough-looking men lounging around. Most young guys would have taken notice of Erin and Piekarski; a pair of attractive women walking into a bar tended to draw attention. But this particular group of thugs was more interested in Vic and Rolf. They became instantly tense and alert.

"Think maybe you folks are lost," the bartender said in a thick Brooklyn accent. He was a gaunt, dark-eyed Italian-

American sporting an old-fashioned mustache, gray at the tips. His slicked-back hair was jet black, but Erin would have bet it was dyed.

"I don't think so," Erin said. "I'm looking for Foggy. Is he here?"

"Who wants to know?" the bartender replied. His eyes were fixed on the newcomers and his right hand, Erin noted, was under the countertop.

"Erin O'Reilly," she said, walking straight toward him. "NYPD. This is Vic Neshenko and Zofia Piekarski." Vic had instinctively drifted to one side and was watching the group of thugs, silently daring them to start something. Piekarski stayed next to him but was looking at the bartender. Her hand had slid nonchalantly down to her belt and was hovering next to her sidearm. Vic, less subtle, was actually holding his Sig-Sauer, and though he hadn't drawn it, he'd thumbed open the safety strap on the holster.

"Holy shit," one of the toughs muttered. "It's Junkyard O'Reilly."

The bartender brought an empty right hand slowly up into view, fingers spread to show he was unarmed. "I'm Foggy," he said. "What can I get for you?"

"We're not here to drink," Erin said. "We need to talk about your son. Would you like to do this privately?"

Santino thought it over. "Hey, Luca!" he called. "Take the boys outside, will you?"

"If you say so, Boss," the biggest goon said doubtfully. He stood up and jerked his thumb in the direction of the door. Then he and the others trooped out.

"How about your muscle?" Santino asked, nodding to Vic.

"He's my partner," Erin said. "He stays."

The mobster shrugged. "Don't matter to me," he said. "You sure you don't want nothing? On the house."

"We can't drink on duty," Erin said.

"Baloney," Santino said, smiling. He had a surprisingly pleasant smile, his weathered face cracking open like a set of shutters letting in a sunbeam. "I've seen plenty of cops, hammered so hard they couldn't see straight. But forget about it. Sit down, why don't you, and let's talk."

Erin and Piekarski slid onto barstools. Vic remained standing, scanning the room for potential trouble.

"Your pal's jumpy," Santino observed.

"You're one to talk," Erin replied. "Or are you going to tell me you were holding a beer bottle when we walked in?"

"I'm a convicted felon," he said. "If you're implying I'm in possession of a firearm, that would be a serious violation of my parole."

"We wouldn't want you to violate your parole," Erin said. "Riker's Island is plenty crowded already, and it's not a nice place to be right now. When's the last time you spoke to Michael?"

"They call him Squeaky," Vic added.

"Vic, I think the man knows his own son's name," Piekarski said.

"I get up there to visit him whenever I can," Santino said. "I had a nice talk with him last week. You can check the visitor logs. Cameras, too, if you want. Listen, Miss O'Reilly, I got respect for you. I know Miss Piekarski, too. Seen her around. She's one of Logan's people out of the Five."

"That's right," Piekarski said. "I was."

"You run with Bobby the Blade," Santino continued.

"One of my best friends," she confirmed.

He nodded. "Bobby's a stand-up guy. And I heard of Toothpick over there."

Vic returned the nod, his expression noncommittal.

"So, with respect," Santino said. "One professional to another. What's going on here? Why are you asking about my boy? You know I won't say nothing against him. And you already got him locked up, so there ain't nothing more you can do to him. So what gives? Is Mikey okay?"

The mobster's voice was casual, but Erin saw the worry hiding at the back of his eyes. He might be a mob boss, she reminded herself, but he was also a father.

"He was in a fight," she said. "He'll be okay, but he's in the prison infirmary."

"How bad is he hurt?" Santino asked.

"Somebody broke his nose and his wrist," Vic said.

"Who?" Santino asked. Anger pushed the worry out of his eyes, leaving them cold and hard, like black marbles.

"Me," Vic said, matching his stare.

Ten seconds of awkward silence followed. Erin got ready, in case Santino decided to do something.

"You must've had a good reason," Santino said at last. "Especially to come here after. Why'd you do it?"

"He tried to shove a shiv into my balls," Vic said. "I got between him and a punk he was trying to knife."

Santino shook his head. "Mikey wouldn't do that," he said.

"Want to bet?" Vic replied. "Because I was there and that's what happened."

"Who was the punk?" Santino asked.

"Why does that matter?" Erin replied.

"It matters 'cause you think it does," Santino said. "If a couple big-shot detectives come into my place to talk about it, then it matters plenty. How come you was mixing it up in a cell-block scuffle anyway? Don't you got better things to do?"

"We were investigating another prison stabbing," Erin said.

"You mean that crooked cop who got shanked."

"That's the one."

"My boy didn't have nothing to do with that!"

"How do you know?" Erin asked sharply. "You just told me he wouldn't do something like that, but my partner and I witnessed him in action."

"Mikey ain't no killer," Santino insisted. "That thing with Bobby last year, that shoulda never happened, but he wasn't the triggerman there neither. He ain't never done nothing like that. He hangs out with some rough guys, but he's just an earner, trying to make a buck same as everybody."

"You knew Matthew Madonna, didn't you?" Erin asked suddenly.

"Material Mattie? Course I did! What's he got to do with anything? He's dead."

"Were you friends?"

"What kinda question is that?" Santino demanded. "We came up in the same neighborhood. We looked out for each other. I trusted him more than my own brothers. So we wasn't friends, we was family, you get me?"

"I hear you," Erin said. "So why would your son be trying to stick a knife into Madonna's kid?"

"Alfie?" Santino was shocked enough that he didn't even try to cover it up. "Not a chance! He and Mikey are like brothers! They love each other!"

"And the Mafia never sends a guy to kill a guy who loves him," Vic said, laying on his trademark sarcasm with his usual lack of subtlety.

"We ain't all like that," Santino said coldly.

"What you're telling me," Erin said, "is that your son would've needed a really good reason to try to kill Alfie."

"A *fantastic* reason," Santino said.

"And you don't have the slightest idea what it is?" she pressed. "You didn't talk to him about this? It wasn't your idea?"

"Miss O'Reilly, I respect you, so I'm gonna be polite and pretend you didn't ask me that."

Erin let it go. "You're the biggest guy in the Lucarellis right now," she said. "Some people would say you're running the Family these days."

"You think a big-shot boss is gonna be wasting time tending bar in a little hole in the wall like this?" Santino asked.

Carlyle had trained Erin well in the art of the technical truth. Santino hadn't said yes and he hadn't said no. The great thing about answering a question with another question was that you didn't have to give anything away.

"The Family's fallen on hard times," she went on. "Lots of guys locked up. More guys having... accidents."

"The world's a dangerous place," Santino said evenly. "It tries to kill all of us. In the end, it succeeds."

"Migliore and DiNapoli?" she prompted.

He held his poker face.

"Were they also friends of yours?" she asked.

"Business associates," he said. "And if you're suggesting I had something to do with what happened to them, I think I'd better have you talk to my lawyer."

"Let's leave the lawyers out of this," she said. "I know you didn't kill them personally. But I also know you have a pretty good idea who did."

"A pretty good idea is a long way from reasonable doubt," Santino said with a hint of a smile.

"Are you sorry they're dead?" she asked.

"Now what kind of a question is that?"

"A pertinent one."

"I'd say it's an *impertinent* one, Miss O'Reilly. Thank you for coming in and telling me about my kid. But now I think it's time for you to go."

"You're throwing us out?" Vic demanded.

"I'm asking you politely to be on your way," Santino said. "And I hope you have a very pleasant day. You look like you could use it."

*   *   *

"That was fun," Vic said once they were out on the pavement. "What an asshole."

"He was polite," Piekarski said. "If you think that was an asshole, you've been off Patrol too long. Assholes swear and throw up on you. And they stink. At least Mr. Santino smelled like he'd showered recently."

"He uses too much cologne, though," Erin added.

"So now we're sniffing the perps," Vic said, shaking his head and giving Rolf a look. "I blame you."

Rolf wagged his tail. His nostrils twitched.

"One thing you can say for these old-school Mafia types," Erin said. "They act nice on the surface."

"But it's all an act," Vic said. "They're vicious sons of bitches once you peel back the manners."

"Of course they are," Erin said. "That man had a gun under the counter and he was prepared to use it."

"Nine-millimeter?" Vic guessed.

"Sawed-off twelve-gauge," Piekarski suggested. "Double-barreled."

"Damn," Vic said. "That would've blown you right out of your shoes, Erin."

"It doesn't matter what kind of gun," Erin said. "He wasn't going to use it on cops. The point is, Santino didn't know about the attempt on Alfie Madonna."

"Or he's one hell of an actor," Vic said. "But I think you're right. He doesn't know his kid as well as he thinks he does."

"I wonder," Erin said.

"What're you thinking?" Piekarski asked.

"Family's really important to Santino," she said. "He reminds me of Matthew Madonna. Mattie wasn't the best dad, but he was really close to his son. The way Santino was talking, I really don't think Squeaky would've gone against him like that."

"Then what the hell is going on?" Vic demanded.

"Someone got to Squeaky," she said. "When I talked to him at Riker's the kid acted like he was on the Oil Man's side, but I don't know if I believe him."

"Jesus," Vic muttered. "How are we supposed to know who's on whose side if these jerks can't even keep it straight themselves?"

Erin was trying to think like a mobster. "Who stands to benefit?" she wondered aloud.

"From what?" Piekarski asked.

"This war. We've lost one bad cop and a pair of Lucarelli captains. Who comes out ahead?"

"Foggy Santino," Piekarski said. "He can run the family now."

"Alfie Madonna," Vic said. "We saved the little punk's life, and somebody's been taking out the Oil Man's henchmen. That must make him pretty happy."

"Alfie couldn't orchestrate something like this," Erin said. "He's not smart enough and he doesn't have the connections."

"Remember what happened to the last guy who underestimated Alfie Madonna?" Vic replied with a sardonic smile. "Alfie made him into a human Pez dispenser."

Erin shook her head. "He's no criminal mastermind," she insisted. "Schultz was the one who planned that."

"You know that for a fact?" Piekarski asked.

"It doesn't matter what I know," Erin said wearily. "Not if we can't make it stick. But this all circles back to Schultz. I'm sure of it."

"How does he benefit?" Piekarski asked.

"When Alfie went to jail, Schultz got put in charge of his late father's real estate holdings," Erin said. "Alfie technically owns them, but he can't do anything with them while he's in prison. The properties keep generating revenue."

"Schultz cashes the checks," Vic said. "And as long as the Madonna brat is alive, even if he's in prison, his lawyer gets to administer his assets. Clever. But that was Vinnie's murder and that's ancient history. What about Johns and those other two mopes?"

"I think DiNapoli and Migliore might just be collateral damage," Erin said. "Once the knives come out, everyone starts fighting. The Lucarellis were already scared and desperate. All it took was one spark to light them up."

"Everyone's settling old scores," Piekarski agreed. "With all the bosses dead or in prison, it's like a kindergarten without any teachers."

"That's some *Lord of the Flies* shit right there," Vic said. "Yes, I have read some books, thank you very much. So you think it all comes back to the Johns murder?"

"I think it comes back to Keane," Erin said. "And Johns."

"They don't have any power," Vic said.

"Or money," Erin said. "So they must have knowledge. Keane knows something about Schultz, something dangerous."

"How do you figure?" Vic asked.

"That's how Keane operates," she said. "He gets compromising information on you, then he gets you to work for him. If you screw him, he can destroy you."

"Scorched earth," Vic said. "It hasn't worked out great for him."

"What does he know?" Piekarski asked.

"I don't know," Erin said. "But whatever it is, it's worth killing for."

"Let's go beat it out of him," Vic suggested. "Metaphorically, I mean. We can't actually beat the shit out of him. Though it sure would make me feel better if we could."

"We can try," Erin said. "But we need leverage on Keane."

"What can we threaten him with?" Vic asked. "He's already in jail for killing a cop. We can't shove a gun up his ass; that's against the law. I don't know what else we can do to him."

"We can't threaten him," Erin agreed. "So we need to offer him a carrot instead of a stick."

"I saw this movie where Clive Owen kills a couple guys with a carrot," Vic said cheerfully. "See, what he does is…"

"Nobody cares, hon," Piekarski said, patting him on the arm.

"Ouch!" Vic said. "I got stabbed in that arm!"

"Sorry," Piekarski said, pulling her hand quickly back.

"Why do people always do that?" Vic complained. "You get hurt somewhere, it's like everyone has this compulsion to touch it."

"Leverage," Erin said with a smile. "We have an instinct to go for someone's weak point, even when it's subconscious."

"What carrot can we offer Keane?" Piekarski asked.

"There's only one thing he wants," Vic said. "And he's not gonna get it. No way. That bastard killed Kira. He's gonna rot behind bars if I have to weld them in place myself. He gets no deal. I don't care if Schultz and Santino and half the friggin' Lucarellis walk. It's not gonna happen."

"It's not up to us anyway," Erin said. "We should talk to DA Markham. He's the one with the authority to bargain."

"And I'm telling you—" Vic began.

"Kira was my friend, too!" Erin snapped. "And for all we know, Markham feels the same as you. But we need to know what our options are. We're going to One PP and we're going to talk to him and you're going to take a page out of Santino's book and *pretend* to be polite. Are we clear?"

"Just when the day can't get any better," Vic said. "We go hang out with another friggin' lawyer. You know what's the only difference between a lawyer and a prostitute?"

"What?" Erin asked.

"A prostitute stops screwing you once you're dead," Vic said with a poker face.

Chapter 16

"The District Attorney will see you now," the secretary said. She was a tired-looking forty-something with a smile you might find on the clearance rack at a discount store. She managed to convey the impression of being both busy and bored at the same time.

"Thanks, ma'am," Webb said. He'd agreed with Erin's idea and had met the others at City Hall. In deference to the setting, he'd made an effort to make himself presentable. It hadn't worked. His coat, hat, and tie had a shabbiness about them that no amount of dry-cleaning could fix. It struck Erin that he and Markham's secretary were two of a kind. The woman wasn't wearing a ring, she noticed. Maybe she could set them up with one another.

That was an absolutely terrible idea. She couldn't imagine why she'd even considered it.

DA Markham stood up and walked around his desk to greet them. He gave them a brilliant politician's smile that almost looked genuine.

"Detectives," he said. "Welcome! It's a pleasure, as always."

"Thank you for making time in your schedule on such short notice," Webb said.

"Nonsense. I've always got time for some of New York's heroes." Markham shook hands with Webb, Erin, and Vic. Then he held his hand down for Rolf.

The K-9 gave the appendage a quick, businesslike sniff and immediately lost interest. Lawyers didn't smell as interesting as bad guys. Bad guys reeked of adrenaline and fear. This man smelled like aftershave and expensive fabric. He probably wouldn't be much fun to bite.

"Have a seat," Markham said. "Can I get you anything? Coffee? Water? Christine has some very good shortbread cookies."

"Coffee would be great, sir," Erin said.

Markham's coffee wasn't anywhere near as good as Schultz's, but it was better than you'd get at most coffee shops. Vic took a bottle of water and sipped it.

"Now," Markham said, settling back in his black leather swivel chair. "What can I do for you?"

Webb glanced at Erin. "Detective O'Reilly, if you'd care to explain?"

"Sir," she said. "We have reason to believe Andrew Keane is in possession of valuable information regarding the ongoing criminal enterprises of the Lucarelli Mafia family. We further believe members of that family are trying to have Keane killed to silence him. There's already been one attempt."

"So I understand," Markham said. "You're referring to the murder of Detective Johns?"

"Yes, sir. He was almost certainly killed by Roy Aiello, a Lucarelli lifer who got himself admitted to the infirmary. He was aided by at least one prison guard, who disabled the security camera, but we don't yet know which one. It's only by luck that Keane wasn't in the room at the time of the attack. He's being kept in isolation now, under guard, but his need for medical attention limits our options a little."

"You believe there's going to be another attack," Markham said. He folded his hands on his desktop, interlacing his fingers. "How important is the information in his head?"

"We don't know," Webb said. "This is just a theory at present."

"What does Keane want?"

Vic stirred restlessly and opened his mouth. Erin decided to intervene before he said something impolite.

"We understand we're not negotiating for his release," she said quickly. "And we don't think witness protection should be on the table. But I was thinking we could get him transferred to another facility, one where he'd be a little more comfortable."

"And less likely to get stabbed to death by Italians," Vic added.

Markham nodded. "My office would certainly be prepared to play ball if he's willing," he said. "But Keane is a cagey operator. He'll drive a hard bargain. I'll need some assurance that his knowledge will be of material assistance in building a major case before I'll give him anything. Do you have any idea who he can give us?"

"I'm hoping Kingston Schultz," Erin said.

"The attorney?" Markham was surprised. "He's not a member of the Lucarellis. He's just their lawyer."

"There's a difference between a criminal attorney and a *criminal* attorney," Vic said darkly.

"Do you have proof he's been engaged in illegal activities?" Markham asked sharply.

"That's what we're trying to get," Erin said.

"Attacking a defense attorney sets an extremely dangerous precedent," Markham said.

"Yeah," Vic said. "We wouldn't want New York's lawyers to be worried we might come after them if they did anything wrong. It might make some other lawyers uncomfortable."

"What are you implying, Detective?" Markham asked. His voice had gone silky-soft and dangerous, like it did when he was about to tear a witness apart in cross-examination.

"Not a thing, sir," Vic said promptly, his survival instinct taking control of his mouth.

"The District Attorney makes an important point," Webb said. "If lawyers get the impression we're out to get them because of their clientele, the legal system breaks down. Then crooks can't get the representation they need—"

"How tragic," Vic interjected.

"—and are entitled to under the Constitution of the United States," Webb finished. "That's why we're proceeding carefully, Mr. Markham. We have not detained Mr. Schultz, nor harassed him in any way."

"What has he done?" Markham asked. "You must be going on something more than suspicion."

"He orchestrated the murder of Vincenzo Moreno," Erin said. "And I think he's behind the recent killing, too. He's protecting his position as the man behind the Lucarelli throne. He's eliminating the only people who can threaten him."

"Conspiracy to commit murder," Markham said. "Yes, that's definitely sufficient grounds to go after him. Do you think Keane can give us anyone else?"

"Hard to say," Erin said.

"All right," Markham said. "I'll have my office draw up some preliminary documents. Don't worry, we won't be offering him the keys to the city, nor even to his jail cell. But I'm sure we can come up with something he'll want. Beggars can't be choosers, after all. We can at least get him out of Riker's. Is there anything else I can help you with?"

"That should just about do it, sir," Webb said, standing up. "Thank you for your time."

"Certainly," Markham said. He got to his feet once more and offered another handshake.

The insistent buzz of a vibrating cell phone interrupted him. Webb reached into his coat pocket and took it out.

"Excuse me, sir," he said, thumbing the screen. "Webb. Hello, Lieutenant. We're at City Hall, in a meeting with the DA. He said—wait, what? When?"

Webb's hand tightened on the phone so hard that Erin saw the flesh under his fingernails turn pale. "We're on our way," he said. "But we're forty minutes out. What? Yes, of course. We can do that."

He shoved the phone back into his pocket. "Follow me," he said to the detectives. Then he turned and jogged out of Markham's office. Erin and Vic shared a worried look and went after him.

"Sorry to run, Mr. Markham," Erin said over her shoulder.

"When duty calls, you answer," Markham replied. "Good luck, Detectives."

They caught up with Webb at the elevators. Rolf was prancing with excitement. He'd picked up the sudden change in Webb's energy and wanted in on whatever was happening.

"Where are we going, sir?" Erin asked.

"Pier Six," Webb said.

"Did they find a body in the river?" she guessed.

The elevator arrived. Webb hurried in and punched the button for the lobby. "No," he said. "We're headed for Riker's Island."

"But that's the opposite direction," she protested.

"Erin, Pier Six is the closest helipad," Vic said. "Apparently our lieutenant is in too much of a hurry to drive."

"Oh," Erin said, feeling foolish. She hadn't had much occasion to ride in helicopters. The last one had been in a blizzard the previous winter and hadn't left her eager to do it again. "What's the big rush?" she asked.

"That was Lieutenant McDowell," Webb said grimly. "She's at Riker's. Something went wrong, some sort of slip. The guard got pulled off Keane's room."

"Oh, shit," Erin said quietly. "Do you mean—"

"McDowell isn't given to hyperbole," Webb said. "So when she said his room is, and I quote, 'a bloodbath,' I think we need to take it more or less literally."

"Looks like we won't be needing that deal from the District Attorney after all," Vic said.

"Is Keane dead?" Erin asked.

"Sounds like it," Webb said. "We'll know more when we get there."

"A bloodbath," Vic repeated. "Are we talking an actual bathtub full of blood? Because there was this one lady who bathed in blood back in the Middle Ages. She thought it'd keep her young. It didn't work."

"Of course it didn't work," Erin said.

"Neshenko, shut up," Webb said. "This is serious."

"I blew that asshole's kneecap off a few days ago," Vic reminded him. "Am I supposed to pretend to be sad someone else finished the job? I should've shot him in his smarmy little weasel face and saved us all a lot of trouble."

"Murder is murder," Webb replied. "And we needed Keane."

"I hope like hell that's not true," Vic said. "Unless you know a good medium who can throw us a séance, we're shit out of luck."

*   *   *

"If you guys are gonna keep coming back, you might as well commit a crime," the gate guard commented. "Then you can stay here overnight. Free of charge."

"Very funny," Vic said. "Asshole," he added under his breath as they hurriedly handed over their guns and got buzzed through into Riker's Island.

"I assume Keane's where we left him?" Erin asked.

"As far as I know," Webb said.

The atmosphere of the prison felt different this time. It was like a hot, muggy, late-summer day just before the dark clouds rolled in. The air had a tense, heavy quality. A storm was just over the horizon and everyone could feel it, guards and prisoners alike. The Corrections Officers they met along the way all had the same fixed, nervous look in their eyes. The guards had broken out the riot gear. The detectives passed half a dozen men fully armored up, shields and batons ready.

"I don't like not being armed," Vic muttered.

"Why not?" Erin replied. "We put seven guys in the hospital and didn't need guns to do it."

"It's fine for you to talk," he said. "You've got Toothy McFang over there to cover your ass."

Rolf, trotting at Erin's side, ignored Vic.

A pale-faced, freckly guard directed them past the infirmary. Erin already knew where they were going, but the COs didn't want anyone wandering around unescorted.

"Where are the inmates?" Webb asked the guard.

"Full lockdown," the guard answered. He swallowed. "It's pretty bad, sir."

"I guarantee, we've seen worse," Vic said.

The CO gulped again. "If you say so."

The Warden himself was standing outside the closet they'd converted into Keane's private room. He was talking to Lieutenant McDowell, who was taking notes on an old-fashioned notebook like the one Erin had given Keane. The door was closed.

"Warden," Webb said. "Lieutenant."

"Lieutenant," McDowell replied. "The Warden was just explaining to me how he can't explain how this could have happened."

"What *did* happen?" Webb asked. "You said Keane had been attacked. You implied he didn't make it. That's all we know."

"Now that you're here, you'd better take a look," McDowell said grimly.

"The room's been sealed," the Warden said.

"Of course," Webb said. He took a pair of disposable gloves out of his trench coat's pocket. "It's an active crime scene. Open it up."

"Do you have a suspect in custody?" Erin asked.

"No," the Warden said.

"What the hell!" Vic said in tones of absolute disgust. "Can't you guys do *anything* right? Everyone's locked up in here together. You've got cameras all over the place. How hard could it be to find one perp?"

"There's nobody left to arrest," the Warden said quietly. Erin found it odd that he hadn't taken offense at Vic's tone, which had been intended to offend. Then she saw the look in his eyes and realized just how shaken the man was.

"Holy God," Webb said as the door swung open, and from the sound of his voice it might have been a prayer, a curse, or maybe a bit of both.

The longer Erin spent around Rolf, the more attention she paid to her own nose. Dogs lived by their sense of smell. Spend enough time with them and you picked up on a little of it. The thick, metallic reek of fresh blood filled her nostrils. It wasn't an inherently bad smell, but once you knew what it meant, it brought a swell of unpleasant memories in on a nauseating tide.

"Jesus Crucified Christ in a wheelchair," Vic said.

Erin just stood in the doorway and stared. This wasn't a closet anymore. It wasn't even a makeshift hospital room. It was a slaughterhouse. Blood and contorted bodies were everywhere she looked.

"How many dead?" Webb asked quietly.

"Five," McDowell said. "Counting Keane, of course."

"Who killed them?"

"As far as I can see, Keane did. They came for him and he was ready. They got him, but he didn't go down easy."

"I don't believe it," Vic said. "He was handcuffed to his bed! One of his knees was missing. He had tubes coming out of him, for Christ's sake! Where... oh shit, I found his IV tube. Damn, I've never seen that before."

"Neither have I," Webb said. "You know what they say: anything's a weapon if you're desperate."

"He ripped out his own IV line," Vic said in tones of dazed professional admiration. "Then he shoved it into that sucker's *eye!* Straight into the brain. Bam, done."

Erin retreated into the detachment of a veteran law-enforcement officer. She forced down the rising bile and made herself think of the scene as a logic problem to be solved. She didn't dare step far into the room, since it would be difficult to avoid walking through blood and contaminating the scene, but she could see plenty from the doorway.

"Looks like they came at him with improvised weapons," she said. "Four inmates. He blocked one with his forearm."

"Classic defensive wound," Webb agreed, looking at Keane. "He used his shackled arm. He must've disarmed his attacker with the other hand and turned the shiv around."

"I'm guessing that was the first guy," Erin said, pointing to a man who'd fallen next to the bed. He'd left a blood trail as he'd dragged himself toward the door, but hadn't quite made it outside. It was hard to get far with a sharpened piece of rebar in the throat.

"He shouldn't have yanked that out of his neck," Vic said. "If he'd left it in, he might not have bled out. Looks like Keane got him right in the jugular."

"The other three all jumped him at once," Erin said. "I think that's when he started using his IV."

"Those two have multiple piercing wounds," Webb confirmed. "Very small ones. They didn't rip the fabric on their jumpsuits, but I can see bloodstains that soaked through. But they did some damage, too."

"Keane's all torn to pieces," Vic said. "He died hard. I gotta say, I'm impressed. Who would've thought the little weasel had that much fight in him?"

"Weasels are vicious animals," Erin said. "Haven't you ever watched a nature show? They'll take on wolves and bobcats."

"Do we have IDs on any of the other four?" Webb asked.

"The Warden's going to get them for us," McDowell said. "It shouldn't take long. They're doing a roll call right now, seeing who's unaccounted for."

"I know one of them," Erin said, pointing. "See that brace on his arm? And the swollen nose?"

"Shit," Vic said. "That's Squeaky Santino! How'd he get out of Solitary?"

"I'm more interested in how he got past a guarded door with three of his friends," Webb said. He turned to the Warden. "Who was posted at this door?"

"Jimmy Rose," the Warden said.

"I assume he's in custody?" McDowell said.

"He's being questioned," the Warden said.

"And he'll be questioned again," Webb said. "By us. Where is he?"

"In a holding cell, separate from GenPop."

"Don't let him talk to anyone," Webb said.

"You're giving orders here?" the Warden shot back. His face had gone red.

"Yes," Webb said calmly. "On matters pertaining to the multiple recent homicides that have occurred in this prison under your watch, I am. If you have a problem with that, you can take it up with Captain Holliday, Precinct Eight."

"I just might go over his head," the Warden said.

"By all means," Webb said. "Talk to the Chief of Police. Or the Commissioner. The answer you get will be the same."

Erin was watching McDowell as Webb was speaking. The other woman nodded ever so slightly.

"I'll see to Mr. Rose's situation," the Warden said. "If you'll excuse me."

He walked stiffly away.

"I think you hurt his feelings," Vic said after the Warden was out of earshot.

"We have five fresh bodies," Webb said. "One man's feelings are low on my list of priorities."

"We also have at least two dirty guards," McDowell said. "I've looked into the Warden's finances and personal background. I didn't see any evidence he's been compromised, but we can't assume otherwise."

"Then we shouldn't let him talk to that guard," Erin said. "Not without one of us."

"An excellent point," McDowell said. "I'll keep an eye on him. Do you have this situation in hand, Lieutenant?"

"Yes," Webb said.

"Good," McDowell said as she headed after the Warden. "Because I'd hate to find more bodies when I come back."

Chapter 17

"I don't believe it," Vic said. He, Erin, Webb, and Rolf were loitering outside the crime scene, waiting for Levine and the CSU team to come work their magic.

"Which part?" Erin asked. "The part where Keane's dead, or the part where he took down four mobsters when he was practically unarmed?"

"All of it," he said. "Mostly I'm just pissed. The whole thing was a goddamn waste. Why'd that bastard have to go and die on us?"

"A little while ago, you were wishing you'd wasted Keane yourself," she reminded him. "At least make up your mind what you're going to bitch about. Pick a side."

"I really could use a cigarette," Webb said.

"Ask one of the inmates," Vic suggested. "Someone's gotta have a pack of black-market smokes."

"Jailhouse tobacco?" Webb shuddered. "I'm not quite *that* addicted."

"I guess we'll never know what Keane's big secret was," Vic sighed. "If all the guys who came after him are dead, we can't trace the hit back to the source. And Keane sure as shit can't tell us anything. Figures he'd give us one last middle finger on his way out. What a son of a bitch."

Erin's head snapped up. "Say that again," she said.

"What a son of a bitch," Vic repeated, laying contempt on every syllable.

"No," she said. "The part about how Keane can't tell us anything."

"Well, he can't," Vic said. "I don't know if you noticed, but he got stabbed. It's kinda hard to talk with half a dozen holes in your lungs, even if you're not dead. Which he is."

"What are you thinking, O'Reilly?" Webb asked.

Erin turned to the door. "I'm thinking about what I gave Keane," she said.

"Careful," Webb said. "Don't touch anything if you can help it."

She nodded and opened the door. "*Bleib*," she told Rolf, who obediently hunkered down to wait for her to come back.

It was like the kids' game where you pretended the floor was lava. Erin stepped gingerly from one bare bit of concrete to the next, moving on tiptoes, keeping her shoes out of the spattered blood. She kept her breathing slow and even, ignoring the sights and smells, making her way toward the bedside.

It took a minute and a half of careful going, but she ended up looking down at Keane. Vic had been right about one thing; it had all been such a damned waste.

"People *died* because of you," she murmured. "And for what? Look at you now."

Being a detective felt awfully futile sometimes. You didn't usually get the chance to stop the bad guys before they committed a crime. Your job was to sift through the wreckage they left behind, in the hope you could give the victims something approximating justice. But one of the harshest lessons twelve years on the street had taught Erin was that justice was an illusion. There just wasn't anything you could do to the worst monsters that could come close to what they'd done to others; not without losing your own soul.

"Did you have anything left in you?" she asked the dead man. "Give me something, you miserable son of a bitch."

Keane, of course, didn't answer.

"Hey Erin," Vic called from the doorway. "Ask him if it's hot enough where he is now. The bastard got a one-way express ticket to Hell."

She didn't answer, concentrating on her surroundings. There was Keane, murdered as savagely as anyone she'd ever seen. There was his first attacker, stabbed in the throat with his own weapon.

"Wait a second," she said. "That wasn't the first."

"How do you know?" Webb asked. He'd joined Vic in the doorway and was watching her.

Erin was looking at another body. "Keane killed this one first," she said.

"I repeat," Webb said. "How do you know?"

She pointed to the dead man's head. "You can't see it from where you're standing," she said. "But this man's got a ballpoint pen sticking out of his left ear."

"Keane killed him with a *pen?*" Vic exclaimed. "That's outstanding! Damn it, why do I have to start liking the guy now?"

"You're missing the point, Neshenko," Webb said.

"The point?" Vic echoed, snickering. "Good one."

Webb rolled his eyes. "What O'Reilly finds significant is that he was holding a pen when they attacked him," he said. "Which means he was probably in the process of writing something down."

"Exactly, sir," Erin said. She didn't see her notebook on Keane's bed. The sheets were soaked with blood, but she ought to be able to see it. She bent down and looked under the bed. Nothing.

"It has to be here somewhere," she muttered. She straightened and let her eyes wander around the room. Keane was cuffed to the bed. He couldn't have gone anywhere, and wouldn't have had time in any case.

"It was his insurance policy," she said. "His leverage. He wouldn't have kept it on his person."

The linen closet's walls were lined with shelves. On those shelves were folded bedsheets and blankets. And one of the piles looked a little disarrayed.

She was still wearing her disposable rubber gloves. She leaned over the bed, careful not to touch Keane's body, and slipped her hand under the folded blankets. Her fingertips found the little notebook.

"Bingo," she breathed, drawing it out and looking at it. There wasn't a spot of blood on it; Keane must have shoved it out of sight before the fight really got going.

"Success?" Webb asked.

She nodded. She flipped open the cover. Page after page was filled with neat block printing. Keane's handwriting had been impeccable, practically as good as a word processor. Somehow, that didn't surprise her.

Erin slowly retraced her steps, leaving the rest of the scene undisturbed. By the time she got to the door, Vic had an evidence bag open and waiting. She dropped the book in and he sealed it. Even though all of them knew they'd crack it open again the moment they got it back to the Eightball, it was important to follow procedure. Lieutenant McDowell would be looking to pounce on any mistake, and chain of custody was vital.

"I need to follow up on McDowell's interviews," Webb said. "Neshenko, can I leave you in charge here?"

"I'm honored by your trust, sir," Vic said.

"Good. O'Reilly, have CSU log this as soon as they get here. Then take it back to the Eightball and check it into Evidence. As soon as you've done that, check it out again and see what Keane was writing. Let's hope it was something useful, and not the next great American novel."

* * *

There were lots of ways to measure time. Clocks were only the most obvious, and not always the most applicable to the human experience. Lieutenant Webb used cigarettes. Recovering alcoholics and addicts tended to think in terms of clean days. Heartbeats, song tracks, relationships, seasons—all were valid.

At the moment, Erin was using coffee. From when she poured a fresh cup from the machine in the Major Crimes break room to the last sip took between fifteen and twenty minutes. By the time she got to the end of Keane's final statement, seven cups had elapsed. Her schedule had also included three trips to the restroom, for obvious reasons.

She pushed her chair back from her desk, tilted the backrest so she was staring at the ceiling, and rubbed her eyes.

"Jesus," she said to no one in particular.

Rolf, misinterpreting her motion, bounced to his paws and started wagging his tail. He loved Erin. She was the best human and the best K-9 handler in the entire world, according to reliable authorities in his own head. But in some cloudy part of his brain, the Shepherd recalled riding around in their Patrol car, pounding pavement in Queens. There'd been more street work, more chases, more biting in the good old days. He didn't understand why they were spending so much time in the office now.

"In a minute, kiddo," Erin told him.

Her tone more than her words connected with Rolf. He sank back to his blanket, gave her a deeply mournful look, and heaved a heartbreaking sigh. Rolf's preferred time measurement was in walks.

"I need to type this up," she said. "Then we'll go for a walk. I promise."

His tail thumped with sullen hope.

Erin lifted her coffee cup to her lips and found only dregs. "Damn," she said. "First, more coffee. I don't know who needs more of an apology, kiddo; you or my kidneys."

She came out of the break room, yet another steaming cup in hand, and found herself face to face with Lieutenant McDowell.

"Sir?" she said.

"Surprised, O'Reilly?" McDowell asked.

"A little," Erin admitted. "I thought you were still up at Riker's, interviewing guards."

"Jimmy Rose is a dead end," McDowell said. "The only thing he's guilty of is bad judgment. He got a radio call to assist another CO. He ran off and found out it was fake. To his credit, he immediately sounded the alarm, but it was already too late."

"One of the hit squad got their hands on a radio tuned to the COs' frequency," Erin guessed.

"My thoughts exactly," McDowell said. "Impossible to say who, of course. Rose should have double-checked the order, or called for relief before leaving Keane's door unguarded, but the call was urgent and the door was locked. The caller claimed he'd had an accident and was injured. Rose panicked."

"What's going to happen to him?" Erin asked.

"That's none of our concern," McDowell said. "Discipline of Corrections Officers doesn't fall under my jurisdiction, even when the Job takes me to Riker's."

"Why *were* you at Riker's Island, Lieutenant?" Erin asked suddenly.

"I was interviewing guards, trying to determine which ones were compromised," McDowell said. "As you know perfectly well."

"But you were there before the attack happened," Erin said.

"That's correct," McDowell said. "I was examining Thorpe, Purvis, and Accardi to try to ascertain culpability in the earlier attack in the infirmary. Accardi is the guilty party in that incident, by the way."

"On what evidence?"

"He has a cousin incarcerated at Otisville," McDowell said. "The cousin got sent up on a narcotics charge a few months ago. The Lucarellis have a strong presence in that prison."

"I know," Erin said. "That's where Icepick Aiello killed Vittorio Acerbo."

"Precisely. Aiello approached Accardi with a proposition. It was your typical carrot-and-stick offer."

"Let me guess," Erin said. "A pile of money if he turned off the security cameras in the infirmary at a particular time and made sure no guards were around. If he refused, his beloved cousin would get his arms broken in the exercise yard."

"That's very nearly exactly what was offered," McDowell said. "Accardi claims he was coerced. He didn't mention money at first, but when I reminded him we'd have a warrant to search his home, his vehicle, and his financial records, he suddenly remembered five thousand dollars."

"That's an easy thing to forget," Erin said with a poker face. "How did you get him to talk?"

"I told him Aiello had already ratted him out in exchange for leniency. It was a lie, of course."

"Obviously," Erin said. "Aiello is old-school Sicilian Mafia. He'd never squeal on an accomplice."

McDowell was watching her closely. "You were sounding me out," the Lieutenant said. "You thought my presence at the prison was suspicious enough to double-check."

"Is that so surprising, sir?" Erin retorted. "I just tiptoed around our last IAB Lieutenant's blood. He was as dirty as they come. Maybe I'm not as trusting as I used to be. If you're mad about that, I'm not about to apologize for it."

"Mad? I'm impressed. You know I'm in a position to do you a great deal of good—or a great deal of harm. I could hit you with exactly the same carrot-and-stick approach that worked so well on that corrupt bastard Accardi. I even told you I'm the one who will decide whether your unit survives. But you didn't let that stand in the way of your job, even knowing it might make me angry."

"With all respect, sir, I spent several months working with the Irish Mob," Erin said. "I saw what happened when those guys got mad. I'm used to dealing with much more dangerous people than you."

McDowell nodded. "Excellent," she said. "Now, Lieutenant Webb tells me you have a booklet containing a message from Keane."

"Properly logged as evidence," Erin said.

"I'm sure it is. What does it say?"

"It's mostly numbers."

"What sort of numbers?"

"Respectfully, sir, I'd prefer either Lieutenant Webb or Captain Holliday to be present before I discuss this further."

McDowell's mouth twisted slightly. "You still don't trust me?"

"I may never completely trust you, Lieutenant," Erin said bluntly.

"And yet you still aren't interested in working for Internal Affairs."

"Not a chance, sir."

"I won't tell you how to address your own career. But by all means, let's see if the Captain is in."

Captain Holliday had only recently returned from a few days off. This wasn't by choice; Holliday didn't take many vacations. But he'd gotten tagged in the arm during the shootout in Major Crimes that had landed Keane and Johns in the prison infirmary, and he'd put a couple of bullets in the dirty cops, so he'd been briefly sidelined. However, now he was back in his office, his wounded arm hidden under his NYPD jacket.

"Excuse us, Captain," McDowell said. "Detective O'Reilly has some sensitive information to share, and she feels that in the current climate of mutual distrust, your oversight would be appreciated."

Holliday raised his eyebrows. His mustache twitched, possibly concealing a thin smile. "I'd be happy to assist," he said. "Do you need me to step out of the office?"

"That won't be necessary, sir," Erin said. She laid her notebook on Holliday's desk.

"What's this?" he asked.

"Bank accounts, mostly," she said. "Tied to shell companies."

"And what are the companies fronting?" Holliday asked.

"I'm not entirely sure yet," she said.

"Why are they relevant?" McDowell asked.

"Because Keane says they're where Valentino Vitelli keeps his money. And he says the accounts connect to Kingston Schultz's real estate empire."

"How do they connect?" Holliday asked.

Erin hesitated, unsure what to say.

"That's a job for our forensic accountants," McDowell said, coming unexpectedly to Erin's rescue. "I recommend we get the ball rolling on this ASAP."

"Agreed," Holliday said. "I'll expect a full report at your earliest convenience, O'Reilly. Shall we say, 0900 tomorrow morning?"

"Yes, sir," Erin said, managing not to sigh. Those two words committed her to several hours of back-and-forth with the Eightball's accountants, followed by more hours of typing. Rolf would still get his walk, but she'd have to dive right back in as soon as it was over. She'd have to call Carlyle. She wouldn't be home for supper, and possibly not breakfast, either.

Chapter 18

Vic, Webb, and Piekarski turned up as the afternoon wore on. Erin was especially glad to see Vic and Piekarski. Vic brought Chinese takeout with him for a late lunch, and Piekarski brought Mina. All work momentarily halted as everyone cooed over the baby. Even McDowell admitted Mina was adorable. Piekarski set up a portable playpen right in the middle of Major Crimes.

Rolf immediately appointed himself Mina's babysitter. He sat just outside the pen, rested his chin on the railing, and stared steadily at the baby for the next two solid hours. He didn't waver and hardly even blinked. The only thing that finally broke the spell was when Piekarski scooped Mina up to change her diaper.

"Looks like Rolf has his retirement all planned out," Vic said with a grin. "He's just waiting for you to pop out one of your own."

"Don't you start," Erin said. "I get enough of that from my mom."

A steady stream of uniformed officers filtered through Major Crimes, ostensibly with minor business for the Captain, but really to hang out with the baby. At last, Holliday had to intervene.

"I swear, the rookies get younger every Academy class," he said, kneeling down and examining Mina.

The infant reached up and batted at Holliday's mustache. She smiled and gurgled happily.

"She's very sweet," the Captain said. "But I think she may be disrupting the precinct workflow."

"We need Zofia," Vic said. "And the City doesn't pay us enough for daycare."

"I'm not in charge of the Departmental budget," Holliday said.

"Neshenko is right, sir," Webb said. "Officer Piekarski is good with numbers. We're deep in the financial weeds right now and she's as good at accounting as my two detectives put together."

"Hey!" Vic said indignantly.

"What grades did you make in Accounting class?" Webb replied.

"I didn't take any Accounting classes," Vic said.

"Your highest level of math, then."

"B-minus."

"Piekarski? How about you?"

"I took Introductory Accounting," Piekarski said. "I got an A."

"O'Reilly?" Webb asked.

Erin shook her head. "B-plus in Statistics was as far as I got."

"I rest my case," Webb said.

"All right," Holliday said. "But no more rubberneckers. The only people on the second floor, starting now, are those with genuine reasons to be here."

Mina succeeded in twining her fingers in the tip of Holliday's mustache.

"And you, of course," he added, gently disentangling himself.

A couple of forensic accountants were working alongside the Major Crimes squad. The whole thing did feel depressingly like a boring school assignment, and Vic said so.

"You'd prefer to be out there getting shot at instead of sitting in this nice, safe office?" Erin asked.

"You got shot in this nice, safe office, as you call it, less than two weeks ago," Vic said.

"You know what I mean."

"I can see the bullet holes from here."

"That happened *once*."

"Most people only get shot at once," Webb said. "Especially if the shots don't miss."

"I guess we're just lucky that way," Erin said.

Piekarski ordered pizza for their supper. They ate at their desks and kept grinding. Erin didn't feel like they were getting anywhere, but the accountants were excited, so that was cause for optimism. Piekarski scribbled notes on the whiteboard. McDowell had set up her laptop at a spare desk and contributed her bureaucratic expertise.

In addition to the financial information, Keane had provided a list of names and a few sidenotes. These were police officers; some assigned to the Eightball, some elsewhere in New York. McDowell grabbed the list with as much enthusiasm as Rolf gave to his bite sleeve. However, as the Lieutenant noted, the word of a criminal wasn't enough to go on. She was opening files on every single named officer and beginning what promised to be a sprawling, long-running Internal Affairs investigation.

A little before eight, Mina started getting fussy and Piekarski bundled her up. She kissed Vic on the cheek, wished him a good night, and left. Vic became noticeably grumpier.

Rolf, bereft of the small, fascinating human, curled up and went to sleep.

As the hours dragged by, Erin tried not to think about Carlyle. He'd be at the Barley Corner, relaxing in the warm, cozy pub. There'd be a soccer game on the big-screen TV. Marian would have whipped up shepherd's pie, or maybe her famous Irish stew. Erin could be there right now, enjoying a pint of Guinness, but instead she was stuck investigating shady dealings in a shabby office.

"Is it enough for a warrant?" she asked Webb around eleven.

"It will be," he said. "Especially if we take it to Judge Ferris."

"Ferris would issue a warrant for a ham sandwich if we asked him to," Vic said. As McDowell looked up from her computer, he hastily added, "Assuming the sandwich had committed multiple felonies, that is."

"The reason he's so reliable is that we've never gone to him with bad or frivolous requests," Webb said. "Let's keep it that way. There's no point bothering him at home. I know he stays up late, but even if we get through all this before midnight—"

"Midnight tomorrow, maybe," Vic interjected gloomily.

"—the banks won't be open," Webb finished. "Anyway, we want as clean a sweep as possible. The better we build the case now, the more airtight it'll be when Schultz challenges it in court. Which he will, I guarantee. That man knows the legal system better than anyone in this room."

"You say that like it's something to be proud of," Vic said.

"If you're fighting battles, it pays to understand the weapons at your disposal," Webb said.

By midnight the accounting squad had tied most of the bank accounts to Valentino Vitelli, and agreed they had enough to freeze the assets while pursuing further action. Some of the other accounts were tied to Alfredo Madonna's real estate holdings.

"That means Schultz," Erin said triumphantly. "Alfie's never done a thing with those. And while he's been in prison Schultz administers them. We've got him."

"Why is this so important to you?" Vic asked. "I thought you liked the guy."

"I do," she admitted. "But he's breaking the law. He's manipulating people into doing what he wants without ever getting his own hands dirty. He's having people killed. It doesn't matter how charming he is, he's still a snake. And he's going down."

"He took Vinnie the Oil Man off our hands," Vic said.

"By having him murdered in a courtroom! He had Alfie do it. Alfie rots in prison, Schultz pulls in the profits from his inheritance, and the worst part is, Alfie still thinks Schultz is his friend! He's betraying everyone around him and they don't even realize it!"

The phone on Webb's desk rang. He picked it up and listened for a moment.

"Thank you, Sergeant," he said. "I'll send someone down."

"What's going on?" Erin asked after he hung up.

"We have a visitor," Webb said. "At the front desk. Sergeant Malcolm says there is, and I quote, 'a polite Italian gentleman' asking to talk to either you or Neshenko. Preferably you."

"I'll go," Erin and Vic said in perfect unison. Rolf raised his head, thumped his tail, and would have said the same if he'd been able to talk.

"Go on, then," Webb said. "You both look like you could use the break."

Rolf was already on his feet. He'd grabbed his leash and was holding it in his mouth, head cocked, ears at full attention.

* * *

Despite their enthusiasm, Erin and Vic were cautious as they headed downstairs. An Italian asking for them was almost certainly connected to the case, but they didn't know how. He might be an ally, an enemy, or something else entirely. He'd have to be crazy to start something in the Eightball's lobby, but they'd dealt with crazy people before.

They found a gaunt, gray-mustached man clad in somber black. Erin's eyes went to his hands first. Hands were the things that would hurt you. But his held only a black hat that matched his old-style suit. His face was grim, but she didn't think he was dangerous; at least, not to her and Vic.

"Mr. Santino," she said.

"Miss O'Reilly," Giovanni Santino said, and bowing slightly in a gesture of old-world respect that reminded her of Carlyle. "And Mr. Neshenko. Thank you for making time."

"Of course," Erin said. "What can I do for you, sir?" She offered her hand, which he gravely clasped, setting his hat on the desk.

He sheathed her hand in both of his own, bowing his head as he did so. His eyes were dark and hollow.

"You know about my boy," he said.

"Yes," she said, belatedly realizing he was dressed in mourning. "I'm so sorry for your loss."

"Thank you," he said. "Is there a place we can speak privately?"

"One of the interrogation rooms ought to be available," Vic said.

Erin shot him a look. "Follow me, sir," she said to Santino. "And don't pay any attention to my partner. It's been a long day for all of us."

She led the way back upstairs to the break room and closed the door behind them. "Can I offer you some coffee?" she asked.

"Thank you," Santino said. His fingers worked their way around the rim of his hat, dancing awkwardly.

Erin handed him a cup, which he took in one hand, keeping his hat in the other. Vic glowered. Rolf watched Erin, taking his lead from her.

"I don't do this," Santino said.

"Do what, sir?" Erin asked.

"Talk to cops."

Erin nodded and waited. It was best not to push when a man like Giovanni Santino came in voluntarily.

"I mean, it's not like this is the first time I've been in a police station or nothing," Santino added after a moment.

"I guess not," Erin said.

Santino's gaunt, grim face cracked into a wry smile. He chuckled dryly. So did Erin. Even Vic snickered.

"I wanted to thank you," the mobster said, the smile sliding off his face again. "For trying to tell me. About my boy. I should've listened, should've done something."

"I'm sorry," she said again. "I didn't know he was going to go after Keane, or I swear we would've done something."

"Who did it?" Santino asked.

"I don't understand," she said.

"Who killed Michael?"

"Keane did. He stabbed him."

"I know that." All traces of good humor were gone from Santino's face. "Who put them in the same room?"

Erin said nothing.

"You can't seriously think we're gonna tell you that," Vic said.

Santino pivoted to face the big Russian. "Why not?"

"Because we're already scooping bodies off the street," Vic said. "The last thing we need is you gunning for some other mope because you're blaming him for your kid getting offed, and piling up a few more. I'm sorry about your son, seriously. I'm a dad myself, so I feel for you. But this is our job. We'll handle it. Oh, and the NYPD doesn't comment regarding ongoing investigations."

"Thanks for that, Vic," Erin said. "Could you give us the room for a minute?"

"What for?"

"Just do it, please."

Vic went off in what she'd call a sulk, but he would insist was brooding. Russians didn't sulk.

"Sorry about that," she said to Santino. "Vic isn't a real sensitive guy."

"Forget about it," Santino said in the finest New York style. "Look, if it's a question of making it worth everyone's while, that won't be a problem."

"I can't take money," she said, holding up a hand. "And unfortunately, Vic's right. I can't give you a name, because I know what you'd do with it."

"You're protecting this guy?" Santino demanded.

"I'm planning on throwing his ass in jail," she retorted. "That's my job, like Vic said."

"When someone kills a Sicilian's son, that Sicilian don't rest while that bastard's breathing," Santino said.

"Mr. Santino," she said. "I know. And I'm truly sorry. If there's anything else I can do to help you, I'll try. But I can't do this."

"You know, I heard something," Santino said abruptly. "On the street. You know Richie O'Malley?"

"We've met," Erin said guardedly. "What about him?"

"He's been asking about you and Cars Carlyle. And he's been hiring."

"Hiring who?"

"Muscle."

"Why?" But even as she asked it, she remembered seeing Richard O'Malley in the Barley Corner, walking into a room full of cops and gangsters just to let her know he hadn't forgotten her.

"Why do you think?" Santino shot back. "We Sicilians may have invented *vendetta*, but you Irish are quick learners. Maybe you don't believe in street justice, but the street don't care what you believe. You and me, we could help one another."

"What are you suggesting?" she asked, suddenly wishing she'd turned on her recording wire.

"If you help me honor my boy's memory, I could maybe help you out with your little O'Malley problem."

Months of undercover experience helped Erin keep a poker face. "I appreciate the offer," she said carefully. "But even if I could say yes, we don't have any firm proof yet."

"Your people need proof," Santino said quietly. "Mine don't."

"But you'd want to be sure you got the right guy," she said.

"You give me your word he's the right one, that's good enough for me. Then you won't have nothing to worry about. Might save your Department some time and money. Good for the taxpayers, good for the mayor, good for the City. Everybody wins."

Everybody except the guy you'd be killing, Erin thought. "I need a little more time," she said.

"I understand," Santino said. "Keep in touch. You know where to find me. And I apologize for barging in like this, distracting you from your work. I know you're a busy woman, so I'll get out of your way now. Thanks again for the coffee."

He put down the cup and offered his hand, which she shook. Then he left, walking past a bemused Vic.

"Well?" Vic asked once he'd watched Santino to make sure the mobster had gone down to the lobby. "What'd our *paisano* want to talk about?"

"Oh, the usual," Erin said, pouring herself a fresh cup of coffee. "Veiled threats, bribe offers, that sort of thing. He offered to kill Richard O'Malley for me."

"He *what?*" Vic was already starting for the stairs. "I'm gonna arrest that son of a bitch right now, before he gets streetside!"

"Forget about it," she said, grabbing his arm. "We'd never make it stick. Even if I'd had a recording, he didn't come out and say it. Everything was implied. You know how these guys talk."

"Yeah," Vic grunted.

"You don't even like Richie," she said. "When he crashed my engagement party, you were ready to beat the shit out of him right there."

"That's different." But Vic relaxed slightly. "What's the O'Malley brat got to do with this?"

"Nothing. It was an exchange."

"Oh, I get it. You give him Schultz, he takes Richie out for you."

"Exactly."

"And you weren't tempted?"

"Vic!"

He grinned. "I had to ask."

"No you didn't. I had plenty of opportunities for crap like that when I was working the O'Malleys. I never did any of it. You know that."

"Do we have to put some eyes on Santino?"

Erin shook her head. "Let's put a note in his file," she said. "If he knew who to go after, he wouldn't have come here. He'd be out on the street, posting a contract if he didn't take care of it himself."

"I heard once that an eye for an eye makes the whole world blind," Vic said. "How come I've never met any one-eyed mobsters? They're really into that shit. It's kinda amazing any of them are still alive, when you think about it."

"Are you done fraternizing with the enemy, O'Reilly?" Webb called from his desk.

"Yes, sir," Erin said. "Unless you're talking about Vic."

"Did you learn anything pertinent to our investigation?"

"No, sir. Mr. Santino didn't know anything."

"Then I'd suggest we get back to work. We want those warrants airtight by morning."

Chapter 19

"You know that nasty feeling in your mouth when you go to bed without brushing your teeth?" Vic said. "How come that only happens if you've been asleep? If you've been up all night, you feel fine."

"I don't feel fine," Webb said. "I feel like I've been run over by a cement truck. I'm too old to keep these hours."

"You could've gone home and let us do the work," Erin said. She rubbed her eyes. "Hell, *I'm* too old for this and you're old enough to be my dad."

"A good leader sets a good example," Webb said. "Or so I've heard. Maybe I should go home and get some sleep. What time is it?"

"Just about nine o'clock," Vic said. "You can't crap out on us now, sir. The workday is just getting started. You'll never make it to quitting time with that kind of attitude."

"Ugh," Erin said. "Have we really been on the clock twenty-four hours?"

"Looks like it," Vic said. "But on the bright side, we're done. You still with us, Big Sister?"

"That's affirmative," McDowell said. Her eyes were, if anything, harder and brighter than they'd been the night before. Otherwise, she appeared exactly the same.

"Can I ask you something, Lieutenant?" Vic asked.

"Ask away," McDowell said.

"Neshenko…" Webb began.

Vic ignored his commanding officer. "Are all IAB Lieutenants vampires?" he asked. "Or just the ones who work here?"

"That depends," McDowell said.

"On what?"

"Your blood type."

There was a short silence. Then Vic grinned. "Good one," he said.

McDowell didn't laugh, didn't even crack a smile. But Erin caught a hint of sparkle in her eyes. She could hardly believe it. Maybe fatigue and caffeine were causing hallucinations.

"We're all set," Webb said. "O'Reilly, want to call Judge Ferris and get him to sign off on the warrants? Then we can go knock on Schultz's door."

"I love serving warrants on lawyers," Vic said. "I'll get my tactical gear."

"I don't think that'll be necessary, Neshenko," Webb said. "A polite approach will probably work best. In fact, while O'Reilly's on the phone, why don't you grab a shower and a shave? You have a change of clothes here, don't you?"

"Is that an order or a suggestion, sir?" Vic asked.

Webb wrinkled his nose. "It's a strongly-worded suggestion. We're all a little ripe, if you'll pardon the observation, Lieutenant."

"Far be it from me to disagree with an accurate assessment," McDowell said.

Erin dialed the courthouse and worked her way through the automated system. A woman answered the phone.

"Judge Ferris's chambers."

"Ms. Lockhart?" Erin guessed.

"Yes," Ferris's secretary said. "Who is this, please?"

"This is Detective O'Reilly, Major Crimes. I have some warrants for the Judge. Is he in yet?"

"I'm so sorry, Detective. Judge Ferris won't be in today. He's in Phoenix."

"Phoenix, Arizona?"

"That's right. His brother is in the hospital."

Erin hadn't known Ferris had a brother. "I'm sorry to hear that," she said. "Do you know when he'll be back?"

"I don't know. It's pretty serious, so he may be gone for a while. They've worked out a system here for divvying up Howard's paperwork while he's away. It's no trouble. Just fax or e-mail me the request and I'll get it taken care of for you. It shouldn't take more than an hour."

"Okay," Erin said. "Thanks. Please let me know when everything's ready." With a mob war brewing, the warrants were urgent enough, but not a desperate rush. An hour wouldn't make much difference, and it didn't seem like she had a choice.

"Of course," the secretary said. "I'll call you as soon as I can."

"An hour," Erin reported once she'd hung up the phone.

"Good enough," Webb said. He rubbed his chin. "I'll grab a shave myself."

"And a shower sounds good," Erin said. "What do you say, kiddo? Want a bath?"

Rolf flattened his ears and lowered his head. He most definitely did not want a bath.

Erin ruffled his fur. "I'm kidding," she said. "You'll be okay for now. But you're getting one before the end of the week."

K-9s tended to get pretty smelly, so they got bathed a lot more often than civilian dogs. Rolf was used to it, but that didn't mean he had to like it. Unconvinced of Erin's sincerity, he slunk after her, trailing a step behind instead of walking proudly at her hip.

* * *

Hot water and a change of clothes weren't as good as a night's sleep, but they'd be a hell of a lot better than nothing. With an hour to burn, Erin decided to go home instead of using the Eightball's showers.

The Barley Corner's breakfast crowd was thinning out when she and Rolf arrived. They slipped upstairs, Erin trying to move quietly so as not to wake Carlyle. Just because she'd been up all night didn't give her the right to kick him out of bed early. She undressed in the bathroom and hoped the running water wouldn't be too loud.

But Carlyle had lasted twenty years in an occupation whose members' life expectancy was more often measured in months. Awareness was more than a habit; it was hardwired survival instinct. When Erin got out of the shower, a towel wrapped around herself, she found the bed warm but empty. By the time she'd dressed and walked into the kitchen, Carlyle was making bacon and eggs on the stove and the coffee pot was bubbling. He'd somehow found time not only to start breakfast, but to get dressed. He was even wearing a tie.

"Sorry I woke you," she said.

"I'm glad of the chance to see you," he replied. "You'd like your eggs scrambled, aye?"

"You know me so well," she said, kissing his cheek. "Sorry I didn't get home last night, either. It was one of those days."

"I heard about the late, unlamented Mr. Keane's misfortune," Carlyle said. "It was all over the evening news. Have you solved it?"

"Pretty much."

"Coffee?"

Her stomach lurched. "No, thanks. I'm swimming in the stuff. Do we have any orange juice?"

"Certainly." He opened the fridge and took out a carton. "What's left to do?"

"Just mopping up, really. We know who was behind it."

"The lawyer?" Carlyle scooped eggs onto a plate and added two strips of bacon.

"Yeah. Schultz."

The toaster ejected a pair of browned slices of bread, which joined the rest of the meal. Carlyle laid the plate in front of her.

"I'd have fixed you the full Irish breakfast," he said. "But I hadn't time."

"Forget about it," she said, spreading butter on her toast. "That's way too many calories for me. You could've had something sent up from downstairs."

"I thought you'd appreciate the personal touch."

She smiled. "It'll be hard to pin Schultz down," she said. "I don't think we can hang the murders on him. Aiello's not talking and the other guys can't."

"Because they're no longer breathing?"

"Yeah."

"Who were they?"

"Squeaky Santino and some of his friends. Stiletto Stilicho, Freddy the Nose, and Buggy Mileno." The other IDs had come in the previous evening.

"Those lads sound a mite familiar."

"They should," Erin said. "It's a narcotics crew we busted together with SNEU a few months back. Lucarellis, of course."

"What happened?" he asked, sitting down opposite her with a cup of coffee in hand. Erin couldn't blame him; he hadn't spent the past ten-plus hours marinating in the stuff.

"A couple of criminal masterminds butted heads," she said between bites. "Schultz and Keane have been operating behind the scenes for a long time. Keane manipulated vulnerable people, particularly cops, by getting leverage on them. He built an empire right inside the NYPD. Working Internal Affairs gave him a unique position. He could choose who to bust and who might be useful. You know all that; we got him for killing Kira Jones after she got wise to him.

"Schultz is different. Like Keane, he'd rather not to get his own hands dirty. I don't think he's ever personally killed anyone. He has a softer touch. He's been quietly taking over the Lucarellis without actually holding a leadership position. He figures out what people want. Then he helps them, or pretends to. But he makes sure he benefits. Vinnie the Oil Man was in his way, so he helped his old family friend Alfie Madonna kill Vinnie. And he snapped up Alfie's inheritance while he was at it, acting like he was taking care of it for the kid. What difference did it make to Alfie? He was in prison, looking at ten to twenty years, minimum."

"I expect there's a pattern of behavior," Carlyle said. "Did he try to get the Madonna lad killed as well?"

Erin had been considering that. "I don't know," she admitted. "It doesn't make sense. Alfie's more use to him alive. If the kid dies, his property goes to his heir, whoever that is. If he doesn't have one, it goes to the state. Either way, Schultz loses out. No, I think that was something else, part of the Lucarelli civil war."

"But the Santino lad was involved in both hits," Carlyle observed.

"I forget how well-informed you are," she said with a wry smile. "I thought you were out of the Life."

"I am. But some of the old lads still come into the Corner. They talk and I listen."

"Squeaky was ambitious," Erin said. "I was hoping to get more out of him, but Keane shut him up for good. We're missing something there. But it doesn't matter right now. The main thing is, Schultz orchestrated the hits on Johns and Keane. We may not be able to charge him with those, but we can definitely get him on conspiracy and racketeering. The numbers guys are sure of it. Keane gave us everything we need to nail him. It's ironic, really."

"What is?"

Erin shook her head at the strangeness of it. "We were only able to bring Keane down because of another cop's dying testimony," she said. "I guess it gave Keane ideas. Do you know what the last thing he wrote was? After all the evidence?"

"I couldn't possibly say," Carlyle said.

"*Bill Ward was crazy,*" she recited. "*But he knew one thing: if you're going down, take as many of them with you as you can.*"

Carlyle nodded. "I'd say he succeeded. I hope if I'm ever backed into such a corner, I can give as good an account of myself."

"Not you, too!" Erin snapped. "The guy was an asshole. The fact that he wrecked a bunch of other assholes on his way out doesn't change that."

"Courage is always admirable," he replied. "Whatever its source. So you've taken Schultz into custody?"

Erin swallowed the last bite of her eggs. "Not yet," she said. "We're waiting on the warrants. That's why I came back here. I had a little time to kill."

He nodded again. "Your friend Judge Ferris?" he asked.

"I wish. We'd already have them in hand and Schultz would be in cuffs. Ferris had to skip town. Some health thing with his brother, out of state. But it doesn't matter. Whatever judge we get will sign off."

"Grand," Carlyle said. "I expect you'll sweep him up before lunchtime. Perhaps you can knock off early."

"I wish," she said again, ruefully. "You'd think a triple shift yesterday means I don't have to run out the clock today, but you'd be wrong. This is the Job. If you wanted a wife to stay home and mind the house, you shouldn't have proposed to a cop."

He smiled. "I'd not have you any other way," he said. "But it's grand to see you now and again. We do have a wedding to plan."

Erin made a face. "Suddenly departmental paperwork doesn't sound so bad," she said. "Can't we just run down to the courthouse?"

"If you'd like," he said. "But I'd rather make our vows in a church. It's old-fashioned, I know, but... Erin, darling? Are you all right?"

She'd frozen with the last bite of toast halfway to her mouth. Rolf was watching her from a respectful distance. Maybe she'd decide not to eat it at the last minute, in which case he was ready to offer an alternative solution. Hoping wasn't the same as begging.

"Courthouse," she repeated quietly. "Warrants. Judges. She wouldn't do that, would she?"

"Who?" Carlyle asked in bewilderment. "Do what?"

"Julia Lockhart," Erin said. "Ferris's secretary. She doesn't know about Judge Barberis."

"Pasquale Barberis?" Carlyle asked. "That judge is in the Lucarellis' pocket. You'd never take a Mafia warrant to him."

"I know that!" she exclaimed. "But Julia doesn't. God *damn* it!"

She sprang up. Her chair clattered backward, landing on the floor with a bang. Rolf was instantly on his paws, stiff-legged and tense.

"You'll be on your way, then?" Carlyle said to her retreating back.

Erin snatched Rolf's leash from the peg at the top of the staircase. "I'll catch you later," she called without turning. She grabbed her phone as she took the stairs two at a time. There wasn't a second to waste.

*   *   *

"Judge Ferris' chambers," Julia Lockhart said.

"This is Erin O'Reilly," Erin said, a little breathlessly. She was trying to talk into her phone while running to her car. "It's about the warrant request I sent you."

"It's being processed." The secretary sounded a little irritated. "I know it's urgent police business; it always is. But I delivered the request immediately. I said I'd contact you when—"

"Who got the request?" Erin interrupted. "Which judge?"

"Detective, we have a procedure for this. Badgering the judge won't get it signed any more quickly, and may annoy them. If you'll just be patient—"

"I'm not going to do any badgering!" Erin interrupted again. "Please, just tell me who ended up with the paperwork." She yanked open the Charger's doors. Rolf hopped up into his compartment and Erin slid behind the steering wheel.

"Just a moment, please." Computer keys clacked. "There's a rotation, but Judge Barberis volunteered."

Erin closed her eyes and rested her forehead against the wheel. "Barberis? You're sure?"

"Yes. I have his acknowledgment of receipt. Now, you'll have to let this run its course. You should be hearing from him any moment."

"Thanks," Erin said bitterly and hung up. She started the Charger, threw it in reverse, and savagely stomped the accelerator. She missed a concrete support column by about an inch and hardly noticed.

Rolf barked. He could feel the thrill of the chase and was more than ready. He shoved his head through the hatch between the seats and willed the car to go faster. He was sure his focus could coax an extra bit of speed out of the engine. His tongue unspooled and hung down over his teeth.

Erin's next call was to her commanding officer.

"Webb," he said.

"We have a problem, sir."

"How novel," he said dryly. "What is it this time?"

"The warrants went to the wrong judge."

There was a very short pause. Then Webb softly said, "Damnation."

McDowell said something in the background.

Webb put his hand over his phone, but Erin still heard his answer. "We think the judge who'll be reviewing our request is working for the Lucarellis. Yes, that's what I said. How do we know? That's a very long story. Okay, here she is."

A moment later, McDowell's brisk, businesslike voice came on the line. "O'Reilly?"

"I'm on my way in," Erin said.

"Who's the crooked judge?"

"Pasquale Barberis."

"How long will it take to convince me he's on the take?"

"Longer than we have."

"What do you think he's going to do?"

"Besides torpedo the request?" Erin was having to divide her attention between the conversation and the busy Manhattan streets. She wasn't doing a perfect job either talking or driving, and was drawing honks from other drivers.

"He might just slow-walk it," McDowell said.

"If he does, it'll be so he can warn Schultz," Erin said. "Then Schultz will destroy evidence and skip town."

McDowell didn't miss a beat. "Go after the lawyer," she said. "I'll go to the courthouse and deal with Barberis."

"You can't arrest a sitting judge!" Erin exclaimed.

"What do you do, O'Reilly?" McDowell asked.

"Huh?" It wasn't an intelligent answer, but Erin was too confused and distracted to come up with anything better.

"What is your profession? Your calling?"

"I'm a cop."

"And what does that mean?"

"I solve cases and take down bad guys."

"That's right," McDowell said. "I'm an Internal Affairs detective. I drag dirty city employees out of the shadows. I'm the Cast-Iron Bitch, remember? It doesn't matter who you are. If you've crossed the line, I will destroy you. So why don't you do your job, Detective O'Reilly, and I'll do mine."

Oddly, Erin felt suddenly much better. It was the feeling you got when you were in the middle of a tough fight and you heard the sirens and knew backup was only seconds away. She didn't feel alone.

"Copy that, sir," she said. "I'm en route to Schultz's office. O'Reilly out."

Less than two minutes later her phone rang. Vic's name stared at her from her screen.

"O'Reilly," she said.

"You're gonna bust the lawyer and you didn't invite me?" Vic demanded. "I'll race you there."

"Street racing is illegal, Vic."

"Not if you have a shield and a siren."

"No siren! We don't want to tip him off if he hasn't already heard."

"We don't have a warrant to arrest him," Vic said. "Not even to search his office."

"We don't need a warrant to detain him," she said. "We can hold him twenty-four hours. And while we have him, he can't be leaving the state or destroying his paper trail."

"Good enough for me. His ass is mine. I always wanted to bust a defense attorney."

"Let's just hope the ACLU never finds out about you," Erin said. "See you there."

* * *

Erin saw Vic's Taurus in one of the police spaces at the corner next to Schultz's office. Vic himself was already on the sidewalk, jogging toward the building. She tapped her horn and waved to him as she passed. He made an exaggerated grimace but slowed to a walk. She grabbed the spot at the next corner, unloaded Rolf, and ran back to meet him.

"I'm gonna enjoy this," he said. "Don't worry, I'm on my best lawyer-arresting behavior. I left my rifle in the car. And I'm dressed for the occasion!"

It was true. Erin stared at him, her mouth dropping open.

"What?" Vic said. "Haven't you seen a guy wearing a necktie before?"

"Not over a T-shirt," she said. "You're supposed to wear a shirt with a collar, if you're going to wear a tie."

"I was in a hurry," he said. "We gonna do this, or what?"

"You're like that guy who sees a sign that says 'No Shirt, No Shoes, No Service,' and walks up to the counter without any pants," she said, shaking her head.

"I don't like wearing a tie on the street," he said. "It gives the bad guys something to hold onto in a fight. This is a big deal for me."

They got into the elevator, which hummed toward Schultz's floor. Erin tried not to imagine Mafia goons waiting at the top with machine guns. They'd be fish in a barrel. Schultz wasn't going to start a firefight with the NYPD, she reminded herself. Besides, he didn't know they were coming. Possibly.

"Are we gonna try to get anything out of him?" Vic asked. "Or just slap the cuffs on him and haul his ass downtown?"

"Let's give him the cuffs," Erin said. "He's not going to talk."

"What do lawyers do to lawyer up?" Vic wondered. "Do they refuse to talk until they're in the room with themselves? What's that saying about guys who defend themselves in court?"

"Something about the lawyer who defends himself having a fool for a client, I think," Erin said.

The doors slid back, revealing a hallway comfortingly empty of Mafia gunmen. Erin, Vic, and Rolf walked quickly to the entrance to Schultz's office suite. A young woman of Jamaican extraction was sitting at the reception desk.

"Good morning, Detective O'Reilly, Detective Neshenko," Schultz's daughter said. She flashed a brilliant smile, but Erin saw something hiding behind the smile she didn't like.

"Good morning, Aayla," Erin said. "Is your dad in?"

"Do you have an appointment?" she asked.

"We're the NYPD, honey," Vic said. "We don't need an appointment and we don't schedule in advance."

"Is there a problem?" Aayla asked.

"Not yet," Vic said. He walked past the desk toward Schultz's private office.

"Please, Detective, you can't go in there," Aayla said.

"Why not?" he asked.

"Do you have a warrant?"

You know damn well we don't, Erin thought. *Because you know Barberis hasn't issued it yet, and he's stalling as long as he can. Just like you are.* "We don't want trouble," she said. "But we do need to see King right now."

"It's no trouble," Aayla said. "But you will have to wait for him to come back. If you would take a seat, we have a selection of magazines."

"No thanks," Vic said. "You guys never have the ones I read."

That's because legal offices don't subscribe to Guns & Ammo *or* Soldier of Fortune, Erin thought. "Aayla, is King here or not?" she demanded.

"I am not prepared to answer any of your questions without a court order," Aayla said. She was no longer smiling.

"Are you prepared to go to jail as an accessory?" Vic shot back. "That'll look real good on your record when you graduate law school. A little practical experience with the legal system. Sort of like being an unpaid intern."

Aayla's eyes flashed. "You don't frighten me, sir," she said. "You have no legal right to threaten me."

"People always think I'm threatening them," Vic said with an utterly unconvincing expression of wounded innocence. "What is it about me?"

Erin fought down her rising impatience. She stared at Aayla, trying to puzzle the young woman out. "You want to help your dad," she said. "I get it. I'd do the same in your position. But you need to think this through. We're not the only ones after him."

"What are you talking about?" Aayla demanded.

"Have you ever heard of Squeaky Santino?"

"That is not a real name," Aayla said. "Who is he?"

"He's a violent felon," she said. "And he killed a crooked cop yesterday."

"So I suppose now you will tell me he is coming after my father? Please, Detective, don't insult my intelligence."

"No," Erin said. "He's not."

"Then what are you talking about?"

"He's dead. Andrew Keane shoved an IV needle through his eye into his brain."

Aayla flinched. "That's horrible," she said.

"Yeah, it was. I know, because I saw him after. Not a pretty sight. But he isn't the guy you need to worry about. His dad, Giovanni; *he's* your problem."

"Why? My father has done nothing to him."

"Giovanni thinks your father manipulated his son into getting himself killed," Erin said. "And he's looking for someone to blame."

It was ninety percent true. If she'd told Foggy Santino that Kingston Schultz was behind the hit on Keane, the elder Santino would probably have gotten to Schultz ahead of the NYPD.

Aayla shook her head. "Even if that were true, there would be no legal case," she said.

"Aayla, you're not listening to me," Erin said as patiently as she could. "Giovanni isn't the kind of guy who goes to the cops. He's a Mafia street hood, with old-school ideas about revenge. He won't call 911. He'll show up in person with an icepick and an attitude."

"You are lying," Aayla said.

"We talked to him last night," Erin said. "Am I telling the truth about him, Vic?"

"Absolutely," Vic said without hesitation. "That isn't a guy I'd want coming after me. I mean, I could take him in a stand-up fight, but he'd get me from behind."

"You know that kind of man," Erin said to Aayla. "Because your dad's firm defends them all the time. They don't forgive and they don't forget. If we don't find King, Giovanni will."

"No, he won't," Aayla insisted. "Because papa is already—"

She stopped short, clamping her mouth shut. But it was too late.

"Because he's already left," Erin said, finishing the other woman's thought. "He's on his way out of New York right now."

Aayla said nothing.

"Thanks for your cooperation," Erin said, spinning on her heel. "Come on, Vic. We need to move!"

Chapter 20

Erin called Webb from just outside Schultz's building, putting him on speaker so Vic could listen in.

"Schultz got away," she said before he could ask.

"A thrilling escape?" Webb asked.

"He was gone before we got here. He was tipped off."

"I wonder who talked to him," Vic said, dripping with sarcasm.

"We'll deal with the leak later," Webb said.

"Lieutenant McDowell's dealing with it right now," Erin replied.

"Do you trust her?" Vic asked.

"Yeah, I do," Erin said, to her own mild surprise.

"You're sure Schultz is gone?" Webb asked.

"His daughter wouldn't let us in," she said. "But she let it slip when we were talking to her. He's running. You want to set some uniforms on the building, just in case?"

"That's a good idea," Webb said. "I'll have the local boys send a unit or two."

"Should we haul the daughter in as an accessory?" Vic asked. "She might make good leverage."

"I'm surprised at you, Neshenko," Webb said. "You have a daughter yourself."

"That's what gave me the idea," Vic said. "If I had the choice between going to prison and leaving Mina behind bars, I'm doing the time myself."

"I don't think we should add hostage-taking to the NYPD's repertoire," Webb said. "Technically, you're probably right and she's helping him. But we don't usually bust family members for that sort of thing unless they're committing other crimes. Let her go."

"Then how exactly do you want us to find this jerk?" Vic demanded. "I'm happy to chase him. Hell, I'd love to. But I need to know where he's going."

"Rolf can't track him," Erin said. "He'll have gotten in a car."

"Do you think he's lying low or skipping town?" Webb asked.

"He's getting out," Erin said.

"How do you figure?" Webb asked.

"If he wasn't before, he is now," she said. "I told Aayla that Giovanni Santino was gunning for her dad. She'll have some way of getting word to him, I'm sure of it. Once he hears the Lucarellis are after him, he'll have no choice but to run for it. They're his best contacts and the people he'd trust to hide him. Without the Mob, he doesn't have any local resources."

"Ordinarily I'd try for a tap on the daughter's phone," Webb said thoughtfully. "But our judicial process appears to be compromised. I'll put out his name and description to the TSA, in case he tries to get on a plane."

"There's gotta be a hundred ways out of this friggin' city," Vic grumbled. "Twenty-one goddamn bridges out of Manhattan. We can't put checkpoints on all of them. Then there's airplanes, helicopters, boats, submarines..."

"Submarines?" Erin echoed.

"I'll put a BOLO on his car," Webb said. "But we can't ignore the possibility of him catching a ride. We can assume he has contacts with the Teamsters."

"So do we," Erin said. "I'll call Corky. If Schultz tries to work through them, he can find out."

"Christ, not that asshole," Vic said. "I thought we were done with him!"

"It's a good idea," Webb said. "And we can put the word out through the media. Then there's traffic cams. We'll find him."

"Yeah," Erin said without enthusiasm. She was sure they were missing something important.

"Come on back to the Eightball after you make your calls," Webb said. "We'll regroup and figure out what to do next."

James Corcoran was delighted to help. "If that lad shows one hair near one of my truckers, you'll be the first to know," he said once she'd explained the situation.

"*Your* truckers?" she replied.

"Oh aye," he said cheerfully. "I don't own them, you ken. They're mine the same way you are."

"You've never had me," she said through gritted teeth.

"And that's something you'll regret when you're old and gray," he said. "It's along the lines of referring to my doctor or my financial advisor. You're my copper, aye?"

"You have a financial advisor?"

"Not as such. A lad needs some savings if he's to have any idea what to do with them. Ta, love."

Shaking her head, Erin hung up. Vic was pacing the sidewalk, scowling and muttering.

"This guy's slippery, Erin," he said. "We're not gonna pick him up at the goddamn Greyhound station and we're sure as shit not gonna grab him behind the wheel of his own car. He has a plan, I'd bet two weeks' overtime on it."

"You're right," she said. "Schultz has been working with the Mob a long time. He's a survivor. He has an exit strategy. I bet he's got a big fat offshore bank account, too."

"He'll be propping his feet up in some non-extradition country by the end of the week," Vic glumly predicted. "Laughing at us and sipping mojitos on the beach."

"You think so?"

"Well, maybe not on the beach," he said. "He'll be in Buenos Aires drinking thousand-dollar wine at some swanky restaurant. He wears expensive suits. I can't exactly picture him in a Speedo."

"No," Erin said slowly. "He'll be thinking about the beach, though. We can't chase this guy, Vic. We need to think ahead of him and cut him off."

Rolf, sitting next to Erin, bent his head sideways and scratched an ear. Things had looked good for a while, but now they'd slowed down again. He had no idea what was going on, and wished the humans would get their act together.

"Where's he going?" Erin asked.

"I told you that," Vic said. "Argentina's my guess."

She shook her head. "Jamaica."

"Because that's where he's from?"

"No. He was born here. But his family has roots there."

"So what? My family has roots in Russia, but there's no way I'd run there if I was in trouble. Russia's a great place to be *from*. I never knew anybody who wanted to go back."

"The Schultzes were rum-runners during Prohibition," she said. "That's how they first got involved with the Mafia. His family smuggled booze up from the Caribbean."

"What's your point?"

"It's just a hunch," she said. "But I think we should check out the waterfront."

"This is New York," he reminded her. "It's all waterfront. We're on a friggin' island. Pick a direction and start walking. You'll get your feet wet sooner or later."

Erin ignored him. She had her phone out again and hit the redial.

"I'm sorry, love," Corky said. "I can't be making a booty call at present. I'm rather busy, and my colleen would be dreadfully sore with me."

"Forget my booty," Erin said.

"Impossible," he said. "Have you seen it? Your backside's the stuff of legends, love. In the old days, lads would write poems in honor of it. How would it go? 'The heavenly swell of Erin's hips demanded attention from my lips...'"

She rolled her eyes again. "Save it," she said. "Nobody likes a kiss-ass. You know all the smugglers in New York."

"Most of them, aye."

"Who operates out of Jamaica?"

"In general, or are you only interested in the lads currently in town?"

"I need to know who might be sailing in the next day or two."

"I'll ask around," he said. "We're still looking for your legal gentleman, aye?"

"Yeah."

"I'll ring you directly. Try not to miss me while I'm gone."

"I think I'll manage," she said and hung up.

"Now we wait?" Vic asked.

"Now we wait," she echoed.

"I hate waiting," he growled.

"Take a lesson from Rolf," she suggested. "Find somewhere comfy and take a nap until the excitement starts."

"That's actually a good idea," he said. "When's the last time you had any sleep?"

"I don't know," she said. "What day is it?"

"Beats me," he said. "What month is it?"

"April."

"Already? What year?"

*　　*　　*

Erin had been driving a few minutes when she abruptly turned hard right at the next intersection. Vic, trailing her in his Taurus, swerved but stuck with her. A moment later, her phone rang.

"What?" she asked.

"Are you lost?" Vic asked.

"No."

"But you're not going to the Eightball."

"Neither are you."

"I'm following you. Where are *you* going?"

"Courthouse."

"Why?"

"I want to see how McDowell is coming with Barberis."

"And you couldn't use the phone?"

"We don't have anywhere else to be at the moment. And I wouldn't mind leaning on the Judge myself."

"Oh, goody. We're already chasing down a defense attorney. Are we gonna arrest the entire New York legal establishment?"

"If you don't want to come, you don't have to."

"I didn't say I didn't want to. This sounds like fun. You know what they call it when you throw a thousand lawyers into the ocean?"

"A good start?"

"Damn right."

They parked next to each other in two of the police spaces at the courthouse and went in.

"I didn't used to think about turning in my guns here," Vic commented as he handed his Sig and backup piece to the guys at the security checkpoint. "Then the Madonna kid did his magic trick with that piano wire and now I wonder."

"We have Rolf," Erin said. "He's better than any gun."

"At close range, sure. Can he throw his teeth?"

Erin handed over her own pistols and walked through the metal detector. Rolf trotted happily beside her, unconcerned. His weapons weren't made of metal.

"Are we really doing this?" Vic asked.

"Doing what?" Erin paused to scrutinize the map in the lobby, looking up Judge Barberis' chambers.

"Providing backup for Internal Affairs against a judge?"

"McDowell isn't so bad."

"Are you kidding? She's a serious hardass."

"So are you."

"That's different. I don't go after other cops."

"Says the guy who kneecapped her predecessor."

"Did you forget Keane had just shot you?"

"That isn't the sort of thing I forget." Erin found what she was looking for, took a second to get her bearings, and set off for the stairs. "I think McDowell's one of the good ones."

"I bet there were good guys in the Gestapo, too," Vic muttered.

"Kira Jones was IAB," Erin said.

"I know. But I still don't trust McDowell. You watch, she's gonna screw us."

"I don't know about that," Erin said. She stopped at Barberis' door. "We probably shouldn't just barge in."

"Why not?" Vic asked. "I do it all the time."

"In tactical gear, with an assault rifle and an ESU team," she said.

"My tac gear and M4 are in the car. I could run back and grab them."

"No."

"It'll only take a minute."

"No."

"You're no fun at all sometimes."

Erin took out her phone and brought up McDowell's number. She fired off a quick text message.

Neshenko and I are at the Judge's door. Is this a good time?

After a moment, her phone showed McDowell's answer.

Come in. Could use you.

Erin showed the screen to Vic, who smiled.

"It's so nice to feel wanted," he said and shouldered the door open.

The secretary inside was a wiry little guy with glasses. He convulsively leaped to his feet as Vic, Erin, and Rolf poured into the room.

"Hey!" he said weakly. "What are you—"

"NYPD Major Crimes," Vic interrupted, brandishing the shield on its chain around his neck. It got tangled with his necktie, but he didn't care. "We have a meeting with your boss."

"Last-minute," Erin added. "Excuse us, please."

"But you can't—" the secretary protested.

The detectives ignored him and went straight to the inner office door. Erin knocked politely. Vic gave it a little less than two seconds, twisted the knob, and shoved.

Pasquale Barberis wasn't a big man, but he had the presence and authority that came with decades serving on the bench of the biggest city in America. He sat behind a desk as massive and imposing as the one in the Oval Office. His chambers were furnished expensively but tastefully. Erin saw lots of dark wood and nice-looking paintings. She wondered fleetingly what her ex-boyfriend would think of it. Luke was an art appraiser and could have rattled off the market value of everything in the room without a second glance.

Opposite Barberis stood Lieutenant McDowell, back perfectly straight, dress blues immaculate, not a hair out of place. Erin could have sworn she felt coldness radiating off the woman. McDowell wasn't exactly frowning, but her stare was as deadly as a double-barreled shotgun. Those twelve-gauge eyes were trained on the Judge as the door swung open and the detectives came in.

Barberis broke eye contact to look at the new arrivals. McDowell didn't.

"Here are my witnesses now, Your Honor," McDowell said calmly.

"Witnesses?" Barberis echoed. "Nonsense." He was outwardly calm, but Erin was used to interrogating poker-faced perps and she knew what to look for. His upper lip was slick with sweat. His eyes were a little too wide. And his Adam's apple was bobbing up and down. This man was tense, even scared.

"As I'm sure you're aware," McDowell said, "Detective O'Reilly spent several months infiltrating New York's underworld. Most of her activities were centered around the O'Malley gang, but she also worked closely with Lucarelli associates Valentino Vitelli, Matthew Madonna, and Alfredo Madonna. Isn't that correct, Detective?"

"That's accurate, Lieutenant," Erin said, startled but playing along.

"They also witnessed the younger Madonna's slaying of Vincenzo Moreno, which took place in the very building in which we are now gathered."

"So did I," Barberis retorted. "It was *my* courtroom!"

"The City's courtroom, sir," McDowell corrected him. "Detective, why did Alfredo kill Mr. Moreno?"

"The Oil Man had his dad murdered," Erin said. "He wanted payback."

"Why were the two of them in that courtroom on that day?" McDowell asked.

"Alfie was being sentenced," Erin said. "Parole violation. He'd leaked word onto the street that he was going to name names in the Lucarellis, so Vinnie the Oil Man showed up to see what he'd say."

"Was it a crime of passion, a spur-of-the-moment murder?"

"No," Erin said firmly. "Alfie planned it ahead of time. The rumors were bait to draw the Oil Man into a place he felt safe and put him off his guard."

McDowell hadn't looked away from Barberis the whole time. Now she turned slightly Erin's direction. "Was Alfredo Madonna capable of devising such a plan on his own, Detective?" she asked.

"No," Erin said again.

"This is all very interesting," Barberis said. "But I don't see what it has to do with me. I wasn't involved in any of this violent thuggery."

"You sentenced him, Your Honor," Erin said.

"That is my job, Detective," Barberis said.

"Indeed," McDowell said. "Detective O'Reilly, who *did* come up with the plan to assassinate Mr. Moreno?"

"Kingston Schultz," Erin said with as much conviction as she could muster.

"What is Mr. Schultz's relationship to Alfredo Madonna?" McDowell asked, returning her full attention to Barberis.

"He's his lawyer," Erin said. "Defense attorney and property manager. He handles Alfie's assets and legal affairs."

"Why would he want his client to commit a very public murder, in front of numerous witnesses, including but not limited to three of the people currently in this room?"

"He wanted to eliminate the Oil Man so he could take over the Lucarelli rackets," Erin said. "And he wanted Alfie out of the picture so he could profit from the kid's inheritance."

"All very interesting, as I've said," Barberis said. "But I really am busy, and I don't have time for this hypothetical speculation."

McDowell's face remained impassive. "This would be the same Kingston Schultz for whom these detectives filed requests for search warrants and wiretaps earlier today," she said. "Warrants which your office has not yet processed."

"As I said, I'm a busy man," Barberis said. "Even without being harassed by the NYPD. I'll get to these requests in due course."

"In the order in which they were received?" McDowell inquired.

"In order of priority," Barberis said.

"I note today you have approved warrants for the financial records of a company suspected of falsifying designer clothing labels," McDowell said. "Likewise, you have approved a search warrant for the dwelling of a suspected flasher operating in Central Park and an arrest warrant for a man suspected of aggravated assault upon a homeless transient in a subway station. In your opinion, are these higher priorities than a man accused of conspiracy, murder, and racketeering?"

"You are not a judge, Lieutenant," Barberis said angrily. "I don't expect you to understand the intricacies of our bureaucracy."

"Oh, but I do, Your Honor," McDowell smoothly interrupted. "Detectives O'Reilly and Neshenko are, at heart, street officers. They understand the rhythm of the street and can navigate it by instinct and experience. I am a bureaucrat. I know how other bureaucrats think and talk. I know how New York's court system operates. And I know when I'm being lied to."

"That's enough," Barberis snapped. "I want you to leave this office right now! I'll be contacting the Commissioner to file an official misconduct complaint the moment you're gone. And that goes for your henchmen, too.

*　　*　　*

I always wanted to be a henchman," Vic said under his breath.

"That is your prerogative, Your Honor," McDowell said. "It may interest you to know that the Commissioner personally charged me with cleaning up corruption in the wake of the scandal involving the late Lieutenant Keane. He told me to, and I quote, 'Get in there with your scrub brush and scrape all the dirt out. I want to be able to eat off the floor when you're done.' I am operating with his direct knowledge and approval."

"I don't care," Barberis said. "I'm not a policeman and I don't fall under your jurisdiction. You're an Internal Affairs cop."

"Indeed," McDowell said. "Which is one reason I've asked these Major Crimes detectives to be present. Any major crime which occurs in New York is, by definition, their responsibility."

"What crime are you referring to?" Barberis demanded. "Are you accusing me of something?"

"I'm looking for an explanation as to why you delayed issuing a warrant to search Kingston Schultz's office, with the excuse of overwork, but somehow found time to place a telephone call to Mr. Schultz's office phone."

"You couldn't possibly know that," Barberis snapped. "No wiretap was approved on my phone, nor on his! I've got the request for that wiretap right here! It's part of the damned warrants that haven't been issued yet!"

Everyone stopped talking for several seconds. Vic pursed his lips and made an almost-soundless whistle. Rolf, feeling the tension in the air, watched Erin closely. This was the sort of situation that turned into biting on short notice and he wanted to be ready.

"Thank you for confirming my suspicions," McDowell said. "With the corroboration of these two decorated detectives, I'm sure it won't be difficult to obtain your telephone records from another judge, one who has not been compromised"

Barberis opened his mouth, but no words made their way out. He licked his lips and glanced at the door.

"I wouldn't recommend it, Your Honor," Erin said. She raised her left hand slightly, displaying Rolf's leash.

"I'm sure you're trying to think of an explanation," McDowell said to Barberis. "Something that will sound completely innocuous, or at least give you some veneer of deniability. However, you're not completely stupid, so you're already considering your options. I expect these detectives will want to escort you to their precinct house and conduct a lengthier interview. You're well aware of your legal rights and will certainly avail yourself of the services of a criminal attorney."

"Probably not Kingston Schultz," Vic interjected.

"Sometime during that process," McDowell continued, "it will occur to you that your best chance will be to flip on Mr. Schultz. Cooperating with us will probably allow you to avoid serving prison time. The most favorable outcome will be if you provide us with information which leads to Mr. Schultz's apprehension and conviction. So I'd advise you to use the new few minutes, as they take you to Precinct Eight, to reflect on how much you know about Mr. Schultz's movements. If we are able to locate him within the next, say, two hours on the basis of your testimony, I feel quite sure you and the District Attorney will be able to come to a mutually beneficial understanding."

"I don't believe this," Barberis said. "Are you seriously arresting me?"

"Of course not," McDowell said. "As you pointed out, I have no jurisdiction to do so. That would be the job of Major Crimes. Will you be needing to handcuff the Judge, Detectives?"

"It's procedure, sir," Vic said with a truly nasty smile. "I wouldn't want to violate procedure during an Internal Affairs investigation."

He took out his pair of handcuffs and let one of the bracelets dangle at the end of its chain. Erin was sure it was for deliberate dramatic effect.

"Pasquale Barberis," Erin said. "You are under arrest for aiding and abetting a suspected felon. I'm sure, as Lieutenant McDowell said, that you know your rights, but Detective Neshenko is correct. We have procedures we need to follow, so if you'd please listen carefully. You have the right to remain silent..."

Chapter 21

"You arrested a judge," Webb said.

"Don't look at me," Vic said. "I'm a henchman. I don't make command decisions. I just... hench."

Webb leaned back in his chair and rubbed the bridge of his nose. "Please tell me it's a clean arrest," he said.

"Perfectly," McDowell said. "The detectives behaved with proper protocol and adhered to departmental guidelines."

"How's our evidence?"

"Getting stronger," McDowell said.

"You should've seen it," Vic said. "She bluffed that son of a— that esteemed member of the legal profession. Faked him into a confession. It was beautiful. She's wasted on Internal Affairs. She oughta be out there with us real cops. No offense, Lieutenant."

"It would be over-sensitive to take offense at a compliment, Detective," McDowell said.

Erin did a double take. The IAB Lieutenant was *smiling*. It did wonders for her face. But a moment later McDowell's muscles reverted to their usual stony stare.

"Oh," Vic said. "Then you're welcome, I guess."

"I assume the Judge lawyered up?" Webb asked.

"Before we even got him loaded into Vic's car," Erin confirmed.

"I offered him a preliminary deal," McDowell said.

"He gives us Schultz, we don't feed his guts to the DA," Vic said. "I don't like it."

"Why not?" Webb and McDowell asked in unison.

"He's a crooked judge," Vic said. "He belongs behind bars."

"Perhaps I should clarify the offer," McDowell said. "I fully intend to recommend to the District Attorney that we refrain from bringing charges against soon-to-be former Judge Barberis in the matter of Kingston Schultz. However, this is not a blanket immunity deal. I further intend to open an investigation into the Judge's past dealings with the Mafia. Once we have the necessary tools, in the form of court orders to examine his finances and case history, I think we'll find a considerable number of discrepancies. If any of those irregularities lead to criminal prosecution, your ambition to lock him up may well be realized."

Vic grinned. "You play the long game, don't you," he said.

"I never stop," McDowell said. "When you're fishing and you hook a big one, Detective, sometimes it pays to let the fish run a little before you reel it in. It's better than to risk snapping your line and losing the catch."

"Do you want to be in the interrogation room, Lieutenant?" Webb asked.

"I don't think that's necessary," McDowell said. "This is your squad's collar, so I expect you and your detectives will be best suited to finishing him off. I'll be happy to observe."

Webb nodded. "All right then," he said. "As soon as Barberis' lawyer and the DA get here, O'Reilly and I will conduct the interview. In the meantime, let's work the phones and see if we can nail Schultz without his help. Then maybe we won't need to cut any kind of deal."

"He won't be a judge anymore, no matter what," Erin said. "And good riddance. But I have to ask you something, Lieutenant."

"Yes?" McDowell said.

"What would you have done if Vic and I hadn't shown up when we did?"

"I would have used the tools at my disposal," McDowell said. "Barberis was vulnerable. Nobody has just one weak point. I would have found a different one and applied pressure."

"Sheesh," Vic said. "You're friggin' relentless. I hope you're never out to get me."

McDowell gave him a slow, level stare. "What makes you think I'm not?"

"Will you look at that?" Vic said, getting abruptly to his feet. "I'm all out of Mountain Dew. Anyone need anything while I'm downstairs?"

"They don't have cigarette vending machines anymore," Webb said sadly. "So no."

As Vic passed Erin's desk, he said in an undertone, "I don't know whether to kiss that IAB lady or hide under my desk where she can't find me."

"She'd find you," Erin whispered back. "But I wouldn't kiss her either, if I were you."

*   *   *

Erin had never been in such a high-powered interrogation room before. She was only a lowly Detective Second Grade. Even Lieutenant Webb was small potatoes compared to District Attorney Markham and Judge Barberis. Lieutenant McDowell was watching from the observation room, with Rolf keeping her company. Erin didn't know Barberis' lawyer, but his suit looked expensive.

"My client admits no wrongdoing," the lawyer said. "But he is eager to do his civic duty in the apprehension of a fugitive."

"I'm glad to hear it," Markham said. "What information is he prepared to volunteer?"

"That is, of course, contingent upon a reciprocal show of good faith by your office," the lawyer said.

Translation: you scratch my back and I'll scratch yours, Erin thought.

"I understand the NYPD believes your client to be in possession of time-sensitive intelligence regarding the whereabouts of one Kingston Schultz," Markham said. "In return for which, Lieutenant Webb informs me they are prepared not to press charges of conspiracy or aiding and abetting."

"No charges of any kind," the lawyer countered.

"Blanket immunity?" Markham inquired, raising a polite eyebrow but otherwise maintaining an impressive poker face. "For all crimes?"

"All *alleged* crimes," the lawyer corrected.

"I can't agree to that," Markham said. "For the simple reason that I'm not aware of the full extent of your client's *alleged* offenses. Suppose, for instance—speaking purely hypothetically—he had committed murder. Helping us apprehend a single non-violent suspect can hardly be expected to balance that out."

"My client has not committed any homicides," the lawyer said.

"That is why I was speaking hypothetically," Markham said.

Why are Webb and I even here? Erin wondered silently. She felt like a spectator at a tennis match, watching the ball bounce back and forth from one side of the interrogation table to the other. And like in tennis, it was rude for the spectators to make noise while the ball was still in play.

"Immunity to all allegations stemming from hypothetical association with the Lucarelli syndicate," the lawyer suggested.

"Out of the question," Webb interjected. "This isn't the Organized Crime Task Force, sir. For all we know, they're engaged in a major investigation of the Lucarellis right now. We can't unilaterally compromise an ongoing investigation."

"A hypothetical ongoing investigation," the lawyer parried.

Every time the word "hypothetical" got tossed out, Erin found herself feeling an increasing urge to grab the speaker by the ears and headbutt him. She resisted.

"Here's our offer," Markham said. "No charges pertaining to Kingston Schultz. No immediate disbarment. Your client is released without conditions, effective immediately upon our apprehension of Mr. Schultz. The matter of his continued employment on the New York Bench to be referred to the proper authorities for due consideration, with endorsement from my office emphasizing his cooperation, assuming we successfully take Mr. Schultz into custody. Take it or leave it. This offer has an expiration date."

*   *   *

Barberis and his lawyer talked for almost an hour. McDowell hung around outside the room where the judge and the lawyer were lurking. Erin and the rest of the squad spent the time trying to find Kingston Schultz and failing. New York was a wide-open city. There were dozens of ways a lone man could get in or out. Erin's suspicion that he might be working with smugglers was all very well, but it didn't get them any closer to finding the rogue lawyer.

"We're counting on Barberis or Corcoran to come through for us," Vic said. "Two of the most trustworthy guys in town. What a joke."

"Informants break cases," Webb said. "You don't have to like them. You don't have to trust them. But they work."

"Corky did back you up in a barfight that one time," Erin reminded Vic.

"I didn't ask him to," Vic said. "He's a jackass."

"He's a reformed jackass," Erin said. "He saved our witness. He's been nothing but helpful... recently. He'll come through for us."

"I almost hope not," Vic muttered. "I'd hate owing that punk another one."

"He's a good guy at heart," she insisted.

"He's a professional criminal, a terrorist, a womanizer, and a redhead," Vic said.

"Those last two aren't illegal," Webb said mildly.

"I don't like him," Vic persisted. "He tried to sleep with your brother's wife, Erin!"

"Okay, I can't defend that," Erin said. "It was stupid and he paid for it."

"So did the rest of us," Vic said. "Just tell me you're not inviting him to the wedding."

"Are you nuts? He's my fiancé's best friend. He'll probably be best man!"

"Oh, really? And who's gonna be your maid of honor?"

"Shelley, I guess. But she's married, so she'd be a matron, technically."

"This would be the same Shelley who's married to your brother? The one Corcoran tried to screw around with?"

"Oh," Erin said. It should have hit her before but she'd been avoiding the wedding planning as much as possible. "Oh, shit."

"And it'll be an Irish wedding," Vic continued, a malicious grin spreading across his face. "So there'll be tons of booze. What could possibly go wrong?"

"Oh, shit," Erin said again.

"What are you going to do about it?" Webb asked.

"I have no idea," she said. "I was worrying about Richie O'Malley crashing the party. I should've been worrying about the people *in* the wedding party. Damn it all."

McDowell came up the stairs. She walked briskly into Major Crimes. All eyes turned toward her.

"We have a deal," the Lieutenant announced.

"Excellent," Webb said.

Erin jumped up. "Thank God. Where's Schultz?"

"Barberis says he doesn't know," McDowell said. "But he'll tell us everything he does know. I'll bring him up."

She hurried back downstairs to fetch the Judge.

"He'll lie through his teeth," Vic predicted. "He's a lawyer. It's what they do."

"He'll tell as little as he can," Webb said. "And yes, he'll probably lie. That's not just a lawyer thing. All perps lie."

"I know that," Vic said. "I can't believe we're giving him a sweetheart deal."

"You heard McDowell," Erin said. "We'll burn him, one way or another. She isn't going to let go of this. She's like Rolf when he's got his teeth in a bite sleeve."

"You *do* like her," Vic said in accusing tones.

"What if I do?" Erin said, shrugging defensively.

"She's the enemy!"

"You'd better hope not," Webb said. "Because she's going to be the one who decides whether you stay in Major Crimes or wind up working dead-end shoplifting cases in strip malls."

"She hates me," Vic grumbled.

"You don't know that," Erin said.

"Of course I do," he said. "Everybody hates me. Especially women."

"That's because you're an insult to your species and your gender. It's nothing personal."

"Thanks."

McDowell returned with Barberis and his lawyer in tow. They went to the break room, which became very crowded once the three of them, Vic, Webb, Erin, and Rolf squeezed in. Vic and Erin sat on the disreputable couch. Barberis, after one look at what was left of its upholstery, decided to remain standing.

"I have the District Attorney's signature on this agreement," the lawyer announced. "So, if there are no further preliminaries, I'd like to get this dealt with so my client can be on his way."

"That's up to him," Webb said, pushing a button on an old-school tape recorder. "Start talking, Your Honor. We're recording this conversation, obviously."

"Kingston Schultz is attempting to leave not only New York City but the United States," Barberis said. He spoke calmly, but avoided eye contact with any of the police. "He is aware of the investigation into his activities. He's likely already attempted to access at least one of his bank accounts to gain traveling money. Once out of the country, he'll make use of his offshore accounts."

"That isn't anything we don't already know," Erin said. "Where's he going? Who's he traveling with? Who are his contacts?"

"I don't control his movements," Barberis said. "You're asking me for information I don't possess."

"Who would he trust to get him out of town?" Erin pressed. "You've worked with Schultz for years. Are there any smugglers he's defended in court? Any that he insisted you use your influence to get out of trouble?"

Barberis hesitated. Everyone in the room noticed it.

"Any lack of cooperation will void that agreement," McDowell said, looking pointedly at the paper in the lawyer's hand.

"A couple of years ago, there was a case that came before my bench," Barberis said. "It was a nothing case, your basic narcotics trafficking. Not a third-strike offense. The defendant might not have even done any time if convicted. But Schultz really wanted this guy to stay clean, to have a good record. I didn't think much of it. We had an overwhelming caseload anyway. Dismissing the charges was quick, easy, and arguably in the City's interests."

"Who was the drug smuggler?" Webb asked.

"*Alleged* drug smuggler," the lawyer predictably interjected.

"Shut up," Vic said. "We don't give a shit and the guy isn't your client, so you shouldn't either."

"I'm doing my job," the lawyer said, bristling.

"That's what hookers and hitmen say, too," Vic said.

"The name, please," Webb said, ignoring the side conversation.

"It wasn't easy to recall," Barberis said. "I handle a very high volume of cases and—"

"It was difficult," McDowell said. "Noted. Every minute you waste increases the likelihood of our fugitive escaping and your deal becoming void."

"Doug Robinson," the Judge said. "He isn't an American citizen, but he held a valid green card at the time and—"

Erin and Vic didn't wait to hear any more. They were already out the door.

"We'll take your car," Vic said as they jogged downstairs. "I'll look him up on the way."

"On the way where?" Erin replied. "We don't know where we're going yet." But she matched him stride for stride. Rolf trotted eagerly beside her, mouth open, eyes bright.

"Since when have we let that stop us?" Vic replied.

Chapter 22

"I need a destination," Erin said. She stopped the Charger on the garage's exit ramp.

Vic's answer, as he glared at her onboard computer, was a continuous stream of profanity.

"I think I'm learning some new words," she said. "But none of them are street names or addresses."

"There's three hundred friggin' Douglas Robinsons in New York," Vic growled. "Give me a second, okay?"

"And those are the ones who actually live here," she said. "What if he's traveling from somewhere else? Barberis said he wasn't a US citizen."

"Then we're shit out of luck," he replied. "But I don't see you coming up with any bright ideas."

"Hold on," she said, taking out her phone.

"Oh, Jesus," he groaned. "You're calling that redheaded bastard, aren't you."

"Corky knows people," she said. "He's exactly who we need right now. You keep looking. Try it your way."

Corky's phone rang, but only once. He picked up almost immediately.

"How's about you, love?" he said cheerfully. "I'm working on our little endeavor, but I haven't anything for you just yet."

"Doug Robinson," she said. "Narcotics smuggler. Do you know him?"

"I've heard the name, aye," Corky said. "He's first mate on a bonny ship, the *Nassau Princess*. Perhaps you know her?"

"Look up the *Nassau Princess*," Erin told Vic. "Corky, any idea where this ship is?"

"Elizabeth Marine Terminal, I believe," Corky said. "I'm in the area right now, as a matter of fact, working the waterfront like you asked. Pressing flesh and flapping gums."

"Good," she said. "Can you find her?"

"Can you find your own arse in a dark nightclub?"

"Enough about my ass!" she said. "I'll take that as a yes. We're on our way. See if you can find out who's on board."

"Grand."

"And Corky, be—"

Her phone beeped as the call cut off.

"—discreet," she finished hopelessly.

"Elizabeth Marine," Vic confirmed. "Jamaican flagged freighter. She's set to sail today, in... shit, forty minutes."

"Find me a route," she said, revving the engine and setting the Charger toward New Jersey.

"You'll want to get on I-78," he said. "You can make it in thirty minutes."

"I can make it in twenty-five," she said, turning on the lights and siren.

Rolf thrust his head between the seats and panted happily. The lights and sounds meant they were in the hunt.

"Jersey," Vic muttered. "Why'd it have to be friggin' Jersey?"

"Elizabeth's the biggest port on the East Coast," Erin said. "It's not that surprising. And it makes sense Schultz would cross state lines."

"Makes it harder for us to track him," Vic agreed. "But I hate Jersey. You want to bring the local boys in on this? Or Port Authority?"

"Call the Port Authority," she decided. "We should have them okay it before we start boarding ships. Besides, maybe they can spare a few bodies to help out."

"Asking permission isn't very piratical," Vic observed.

"Then it's a good thing we're cops, not pirates," she said.

"Being a pirate would be a lot more fun."

"I still don't think you have a cutlass."

"I could get one. You gotta give me some advance warning if we're gonna do stuff like this."

*　　*　　*

It took Vic half the drive to get through to someone in the Port Authority who could help, and most of the rest of the trip to explain what was going on. No, they didn't have a warrant yet. No, it wasn't a hot pursuit situation. Yes, they understood he'd need to talk to his superiors. Yes, he'd be happy to hold for a supervisor. Yes, it was fine if the Port Authority sent a report to One PP; in fact, Vic wanted that to happen. Yes, uniformed backup would be appreciated. No, they didn't anticipate the use of deadly force, but you never knew. No, a tactical team shouldn't be necessary.

By the time Erin swung onto Corbin Street and came in view of the massive cargo cranes and man-made canyons of shipping containers, Vic looked ready to take a power drill to his own forehead. He finally hung up and slumped back in his seat.

"Goddamn bureaucrats," he said. "If we made the perps deal with them instead of us, it'd be an Eighth Amendment violation. You want to do me a big favor and shoot me?"

Rolf licked his ear.

Erin pulled into the terminal, showing her shield to the guards at the gate. She thought of asking whether anyone unusual had come through, but decided it would be a waste of time they didn't have. As she'd told Vic, this was the busiest port facility on the eastern seaboard. There were plenty of ways in. Whether or not these guys had noticed anything was a long shot at best. Besides, if James Corcoran could get in, how secure could it be?

"Speak of the devil," she murmured, spying a familiar shock of flaming red hair in the midst of a trio of Port Authority policemen: two old fat guys and a skinny rookie. She parked and got out, raising a hand in greeting.

"I don't believe this," Vic said. "Are you an honorary cop now?"

"Nay, lad, I work for a living," Corky said. "I'm an official representative of the Longshoreman's Union, you ken."

"Bullshit," Vic snorted. "You're a career criminal with a rap sheet as long as my dick."

"That's not so very long, when you come down to it," Corky said, glancing at Vic's trousers and winking. "And I'm providing full and willing cooperation with the New York Police Department, so it's you being rude, aye? And with precious seconds ticking away."

"Lady, what the hell is all this?" one of the older uniforms asked Erin.

"I'll explain later," she said. "Where's the *Nassau Princess*?" As she spoke, she was strapping Rolf's body armor around him. She was already wearing her own Kevlar vest.

"Follow me," Corky said. "We'd best hurry. They're casting off minutes from now."

"Can't we stop them?" Erin asked one of the cops as they started to run. "Or at least delay them?"

"Not without a court order," the cop wheezed. "Screws up all the timetables. Lots of ships through this channel." He looked like he didn't get much exercise and had been hitting the snacks a little too hard.

"It's like air-traffic control," explained the younger, fitter officer. "You need patterns, or ships run into each other. Ever hear of the Halifax Explosion?"

"Wasn't that the blimp that blew up back in the Thirties?" Vic asked.

"That's the Hindenburg," Erin said.

"That was in Jersey," the young cop said. He was keeping up easily and seemed bright and eager. He'd be useful if he didn't do something enthusiastic and stupid. "The Halifax Explosion was in Halifax."

"Hell, even I can figure that out," Vic grunted. "Slow down, you goddamn Mick!"

"Speed up, you bloody Russkie!" Corky called over his shoulder. "They'll not wait on you!"

"A freighter full of explosives ran into another ship in Halifax Harbor," the young cop explained, not even breathing hard. "It blew up and took out basically the whole city. Killed seventeen hundred people. That's why we can't just run freighters every which-way. Gotta stay in your lane or bad shit happens."

"Copy that," Erin said. "Where the hell is this boat?"

"Ship, ma'am," the young cop corrected her. He pointed. "There."

The *Nassau Princess* was a weather-beaten old steamer. She looked tiny next to some of the big bulk freighters. It was impossible to say what her original color had been, but she was now primarily rust-tinted. She didn't look like the kind of ship Erin would want to be on in a storm, but she was probably seaworthy enough. Smoke was belching from her stack, which meant her engines were running. A couple of seamen on the pier were in the act of casting off her lines.

"Stop! NYPD!" Erin shouted, but at that moment the ship's horn gave a deep-throated note that made the fillings in her teeth vibrate and drowned out all other noise. The *Princess* shuddered and began to move.

Corky was about twenty yards ahead of the cops. The ship was still almost touching the dock when he got there, so he simply grabbed the rail and vaulted aboard.

"Shit," Erin muttered and poured on extra speed. Rolf loped alongside. He knew Erin wasn't nearly as fast as he was, but he didn't hold it against her. She was doing her best.

By the time she and the K-9 got to the pier, they were looking at a five-foot gap. "*Hupf!*" she said and jumped. It wasn't a long or difficult leap, but the stakes were high. If she slipped, she'd go into the filthy water where she stood a high chance of being crushed against the concrete pilings if the ship slewed sideways, or maybe chopped into chum by the propeller.

Rolf coiled and sprang, easily clearing the gap. Erin wasn't as graceful, but she wrapped her arms around the railing and rolled over it. She looked back and saw Vic a few running strides behind her, together with the eager young officer. The other two cops, fatter and slower, were lagging.

Vic and the youngster jumped side by side. The kid made it with room to spare, but Vic's foot caught an oily patch on the pier. His shoe slipped just as he leaped. Erin saw his eyes go suddenly wide and knew he wasn't going to make it.

She held onto the railing with her left hand and stretched her right out as far as it would reach over the widening gap. Vic flung out his arm. His hand found her forearm and clutched. She tightened her grip around his wrist and hung on, gritting her teeth. Vic's body, all two-hundred-plus pounds of it, crashed against the side of the ship. It felt like he was yanking her shoulder clean off. Erin gasped in pain but didn't let go.

Vic grunted as he slammed into the plate steel. He planted his feet against the ship and brought up his other hand, grabbing Erin's arm.

Her eyes watering with strain, Erin concentrated on not letting go. She realized there was simply no way she could hoist him over the railing. He was too damned big. But she couldn't let him fall either.

"I got you, buddy," the young cop said. He'd seen what had happened and hurried to help. He leaned down and took one of Vic's arms. The weight dragging Erin down was abruptly halved. Between the two of them, they got Vic up and onto the deck.

"Thanks," Vic said. His pants were torn and he had blood on his knee where he'd scraped the rusty side of the ship.

Erin rubbed her shoulder. "You're really heavy, you know that?" she said.

"You're welcome, pal," the other cop said. "You good?"

"I'm good," Vic said, turning their clasp into a handshake. "Good to meet you. I owe you one. Vic Neshenko."

"Gus Detweiler," the kid said. "Forget about it. Now can someone please tell me what's going on?"

Erin glanced toward the stern of the ship. She saw the other two Port Authority cops standing forlornly at the water's edge, watching them go. So much for the reinforcements.

"We're looking for a mob boss," she said. "We think he's on board."

"Great!" Detweiler said. His eyes were shining. This, his body language said, was exactly the sort of shit he'd become a cop to do. He'd been waiting his whole life for this day.

"Take it easy, kiddo," Erin said. "Let's try not to get anybody hurt."

She drew her gun as she said it, which made her feel like a bit of a hypocrite. Corky came back to join them.

"What's the ballyhoo?" he asked. "I thought we were conducting a heroic pursuit, and here's the lot of you just standing about. You'll give coppers a bad name."

"I almost died, dipshit," Vic growled.

"Get in line, lad," Corky retorted, unimpressed. "I spent a few dull weeks in hospital with tubes crammed up my nethers not so long ago. If you're not in spitting distance of death, I'd hardly call it living."

"Is this guy really a perp?" Detweiler asked.

"Reformed perp," Corky said cheerfully.

"This isn't really the time for this conversation," Erin said. "He's with us and he's okay. We're looking for Kingston Schultz. He's a black guy about sixty years old, graying hair. He's wanted for conspiracy and racketeering. We don't know if he's armed."

"Copy that," Detweiler said, drawing his own sidearm. "Any other suspects?"

"The first mate's a known drug smuggler," she said. "Maybe the rest of the crew, too. Now, we need to make an organized search and—"

"Hey, man, what do you think you're doing?" a Jamaican voice demanded.

All heads turned toward a nearby door, which had just opened to reveal a sailor with a truly impressive set of dreadlocks. He hadn't expected to run into any strangers on board and the presence of three men, a woman, and a dog had surprised him.

"NYPD," Vic said. "You just stay right there, buddy, and keep your hands—"

The man dove backward out of sight. "Hey boss!" he yelled. "It's the police!"

"Dammit," Vic snarled, charging after him.

Other voices rose in a confused babble from somewhere inside the ship. Something heavy and metallic crashed into something else with an echoing clang, accompanied by a startled curse from Vic.

Erin swore under her breath and went after him. Rolf and Detweiler were right on her heels. She'd lost sight of Corky. There was no time to worry about the Irishman. She plunged into the interior of the *Princess*.

The corridor was very dark after the bright sunlight. Erin blinked rapidly, trying to accustom herself to the shadows, and stumbled over a round cylinder. She recognized it as a loose fire extinguisher even as it rolled away. The sailor had probably thrown it at Vic as an improvised weapon. She couldn't see either Vic or the Jamaican.

"*Such!*" she snapped.

Rolf lunged forward, hauling on the leash. Erin followed, trusting his nose. She didn't know who he was tracking, but figured he'd latch onto the freshest scent. She smelled engine oil, salt spray, and Vic's cologne. He must buy the stuff by the quart. Erin hardly needed Rolf for such a strong scent trail. Her own senses were nearly up to the task.

"Stop running, asshole!" Vic shouted from somewhere ahead. But his quarry must not have listened, because Erin could hear the clatter of shoes on metal. It echoed, seeming to come from all directions at once.

The inner workings of the *Princess* were a labyrinth of rusty metal bulkheads. The ship was a lot bigger than it had looked on the outside. Rolf scrambled down one passage after another, snuffling eagerly. Erin saw no option but to keep after him, and Detweiler was sticking with her. They seemed to be moving toward the stern of the vessel, where the bridge was located.

A door swung open as they hurried past. Erin tried to stop, but Rolf was in full pursuit mode and pulled her a couple steps farther. A crewman came out, opened his eyes very wide, and took a swing at Detweiler.

The kid was quick, Erin had to give him credit for that. Even taken unawares from the side, he reacted fast. He twisted his upper body, the sailor's fist passing harmlessly an inch from his cheek. He grabbed the man's shoulder with his left hand and pulled. The sailor, off balance, toppled and slammed his head against the opposite bulkhead. The guy went down in a heap, the fight over before anyone really realized it had started.

"Sorry," Detweiler said, then barked a laugh at the absurdity of what he'd just said.

"Good move, kiddo," Erin said. "He okay?"

Detweiler knelt beside the downed man. "He's out, but breathing," he reported.

"Cuff him and leave him," she said. They didn't have the manpower to spare guarding a prisoner, and she didn't want the man coming to and chasing them.

Detweiler reached into a hip pocket and came out with a zip-tie. He whipped it around the stunned sailor's wrists and pulled it tight, which took only a few seconds. Then he rejoined Erin, who was already moving again.

"Nice trick," she said.

"That's from my Training Officer," Detweiler explained. "He said I've only got one pair of cuffs, and what if I end up with a dozen perps? Zip-ties are cheap and they don't weigh much. I always carry a few."

Erin smiled to herself. She'd just learned a useful tip from a rookie. It paid to keep an open mind. Wisdom came from unexpected sources.

Somewhere ahead, a God-awful racket burst out. Several unfamiliar voices were shouting. So was Vic.

"Hands up!" he yelled. "You're all under arrest!"

He started to say something else, but the words turned into a grunt. Then there were noises that reminded Erin of the moment right after the snap in a football game, when a bunch of big guys ran into one another.

Rolf forged ahead, up a flight of metal stairs and through a doorway. Erin followed and found herself on the ship's bridge. Vic was on the floor, wrestling with a big Jamaican. Another sailor, the one Vic had been chasing, was sitting against the nearest wall, rubbing his head and looking dazed. A third man was advancing on the struggling pair with a pipe wrench in his hands. At the helm stood a fourth guy, clad in dirty trousers, a tank top, and an oddly pristine white captain's hat.

Erin wasn't close enough to jump the guy with the wrench before he had the chance to brain Vic, but she didn't want to shoot him either. "*Fass!*" she ordered Rolf and let go of the leash.

The Shepherd sprang, covering the intervening space in a single bounding leap. The wrench-wielder was just raising his weapon when Rolf hit him squarely amidships. Man and dog tumbled in a heap, Rolf on top. The wrench clattered across the deck.

"Everybody freeze!" Erin roared, wrapping both hands around the grip of her Glock and leveling it.

The captain's hands came up, but he was holding a weapon in them and it was pointed at her. It wasn't a firearm, she realized; it was a speargun, loaded with a wickedly barbed projectile.

"Please get off my boat, ma'am," the captain said. "You have no right to be here."

"I have a shield that says I do," Erin countered. "NYPD Major Crimes."

"We are not in New York, ma'am," the captain replied.

Vic managed to roll on top of his opponent and put him in a headlock. The other man was punching Vic around the kidneys, but the big Russian didn't seem to mind. He tightened his grip and began applying steady, relentless pressure.

Rolf, meanwhile, had the wrench guy's arm in his jaws. The K-9 was exercising restraint, which meant he'd punctured the arm with his teeth but hadn't broken the bone. He wanted his target to know that breakage was still very much an option, however. The man, getting the message, wasn't resisting.

"It doesn't matter, if we're in New York, sir," Erin said. "I'm here with an officer from the Port Authority. You're still in the bay. He has jurisdiction until you hit international waters, and you're miles away from those. Isn't that right, Officer Detweiler?"

"That's right, ma'am," Detweiler said. He was breathing hard but sounded excited rather than tired or scared. His gun was also trained on the captain. "Drop the weapon, sir."

"I think not," the captain said.

"You've only got one shot," Erin reminded him. "There's two of us pointing guns at you."

"I am sure that will be a great comfort to the one who survives," the captain replied.

Erin wondered whether her vest would stop a speargun at close range and decided she didn't want to find out.

"What's the point of this?" she asked. "You're not smuggling drugs *out* of New York. It's not like you have any contraband on board."

"Then why are you here?" he demanded.

"All we want is Kingston Schultz," she said. "We didn't come looking for a fight. Which one of you is Doug Robinson?"

"I think it's this guy," Vic said, giving his opponent an extra squeeze. "I saw his mugshot."

Robinson's face was turning very dark with trapped blood. He flailed ineffectually at Vic, but his efforts were weakening.

"Give us Schultz," Erin said. "Then I'll be willing to forget you threatened a cop."

"I think not," the captain said again.

"Detweiler?" Erin said without taking her eyes off the captain.

"Ma'am?" the kid replied.

"How many bullets do you have in your gun?"

"Seventeen, ma'am."

"If this man shoots me, I want you to empty the clip into him, center mass. All seventeen rounds. Understood?"

"Copy that." Detweiler's voice was steady. So were his hands.

"We don't want to hurt you, sir," she told the captain. "But we're not leaving without King Schultz."

"Mr. Schultz is not my friend," the captain said.

"Then why are you protecting him?" Erin asked, inwardly rejoicing. He'd just implicitly admitted Schultz was in fact on board. Up until then, it had just been a guess.

"He is my wife's cousin. He is family."

Shit, Erin thought.

One of the most common and most hated calls cops responded to was the so-called "domestic." No matter how bad a situation was, add family to the mix and it got even more explosive. Domestic disputes could turn violent with no warning. Family members might try to kill one another, or one of them might try to kill the cop, or they might all gang up on the police, their family quarrel forgotten in the face of a common enemy. Blood ties were a primal, tribal thing. They made people stupid.

"Listen," she said, trying to keep her tone calm and level. "Mr. Schultz is in serious danger. Mob guys are trying to kill him. We can protect him, but we need to find him."

"I think we will take our chances on the sea," the captain said. "The only gangsters we find on the water are pirates, yes?"

"I *knew* I should've brought a cutlass," Vic muttered. He'd finished choking his opponent out. Doug Robinson was slumped on the deck, unconscious. Strictly speaking, NYPD officers weren't supposed to apply choke-holds. It was too easy to hold on too tight or too long and kill the suspect. In the heat of the moment, Vic seemed to have forgotten the rulebook. Fortunately, he'd had enough sense and self-control not to asphyxiate the poor bastard. Vic rolled his assailant onto his stomach, knelt on top of him, and quickly cuffed him. If he even noticed the speargun pointed at Erin, he gave no sign of it.

"Drop the weapon, sir," Detweiler said. "We don't want to kill you, but we can and we will if you make us."

The captain smiled. His teeth were very white and very bright, matching his hat. "This is one of those things we see in the movies. A Mexico standoff, yes?"

"Mexican standoff, dumbass," Vic said. He was on his feet, his Sig-Sauer in hand. Now there were three handguns pointed at the captain, who remained remarkably unperturbed with his single spear.

And that was the problem. It was really hard to make a man surrender if that man honestly didn't care whether he lived or died. He'd decided to take a stand on principle. This man clearly felt like his home and family were being threatened, so he was going to do everything in his power to defend them. It was admirable, in an annoying way.

"What's your name, sir?" Erin asked. It was time to negotiate.

"Captain Bailey," he said. "Adam Bailey."

"Captain Bailey, I'm Erin O'Reilly," she said. "And I think we got off on the wrong foot here. We don't care what you're hauling, or whether any of it is legal."

"I am carrying machine parts," Bailey said. "Every plate and screw is legitimate, Mrs. O'Reilly."

Mrs.? Erin thought in momentary confusion. Then she realized he must have noticed her engagement ring and assumed she was already married. That indicated a perceptive man, to pick up a little detail like that in the middle of a fight. It made him more dangerous than she'd thought.

"I'm sure your cargo's totally legit," she said. "And I promise, you won't have any trouble with it. I apologize for the misunderstanding, for barging in like we did. But no harm done."

"Bullshit," Vic said under his breath. "They tried to crack my head in with a friggin' wrench!"

"Like I said, it was a misunderstanding," Erin said, willing Vic to shut up. "Your crew thought your ship was being attacked, so they fought back. There'll be no charges brought against any of them. You have my word. But we're not leaving this ship without Kingston Schultz."

"Then you will be riding along all the way to the Caribbean," Bailey said, smiling again. "Perhaps we should get used to each other. I can teach you a few things about sailing, perhaps, and you can earn your passage?"

"A Jamaican vacation sounds kinda nice," Vic said. "But Zofia's gonna be pissed if I run off without her and Mina. I'll have to take a hard pass on that."

"Then we are at a standoff, as I said," Bailey said.

"And I remind you, Captain, you only have one shot," Erin said. "The moment you fire, this standoff is over and you're dead where you stand. You still have choices right now. In the end, you won't have any."

"But in the meantime, we have time," Bailey said. "It is a long voyage."

"Speaking of which," Vic said. "I'm not a sailor, I'm just a dumb street cop, so maybe I don't understand this stuff, but while you're pointing that friggin' harpoon at my friend, who's steering this thing?"

Bailey's smile faltered. Perhaps, Erin thought, she'd given him too much credit for perception. At that moment, the deep thrumming boom of a ship's horn rolled through the air. The *Princess's* horn had been loud, but it was a whisper by comparison. This sound reached down Erin's throat, grabbed her stomach, and tried to shake her apart from the inside out. She could feel her eyeballs vibrating in their sockets. The noise went on and on, resonating in her bones.

While Bailey had been neglecting the helm, the little freighter had continued on its way, meandering through one of the busiest shipping channels in the United States. Despite the thriving commerce in the area, there was a great deal more open water than shipping. They would have needed to get really unlucky to blunder directly into the path of another ship.

That was the thought that ran through Erin's head when she looked out the cabin window and saw the gigantic, nightmare shape of the bulk cargo ship bearing down on them. It was so big that it drove conscious thought out of her mind. It was like seeing Godzilla stomping toward downtown Tokyo. The bridge on the *Nassau Princess* didn't even come halfway to deck height of this monster.

"Fuck me," Vic said. At least, that was the shape his lips made. With the throbbing horn-blast still deafening her, Erin wasn't aware of any sound leaving his throat.

All the expression and most of the color drained out of Bailey's face. He dropped the speargun and seized the wheel, spinning it frantically to the right with one hand. With the other he jammed the throttle lever all the way forward.

Erin felt the change in the rhythm of the *Princess's* engines through the soles of her feet. The old ship gamely gave everything she had, kicking up her speed by a couple of knots. The rudder locked hard to starboard and the rusty little freighter began to creep out of the path of the bigger vessel.

It wasn't going to be enough. Nowhere close. Erin did the math in her head and came up with the wrong answer. The big cargo ship would be trying to swerve, slow down, or both, but Erin knew those things didn't turn or stop on a dime. Inertia was a harsh mistress. The collision was inevitable. They had fifteen seconds at most until impact.

"Get outside!" she shouted. "Rolf! *Pust!*"

Rolf, oblivious to the impending calamity, immediately relaxed his grip and trotted toward Erin, wagging his tail and giving a doggy grin. He expected his rubber Kong ball, but that was the least of Erin's concerns at the moment.

Captain Bailey had come to the same conclusion as Erin. He snatched the intercom microphone up from the control board and yelled into it.

"Abandon ship!"

Time went out of whack, seeming to move with gluey slowness and liquid speed simultaneously. Erin shoved her Glock into its holster and lunged for the exit. A door to her right led onto the deck, so that was where she went. As she ran, she grabbed the man Vic had thrown against the bulkhead. He was up now, but still dazed, and stumbled after her. Rolf was at her side. Behind her, Vic had somehow hoisted the comatose body of Doug Robinson onto his shoulders in a fireman's carry. He staggered under the weight, trying to haul the man outside with him.

Bailey went for the last man in the cabin, the one Rolf had bitten. This guy wasn't in as bad shape as Robinson. His arm was lacerated, but he was otherwise unharmed and able to stand. Bailey took him by the other arm and half-dragged him toward the exit.

Erin flung the door open and made it three running strides onto the deck. The cargo ship's bow loomed over them. The arrowhead shape of the prow blotted out the sun high overhead, leaving the deck in shadow. To her horror, she realized she was looking straight up at the oncoming ship. It was like being run over by a skyscraper. Then it hit.

Erin was conscious of a grinding crash, a slow-motion earthquake. The deck lurched under her, tossing her like a ragdoll. The entire ship heeled over hard. One moment she was horizontal, the next she was sliding down a forty-five-degree incline. A chaos of sound and motion engulfed her. She lost her grip on the guy she'd been helping and watched him shoot straight under the railing and into the bay. Rolf, claws scrabbling helplessly, followed him in with a splash. Erin knew it would be her turn next.

For a fleeting moment she considered grabbing for the rail, but what good would that do? The ship was doomed. The *Nassau Princess* was being driven down into the mud of the channel. Her best chance, maybe her only one, was to get clear of the wreck before it sank. She folded her arms across her chest, pointed her toes, and took a deep breath as she was launched over the side.

It was a sunny, warm April day, but the water was bitter cold. The shock of it nearly drove the breath from Erin's body, slamming icy spikes into her. She gasped and took in a mouthful of salt water. She went under, bubbles boiling off her clothes. The water was clear and aqua-colored, but as she went deeper, the color quickly changed to a dark muddy turquoise. Pressure clamped iron bands around her forehead and tried to ram her eardrums into her skull. She kicked and extended her arms, fighting for the surface.

The NYPD required its officers to pass a basic swimming test. New York might be a city, but it was an island city and it was possible a cop might need to go into the water at some point. However, the swimming test was almost a joke. It wasn't like they expected officers to be Olympic divers. Erin knew how to swim, but was no expert. And even an expert would have trouble staying afloat fully clad, wearing shoes and a gun belt.

Her clothes and equipment dragged her down. Her Kevlar vest, meant to protect her, was an anchor strapped to her chest. Erin doggedly swam toward the light. The pressure gradually lessened, the light increased, and suddenly she broke the surface, spitting water and sucking in oxygen.

Sounds roared back on her. It was like a train derailment. The *Princess* was nearly capsized, her hull showing a dreadful gash. The bulk freighter was plowing straight through, ripping the smaller vessel almost in half. Erin was less than twenty yards away, treading water for all she was worth. She began swimming away from the disaster, trying to get somewhere safer, which at that moment meant literally anywhere else.

A short distance from her, a dark head thrust itself from the water. Rolf was dog-paddling toward her, fur plastered to his scalp. He was having no trouble at all keeping afloat, in spite of his own bulletproof vest. His tail worked as a rudder, steering him in the direction of his partner.

"Vic!" Erin shouted hoarsely. The salt water had left a foul taste in her mouth and a raw feeling in her throat. "Vic!"

Something was splashing away to her left. There was Vic, flailing at the water with one hand. With the other he was still stubbornly clinging to Robinson's unconscious form, somehow keeping the man's head above water. The Russian's face was red from exertion. He couldn't even spare the breath to swear.

More heads were visible, members of the Jamaican crew. Captain Bailey was recognizable by his hat, which by some miracle was still on his head. He and two of his buddies were trying to make their way toward the nearest shore, which was frighteningly far away. Erin hadn't realized just how wide Newark Bay was. When you were driving over it on a bridge, it didn't seem nearly so big.

Then two thoughts struck her in rapid succession, as cold and sharp as the icy water. "Corky!" she called. "Detweiler!"

The only answer was the tortured squeal of metal that was the *Nassau Princess*'s death rattle as the wreckage slipped below the waves.

Chapter 23

The bulk freighter kept right on going. It didn't have a lot of choice in the matter. It couldn't stop, and if it turned it would ground itself and block the channel. Erin saw several faces peering over the side as it sailed past, their eyes wide with shock.

A swell of water, the bow wave of the massive ship, picked her, Vic, and Rolf up along with the rest of the flotsam and washed them effortlessly away from the sinking ship. Erin tried to swim against it, but it was like fighting a riptide. She got farther away with every stroke.

"Corky!" she called again, hopelessly.

Faint voices carried over the water from the shore, an excited babble of bystanders and dock workers. Sirens were blaring somewhere in the distance.

Vic swam toward her, struggling to within a few yards. "You okay?" he asked in a tight, breathless voice. He was still lugging Robinson.

"Yeah," she said. "You good?"

"Christ, this guy weighs a ton," Vic muttered. "I gotta start beating up the little ones. Wake up, dumbass!"

"Hear the sirens?" Erin said. "They're on their way."

"Great. You think they have a squad car that can float? Or are they just gonna sit on shore and watch?"

"The Harbor Patrol has boats," she said, swimming to Vic's side and trying to help keep Robinson's head above water. "Did you see Detweiler? Or Corky?"

"I didn't see Corcoran after I went inside," Vic said. "Detweiler? I could've sworn the kid was heading back belowdecks."

"Oh my God," Erin murmured. "Then he didn't get out."

"Looks that way," he said grimly. "I know he's a rookie, but why would he do something that stupid?"

"I have no idea," she said. "Maybe he got confused or panicked. And Corky... Oh, God. What am I going to tell Carlyle? And Teresa?"

"You don't know he's dead!" Vic said with sudden fierceness. "Nobody's dead until the body's laid out in the friggin' morgue! And if you don't want it to be *your* body, keep your head in the goddamn game! Look, if you can hold onto this lard-ass for me, I'll go back and see what I can do."

"Don't be crazy, Vic," she said. "That ship's sinking. If you try to get on board, it'll just suck you down with it. Then Zofia will kill me."

The *thwop-thwop-thwop* of rotor blades cut through the other noises. The water around them was abruptly pushed away in a circle by the prop wash of a helicopter that came in low and hovered above the floating detectives. Erin saw the NYPD logo.

"See?" she said, holding stubbornly to hope. "They're coming for us."

"Yeah," Vic said. "They're up there, and we're down here."

The copilot waved to them and pointed to the shore. Erin followed his gesture and saw a Harbor Patrol boat homing in on them.

It wasn't a moment too soon. Her muscles were cramping from cold. Her clothes felt like they were made of lead, dragging relentlessly at her limbs. She'd lost one shoe somehow, which was actually enough of a relief that she kicked off the other one to join its mate at the bottom of the bay. And Vic was right; Doug Robinson was really heavy. She felt a dragging, icy despair sapping her strength. How could Corky, with his bright smile and careless wit, be gone just like that? Here at the end, when they should have already won?

It only took the boat a few minutes to come alongside, but it felt much longer. By the time two pairs of strong, helpful hands reached down and plucked her out of the water, Erin's teeth were chattering. She was shivering uncontrollably. Robinson came up next and was laid on the deck like a beached whale. Then Vic was brought up, gasping and cursing alternately. Finally, one of the crew got hold of Rolf by the handle on his K-9 vest and hauled him in. The Shepherd braced his paws and shook himself so vigorously that everyone on the boat got spattered.

"How many on board?" the boat's commander asked.

"I don't know," Erin said, forcing the words through trembling lips. "At least four other crew, another cop, and two civilians. So seven could be in the water."

"Copy that," he said, relaying the information into his radio.

"This is Air Three," the answer came from the circling helicopter. "I have two swimmers and two more hanging onto something, looks like driftwood. Come to my location."

"Copy that, Air Three."

Someone wrapped a blanket around Erin's shoulders. She clutched it gratefully. Rolf padded over to her, leaving wet pawprints in his wake, and lay down beside her. It had been a tiring day and he hadn't even gotten his Kong ball.

"Crazy shit, huh?" Vic said, wrapped in a blanket of his own.

"I dunno," one of the Harbor Patrol said. "I was on duty back in '09 when Sully did that crash-landing in the Hudson. Now *that* was a wild day. It ain't every day an Airbus comes down on you. This ain't nothing."

Erin craned her head to see where they were going. The *Princess* was nearly out of sight already; only a thin sliver of bow remained thrust defiantly upward, like a drowning man clutching at the sky. As she watched, it slid out of view, leaving scattered jetsam coating the waves. Among the detritus she saw something red-tinted. It looked like a man's head, ginger hair plastered to his skull.

Incipient hypothermia forgotten, she sprang to her feet and waved. "Corky!" she screamed. "Corky!"

He raised his head and waved back. He was draped half over a slab of wood. Next to him was another man, darker-haired and darker-skinned.

The motorboat slowed as it approached, turning so the crew at the back could retrieve the survivors.

"Permission to come aboard, lads?" Corky asked.

Erin felt unexpected tears prickling the corners of her eyes as James Corcoran was helped into the boat. He sported a gash across his forehead, but seemed otherwise unharmed.

"I thought you were dead," she said, wrapping her arms around him. "You crazy bastard! Where did you go?"

"It's you ran off without me, love," he said with his familiar roguish smile. "And without even a fare-thee-well! I thought I'd see what I could find on my own. And it's just as well I did. Look who I brought with me."

At that moment the Harbor Patrol hoisted a dripping, bedraggled Kingston Schultz onto the deck. The lawyer was wearing one of his expensive suits, but he'd lost his necktie somewhere along the way. His hair sent rivulets of water down his face and shoulders.

"Where'd you find him?" Erin asked.

"In his cabin, of course," Corky said. "First place to look, aye? We had us a bit of an adventure, didn't we, lad?"

"Indeed," Schultz said. "Miss O'Reilly. What an unexpected surprise."

"Aren't all surprises unexpected?" Vic interjected. "That's what makes them surprises, buddy. You're under arrest."

"I imagined that would be the outcome," Schultz said ruefully. "My first assumption when I encountered Mr. Corcoran was that he was there to dispatch me, so I admit to a certain amount of relief at this outcome. Though I had not anticipated a swim, or I would have dressed more appropriately. The waters off Nassau are much warmer this time of year."

"I'm afraid you're not going to Nassau," Erin said. "Vic's right, Mr. Schultz. You're under arrest for racketeering and conspiracy. But you know that already, because Pasquale Barberis told you. Just like he told us where to find you. That's something you might want to think about when the DA talks to you."

"I have a great deal to consider, Miss O'Reilly," Schultz said with quiet, damp dignity. "I would take it as a kindness if you would refrain from binding my wrists until I have restored some circulation. It is not as if I could run anywhere at present, and you can see I am unarmed."

"You had Keane killed," Erin said.

"I am surprised the thought troubles you," Schultz said. "You hated him, unless I am very much mistaken."

"So what?" she replied. "I hate a lot of bad guys, but that doesn't mean I get to kill them."

"I think you will have a great deal of difficulty proving your accusation," Schultz said.

"We'll see," Erin said grimly.

"How in the hell did you get off that boat?" Vic asked Corky.

"Rather well, I thought," Corky replied. "Buy me a pint and I'll spin you the tale. It'll be well worth it, I assure you."

"We got two more in the water, sir!" a man called from the starboard gunwale.

Erin hurried over in time to see, to her astonishment, a drenched Officer Detweiler coming out of the bay. The kid was very much the worse for wear. His uniform shirt was torn almost off his lean shoulders, he was covered with scrapes and contusions, and his hair was a mess. But he came up grinning alongside one of the *Princess's* sailors.

"I couldn't leave him down there, tied up," Detweiler reported. "He wouldn't have stood a chance. You good there, buddy?"

"Yeah, man," the sailor said, returning Detweiler's grin. "And I'm grateful. No hard feelings about taking a swing at you, hey?"

"None," Detweiler said. "Detectives, this is Baron Reid."

"You remembered him and went back for him," Erin said, amazed.

"Well, yeah," Detweiler said. "I was the one who put him there. I had to go back for him. I mean, heck, anybody would've done the same."

"You really think that, don't you," Vic said, shaking his head slowly. "This kid's something else, Erin. What do you think we ought to do with him?"

"Write a letter of commendation to his commander, for starters," Erin said. She put out a hand. "Good work, Officer. Damn good work."

Delighted, Detweiler shook hands with her. "Do you guys do stuff like this all the time?" he asked.

"We mostly do paperwork," Erin said. "But yeah, this kind of thing does seem to happen to us a lot."

"Then sign me up," he said. "What do I have to do to get a gold shield?"

"Looks like you hit your head on something on your way out," Vic said, pointing to an impressive lump on Detweiler's scalp. "That's a good start if you want to work with us. It helps to be a little brain damaged."

"We'll talk later," Erin said. "If you're serious about transferring from the Port Authority."

"Heck yeah!" Detweiler exclaimed. "This is why I became a cop!"

"Nutjob," Vic muttered. "I like this kid. He's got potential."

*   *   *

It was well past quitting time when Erin, Vic, and Rolf dragged Kingston Schultz and their own battered bodies into the Eightball. But as Vic pointed out, only civilians went home at five. Cops stayed until the job was done.

"And since the Job's never done... do the math," he added.

They processed Schultz and left him in a holding cell. He was remarkably quiet and calm. He hadn't said anything since coming off the boat except to politely ask for his lawyer and his telephone call. He'd used the call to contact Aayla and to ask her to line up an attorney.

Webb and McDowell were waiting for them in Major Crimes. Erin was distinctly conscious of her disheveled appearance. She looked like what she was: a cop who'd been shipwrecked and dragged out of Newark Bay. She'd changed into her emergency clothes in the locker room, so she'd be making her report clad in NYPD sweats. Vic, unfortunately, had run out of his backup clothes, and all the other officers currently on duty were too small to lend him anything. He was filthy, bloodstained, and still damp.

"Kingston Schultz is in custody," Erin said. "He lawyered up right away, so there's no point trying to interrogate him."

"Do you really think that's the main issue here, O'Reilly?" Webb asked. He didn't even look angry. He mostly just looked tired.

"It was a fluid situation, sir," she said.

"That's one way of putting it," Webb said. "You sank a ship. In a major shipping lane outside a very large, very active port facility."

"We didn't sink it, sir," Vic said. "That other ship hit us, and we weren't even behind the wheel. Captain Bailey's the guy you want to talk to. He was supposed to be steering the thing."

"Ah, yes," Webb said. "Captain Bailey. Where is he?"

"Somewhere in Jersey," Erin said. "Local law is trying to run him down. He managed to swim to shore. They picked up the rest of his crew, but he slipped through. The Port Authority boys have the ones who got caught, but they agreed to give us Schultz."

"You *sank* a *ship*," Webb said again, laying emphasis on the words. He planted his elbows on his desk and buried his head in his hands. "Do you have the slightest idea how much trouble that's going to cause?"

"It's a new one for me," McDowell said. "I've handled complaints regarding officers who've wrecked squad cars, motorcycles, civilian automobiles... I worked one helicopter crash and even a mounted officer who managed to ram a horse-drawn carriage with his own horse. But never a shipwreck."

"Did you have permission to board?" Webb asked.

"There wasn't time to ask, sir," Erin said.

"So you boarded a moving vessel, without permission, got in a fight with the crew, and then collided with another ship?"

"Pretty much, sir."

Webb hadn't raised his face from behind his hands. "That's not police work, O'Reilly. That's piracy."

"I'm telling you, *cutlass*," Vic said out of the side of his mouth.

"Not helping, Vic," Erin replied.

"These detectives are government employees," McDowell said. "They're not operating as free agents. So technically they'd be privateers, not pirates. It's an important point of international law."

"Is that relevant, Lieutenant?" Webb asked.

"Only if the Jamaican government files a protest through official channels," McDowell said. "Which they'd be well within their rights to do. My understanding is that most if not all of the crew are Jamaican nationals. So it could be argued you've perpetrated an act of war against Jamaica."

"Wait a second," Vic said. "I never even fired a shot and you're telling me I declared war on some piddly little Third World piece of shi—piece of crap country? That's a load of... a load of garbage!"

"Relax, Neshenko," Webb said. "I don't think Jamaica's declaring war on the United States of America over this. I doubt it'll even rise to the level of an international incident."

Erin nodded, but she felt a tightness in her guts. McDowell was looking over their shoulders on this case. It had been vitally important to do everything properly and by the book. Sinking a foreign cargo ship probably broke a large number of rules. She respected McDowell, even liked her a little. But the Cast-Iron Bitch couldn't be expected to overlook something so blatant.

"I suppose it's a blessing nobody else got killed," Webb said. "Maybe even a miracle. There's going to be a major inquiry to determine fault in the collision. It'll take months. Maritime insurance companies will get involved. And then there's the question of salvage. It'll be a bureaucratic nightmare. You'll certainly be asked for testimony and written reports, so you'll want to talk to your Union lawyers as soon as possible."

"Oh goody," Vic muttered. "More lawyers."

"But that's all in the future," Webb said. "In the meantime, is there anything else I should know about what happened out there?"

"Officer Detweiler of the Port Authority performed heroically," Erin said. "He went into a sinking ship, alone, to rescue a trapped crewman. I want that reflected on his record."

"Of course," Webb said. "Write it up and I'll have your report forwarded."

"James Corcoran is personally responsible for rescuing and detaining Mr. Schultz," Erin added.

"This is the James Corcoran who was formerly employed by Evan O'Malley?" Webb asked.

"Yes, sir. I'd like to recommend a civilian commendation for him for valor."

Vic rolled his eyes so hard they practically clinked like marbles, but he didn't say anything.

"Where is Mr. Corcoran now?" Webb asked.

"At Bellevue, getting stitches," Erin said. "He suffered a laceration on his forehead in the course of his rescue."

"I'm sure we can think of some appropriate way to recognize Mr. Corcoran's... unique contributions," Webb said. "Now, on to the main business. Do we know, for a fact, that Schultz is behind the murders of Keane and Johns?"

"It's effectively confirmed by Keane's dying declaration," McDowell said. "I've been examining his notes. We have enough to nail him, even without Barberis' testimony."

"Which we have," Webb added.

"I think Schultz may try to flip on Barberis," Erin said. "I planted the seed in him."

"You told him Barberis sold him out?" Webb guessed.

She nodded.

"Excellent," he said. "We'll see how that develops. With any luck, they'll do the usual bad guy thing and tear each other apart."

"There'll still be some aftershocks in the underworld," Erin said. "The Lucarellis are at one another's throats. And there's practically nobody left to get them under control. I suppose Giovanni Santino is the biggest boss still standing."

"That's a problem for another day," Webb sighed.

"There's one thing I don't get," Erin said.

"Only one?" Vic replied. "That's a good day for me."

"Alfie Madonna," she said. "Schultz didn't send Squeaky and his buddies after him. Buggy Mileno knew who was behind the hit attempt, but Keane killed Buggy. So who was it?"

"His father?" Webb guessed.

"No," Erin said. "Giovanni didn't know about it. He was shocked when he heard. There's another player in this, one we haven't identified."

"It's a dead end," Vic said. "With all the hitmen dead, good luck on that."

"I know," she said. "But I don't like leaving a loose end."

"Cases are like Persian carpets," Webb said. "You can leave one loose thread. It reminds us we're imperfect mortals."

"I'm well aware of our fallible human nature," McDowell said. "On that subject, I'll be continuing to probe Riker's Island's Corrections staff. I hope to identify any other guards who have been compromised by organized crime."

"It'll be like termites," Vic said. "You want to get rid of the whole nest, you gotta use poison gas, or maybe burn the place to the ground."

"You're probably right," McDowell said. "But we have to try. It's the Job, isn't it?"

"Speaking of which," Webb said. "I understand you have a report pending on the conduct of the Major Crimes unit."

"That's correct," McDowell said. "Do you have something to add to it?"

"Only that I take full responsibility for the detectives in my unit," Webb said. "And that I have complete confidence in every one of them. I'd trust my safety, and that of this city, to them without reservations or second thoughts."

"Even though they wrecked a cargo ship today?" McDowell asked with a sardonic lift of one eyebrow. "You seemed pretty unhappy about that."

"I'm unhappy about my receding hairline and my expanding waistline," Webb said. "And I complain about them, too. But they're inevitable. Neshenko and O'Reilly did what was necessary. Nobody died. They're damned good detectives."

"Noted," McDowell said dryly. She stood up. "Thank you for reminding me of my other duties. I have a great deal of paperwork to attend to. And thank you all for your cooperation. I understand it's always difficult to do good work with someone breathing down your neck. I'll forward a copy of my report to you when it has been completed. You have a right to know what I'm saying about you. Good day."

"Sir, you nearly made me blush," Vic said once McDowell had left. "And I think Erin's a little misty-eyed over there."

"If my eyes are cloudy, it's from exhaustion," she said. "This has been one hell of a day."

"Sounds like you need a little quiet, restful time sitting down," Webb said. "I prescribe some paperwork."

"Are you planning to administer it orally?" Vic asked. "Or anally?"

"What was that, Neshenko?"

"I said, I'm thrilled at the prospect of picking up some overtime, sir," Vic said.

"Wasn't it nice when McDowell was here?" Erin said. "Vic had to censor himself."

"It was actually kind of strange," Webb said. "Like being in the Twilight Zone."

Chapter 24

It was almost a relief when Erin saw the e-mail from Lieutenant McDowell in her inbox on the last day of April. Whatever the squad had been doing the past few days, wrapping up the Riker's Island case, she'd been aware of the looming threat from Internal Affairs. She'd told herself McDowell liked them, that the Cast-Iron Bitch had shown herself to be reasonable at heart, but none of it was any good. She'd done her best possible work and tried not to think about it, but trying not to think of something was always doomed to fail, even with alcoholic assistance.

McDowell could kill the Major Crimes unit. She could recommend Erin for traffic duty, bust her back to Patrol Division, or throw her off the Force altogether. She could—Erin could hardly bear to think about it—take Rolf away from her. And there wasn't a damn thing Erin could do to stop her.

Now, more than a week after the wreck of the *Nassau Princess*, Erin stared at the e-mail and hesitated. It was a childish impulse. Ignoring it wouldn't make it go away. McDowell had forwarded it to her as a courtesy; other e-mails were, at that moment, waiting for Webb, Holliday, and the Commissioner to read them if they hadn't already.

Anything was better than waiting under an axe to see if the blade would come down on her. Erin clicked on the message. It contained two attachments: a cover letter and the report itself. She sucked in a deep breath and opened the letter.

Detective Second Grade Erin O'Reilly was recruited into Major Crimes at the recommendation of Lieutenant Andrew Keane. Lieutenant Keane was aware of disciplinary proceedings against Detective O'Reilly for insubordination and interference with a homicide investigation. He believed her actions indicated a lack of moral fiber and a vulnerability to exploitation. This was part of his ongoing efforts to subvert the NYPD and create a network of corrupted, vulnerable officers under his personal control. This control extended to criminal enterprises including but not limited to narcotics trafficking, extortion, black-market smuggling, racketeering, and murder.

Other Major Crimes detectives were likewise apparently compromised. Detective Third Grade Viktor Neshenko has been repeatedly cited for excessive force and insubordination. Lieutenant Harold Webb has struggled with alcoholism and depression. Detective Third Grade Kira Jones was believed compromised by improper association with gang members, in addition to Lieutenant Keane believing her sexual orientation made her vulnerable to potential blackmail.

Lieutenant Keane was proven wrong on all counts. Precinct 8's Major Crimes unit showed itself impervious to blackmail or outside leverage. When its detectives became aware of Lieutenant Keane's machinations, they mounted a clandestine investigation culminating in Keane's arrest and the dismantling of his organization. They acted with conspicuous bravery, even heroism.

However, heroism often masks underlying problems. Any situation requiring heroes is inherently out of control. It would be useless to deny that conditions at Precinct 8 show irrefutable evidence of a comprehensive failure, one which requires swift resolution.

Lieutenant Webb, Detectives O'Reilly and Neshenko, and Officer Zofia Piekarski should never have been placed in such a position. Their job, by definition, is the investigation of major crimes against the citizens of New York. In pursuance of this duty they had a right to expect the full support of the Department. They needed to be able to trust the command structure of the NYPD, including its Internal Affairs Bureau.

This trust has been broken. Internal Affairs, and by extension the NYPD, failed them utterly. Once they learned of the systemic corruption within the Department, they did not feel they could trust other Internal Affairs officers. They believed, with some justification, that numerous officers were already compromised. They were forced to rely on their own resources.

As a direct result, numerous people have died. Among these are officers of the NYPD, of both the corrupt and upstanding varieties. Detective Kira Jones was murdered in the line of duty by Lieutenant Keane. Keane himself was slain by order of his former criminal associates, as was his subordinate Detective Johns. There have been other casualties as well. All these might have been avoided had Lieutenant Webb and his squad known whom to trust, and had they not been betrayed by the very organization whose sworn duty it is to oversee and shield them from corruption.

The failure is ours.

Rebuilding trust is a fragile and hazardous undertaking. It will require time, expense, and effort. It is my recommendation that the entirety of Precinct 8's Internal Affairs unit be disbanded and replaced with outside officers. Additionally, I have uncovered evidence of potential corruption on the part of several Patrol officers in this Area of Service. Those names remain classified pending a more thorough investigation. Those officers who have been deemed at risk, but not criminally compromised, have been referred to their commanding officers for disciplinary action, including potential transfer or termination.

Undercover work is possibly the most dangerous and difficult assignment for a police officer. Its danger lies not only in the physical peril of working in close proximity to violent criminals. There is also the moral hazard of deliberately cultivating friendships with those same criminals, associating with them and participating in their lifestyle. Of necessity, these friendships are not entirely artificial. To be convincing, the undercover officer must fully commit to the role. Additionally, the officer cannot count on being able to summon backup or reinforcements. He or she often operates entirely alone, in complete isolation.

To function within this demanding environment requires the officer demonstrate outstanding dedication and integrity in the face of mortal danger and severe temptation. The officer often finds it almost as difficult to reintegrate into a more normal law-enforcement role as to maintain the illusion of criminality.

Detective O'Reilly walked this dangerous line for several months. It is likely her experience of operating independently, beyond the safety net of immediate assistance from fellow officers, equipped her with the necessary skills and mindset to function in the environment of corruption fostered by Lieutenant Keane.

It is the recommendation of this investigation into Precinct 8 that Detectives O'Reilly and Neshenko be commended for their unstinting dedication to duty in the face of serious internal and external opposition. They have acted with courage, competence, and integrity.

It is further recommended that Detective Erin O'Reilly be advanced to Detective First Grade; Detective Viktor Neshenko be advanced to Detective Second Grade; Lieutenant Harold Webb receive a letter of commendation; and Officer Zofia Piekarski be promoted to Detective Third Grade and transferred to a permanent position appropriate to her new rank.

Detective Kira Jones is recommended to be posthumously awarded the Medal for Valor for outstanding personal bravery, performed intelligently in the line of duty at great personal risk, ultimately at the cost of her own life.

Respectfully submitted by
Fiona McDowell, Lieutenant, Internal Affairs Bureau, NYPD

"Wow," Erin said, pushing her chair back. Rolf perked up, but when she showed no signs of springing into action, settled his chin back onto his paws.

"What's the matter?" Vic asked. He'd been making a vending machine run and was on his way back to his desk, Mountain Dew and Twinkies in hand.

"Those things will kill you faster than my Camels," Webb observed, glancing at the snack cakes.

"Check your e-mail," Erin said.

"Oh, so we're being mysterious now?" Vic settled himself, took a sip of Dew, and started reading.

Two minutes later he was back on his feet. "What the *fuck* is wrong with these people?" he exclaimed. Erin and Webb jumped. Even Rolf sprang up, coming to full attention this time.

"Neshenko!" Webb snapped, recovering. "You nearly gave me a heart attack! What are you talking about?"

"IAB," Vic said. "McDowell. That crazy bitch is *promoting* me!"

"You say that like it's a bad thing," Erin said.

"It *is* a bad thing! She's gone nuts! Don't you think that's a bad thing?"

"This is like that Groucho Marx line," Webb said. "About how he wouldn't join any club that would have him as a member. Relax, Neshenko."

"It'll be fine," Erin said. "Making Second Grade isn't really any different. You'll get paid a little more and your pension will be bigger. Nobody expects you to run anything."

"You'll just be able to boss junior detectives around," Webb added.

"That's another thing!" Vic said. "Zofia's getting her shield."

"I thought that'd make you happy," Erin said. She still felt dazed by what she'd read.

"It'll make Zofia happy," he said. "She'll be over the friggin' moon. But didn't you see? She'll be transferred to a permanent position, God only knows where. She'll probably end up in Queens, working with those losers that gave you such a hard time."

"We have a long-running vacancy in this squad," Webb said mildly. "If Detective Piekarski wants to apply for it, I'll see her name receives due consideration."

"Really?" Vic stared at him. "I thought you didn't like us serving together."

"I'm getting used to the idea," Webb said. "If Captain Holliday is okay with it, I think we can give it a shot."

"What do you think of this whole business?" Erin asked Vic.

"I told you, they're nuts," he said. "I guess McDowell's okay. I'd want to see her in a barfight before I make a final call. But I don't get it. I thought she was here to bust our balls."

"That's where you're wrong," Webb said. "She's here to clean up the Eightball and get this house in order. I imagine the PC thought she'd dig out a few of Keane's guys and call it good, but he underestimated her. She ended up blaming IAB and the NYPD itself."

"She's ruthless," Erin said. "I guess that includes being ruthless with herself and her own people."

"She won't shift blame," Webb said. "And she's right. We got hung out to dry. You two, particularly. You shouldn't have had to go it alone."

"We didn't," Erin said. "We had friends backing us every step of the way. Friends with shields, and friends without them."

Vic sighed. "Like Corcoran," he muttered. "I still hate him, but I guess he's not so bad."

Knuckles rapped loudly on wood. All heads turned in the direction of Captain Holliday's office, where the Captain stood in the doorway.

"I hope I'm not interrupting important police work," he said.

"All police work is important, sir," Vic said.

"At ease, Neshenko," Holliday said. "I don't see anyone from IAB on the floor at the moment. What do you think of our Internal Affairs Lieutenant?"

"Like I just told Erin, she's okay," Vic admitted. "If we gotta have a hall monitor, we could do worse."

"Good," Holliday said. "Because you're stuck with her. She'll be filling the slot while the unit is rebuilt and maybe beyond."

Erin nodded. She could live with that.

"I just wanted to congratulate all of you on your accolades," Holliday went on.

"What's an accolade?" Vic whispered to Erin. "Is it some kind of car? Cadillac, maybe?"

"You're thinking of the Escalade," Erin replied in an undertone. Then, louder, "Thank you, sir. Sorry about all the headaches."

Holliday's mustache twitched in a hint of a smile. "That's what precinct captains are for," he said. "You've had quite a time of it. You solved two prison murders, brought down a corrupt judge, arrested a crooked lawyer, saved your squad, got in I don't know how many fights, and sank a drug-smuggling ship."

"We didn't sink the ship, sir," Vic insisted. "We were on board, but it wasn't our fault."

"Noted," Holliday said. "In any case, I'd say you've earned your recognition. So let me be the first to address you properly, Detective Second Grade Neshenko."

Vic stiffened to attention, almost in spite of himself. "Thank you, sir," he said.

"Detective First Grade O'Reilly," Holliday said.

"Sir," Erin replied, straightening her own spine.

"It's too bad we can't promote Rolf," Holliday added, glancing down at the Shepherd. "I'd say he's earned it too."

Rolf, hearing his name, cocked his head. His ears tilted to the side in that quizzical way beloved by German Shepherd owners the world around.

"That's okay, sir," Erin said. "He knows he's a good boy. And that's the highest honor any dog can have."

She picked up his rubber ball. His eyes followed her hand intently.

Erin flicked her wrist. Rolf caught the ball before it could come anywhere close to the ground. His jaws closed on it with a wet, muffled squeak. His eyes went soft and he sank to the floor, an expression of canine bliss stamped on his furry face.

If Rolf had been able to talk, he would have told the detectives he'd gotten the best deal. Promotions? As Erin would say, forget about it. He'd take a rubber ball and an ear rub any day.

Here's a sneak peek from Book 28: White Lady

Coming 6/30/2025

"It has now been seventy-two hours since anyone saw Laurel Peterson. Hopes for her safe return are growing dim, but her family refuse to despair. Her mother, Andrea, has written the following heartfelt message for Laurel's captors."

Holly Gardner's face held just the right mix of sympathy and professionalism. The newswoman's makeup was flawless, emphasizing model-perfect cheekbones and bright blue eyes. Her hair was a lustrous golden blonde that must have come out of a bottle; no real hair had that sort of glow.

"For Christ's sake, turn that off," Vic Neshenko growled, throwing a crumpled napkin at the television. "I can't stand that bitch."

"You're the one who wanted to put a TV in the break room," Erin O'Reilly reminded him. But she picked up the remote and clicked the power button. The too-beautiful face of Holly Gardner, Channel Six News, disappeared mid-heartfelt-plea.

"Yeah," Vic said. "So I could watch sports on my coffee break."

"You don't even drink coffee."

"And I don't watch the news," he said. "Can you believe that crap? It's all bullshit."

"You're saying Laurel Peterson hasn't been kidnapped?" Erin replied. "It's front-page news all over the country."

"That's what I mean," Vic said. "This is one lousy missing persons case. And nobody saw her get snatched, so maybe it isn't even a kidnapping. Why is it getting so much play?"

"She hasn't been found yet," Erin said.

He waved a hand irritably. "Of course not. But why do people care so much about this one girl?"

She shrugged. "Sometimes a case goes viral. There's no rhyme or reason to it."

"That's where you're wrong," Vic said. "Let me put it this way. Suppose I got abducted. Would that be all over the country?"

"Who'd want to kidnap you?" Erin retorted. "No offense, but you're a useless, ugly Russian meathead."

"None taken," Vic said. "Whereas Laurel Peterson is what, exactly?"

Erin shrugged again. "A young, pretty woman."

"A young, pretty, *white* woman," Vic said. "You've seen her picture: the homecoming queen glamour shot. I know you know the one; it's staring at you off every goddamn newspaper on the East Coast and they show it all the time on TV. It's Missing White Woman Syndrome, that's what it is. If she was old, or ugly, or Black, or Hispanic, you can bet we'd have never even heard her name. But because she's this wholesome, all-American blonde beach babe, all of a sudden her life's worth more than everyone else's. How many missing persons reports have we had since little Laurel dropped off the face of the Earth? Just in New York?"

"I have no idea," Erin said. "What's eating you, Vic? We didn't even catch the case. Missing Persons is handling it. And they've got the Feebies to run to if they get stumped. The Feds are consulting and you know what they're like when you try to tell them anything."

"Yeah, I guess," Vic said. He pulled the tab on his can of Mountain Dew, waited for the fizz to die down, and took a sip. "It's not fair, though."

"Show me something that is," she said. Lieutenant Webb had brought donuts that morning. The box was almost empty, but Erin found her hand wandering toward it.

Rolf, standing at her hip, watched her hand closely. He loved his partner's hands. They gave food, caresses, and the best of all things, his rubber Kong ball. At the moment, there was a definite possibility the human hand might dispense a donut. If it did, the German Shepherd intended to be on the receiving end.

"You know why serial killers target young white women?" Vic asked.

"You know the Lieutenant doesn't like us calling them that," Erin said. "Not until there's no doubt. You want to talk about going viral? Tell a reporter we think there's a serial killer out there and we're talking media circus."

She took the second-to-last donut out of the box and raised it to her lips. Then she paused, broke off a piece, and dropped it. The fragment didn't get anywhere close to floor level. Rolf's head twitched in a movement too fast for the eye to follow and the morsel disappeared as completely as Laurel Peterson.

"You're right," Vic said. "But I'm speaking generally. I don't know if Laurel's been grabbed by the Long Island Strangler or whatever they'd call the bastard. That's not the point I'm trying to make. I'm talking about the guys who kill girls. Serial killers are sad little punks who can't get it up the normal way. I read a book about it."

"*You* read a *book?*"

"Shut up and listen. They kill out of displaced sexual inadequacy. And who do they target? The beautiful people. The people the tabloids talk about. Gorgeous blondes. The media *creates* serial killers by taking these women and plastering their faces all over the place like goddamn celebrities. Then these punks get to feel famous by association. It makes them feel powerful. And that's sick."

"You might have a point," Erin said. "But none of that is going to help Laurel."

"You really think she's still alive? You know the odds. After three days missing, the only way most kidnapping victims come home is in a body bag. If Laurel's family's lucky, they may find the body. If they're really lucky, they won't have to ID it. The funeral's gonna be closed casket. I bet *those* pictures don't show up on the six o'clock news. They'd spoil peoples' appetites for dinner."

Vic took another morose sip of Dew. "This is a hell of a world to grow up in," he added. "Especially if you're a girl."

Understanding dawned on Erin. "You're thinking about Mina."

"You leave my kid out of this," Vic said.

She laid a hand on his arm. "You were talking about odds," she said. "What are the odds of being snagged by a serial killer? They're astronomical. Mina's going to be fine. Hell, she's only a couple months old anyway. You won't have to worry about her with ordinary boys for another fifteen years, let alone psychos."

"Twelve," he gloomily corrected her. "You wouldn't believe how fast kids grow up these days. Maybe if we're really lucky she'll take after me instead of Zofia. Then I won't have to worry so much. Zofia's a lot prettier than I am."

"Now that we can agree on," Erin said. "Come on, Vic. Break's over. Let's get back to work. And forget about Laurel. There isn't a damn thing you or I can do for her. Like you said, the poor girl's dead. She's probably been dead for days."

"It's gonna be made into one of those goddamn True Crime stories," Vic predicted. "Wait and see. And that Gardner chick is gonna be the one doing the interviews. Somebody oughta shove that microphone right down her throat."

"You're probably right," Erin said. They left the TV off and returned to the Major Crimes office and their normal, everyday diet of murder and mayhem.

They tried to ignore Laurel Peterson, Holly Gardner, and the rest of the media nonsense. And they managed it pretty well for the next three days, until the corpse was found in Central Park.

*   *   *

"Are we sure it's her?" Erin asked.

"Pretty sure," Lieutenant Webb said. The Major Crimes squad was walking briskly along the paved path that wound through the park. Rolf and Erin, who went for regular jogs on this very path, and had run it only a few hours ago, were moving easily. Zofia Piekarski and Vic, who kept in shape, had no trouble keeping up. Webb, who smoked better than a pack a day and carried an extra forty pounds around his midsection, was breathing hard.

"I don't believe it," Piekarski said. "This girl gets snatched, the kidnapper holds her for six days, then he ditches her just like that?"

"I guess he got tired of her," Vic said.

"But no ransom demand," Piekarski said. "No communication with the family. Nothing!"

"He wasn't looking for money," Erin said grimly. "How much farther?"

"Over there," Webb wheezed, pointing to a white tent about thirty yards off the trail. A small crowd of New Yorkers clustered as close as they dared.

"That's one of ours," Vic said, recognizing the style of the tent. It was the kind used by the Crime Scene Unit to protect a scene from rain, wind, sun—and prying eyes.

"CSU's been here about an hour," Webb said. "A jogger saw the body and phoned it in around quarter to eight."

"Jesus," Erin murmured. "I was running on this path at six-thirty. I went right past the spot and didn't see a thing!"

"It's in the trees," Piekarski said as they veered off the trail and walked toward the site. "It probably wasn't obvious."

"I'm a cop!" Erin said. "I should've seen something! And you," she added, giving Rolf a stern look. "What's your excuse? Did you forget how to use your nose?"

Rolf cocked his head, not understanding the question. He was trained to seek out humans, both living and dead, but hadn't been on duty that morning. Erin had taught him to disregard interesting smells while running, as otherwise he tended to pull sideways and break her rhythm. Central Park was replete with the odors of dead and rotting things. It was amazing the humans didn't seem to notice them.

"My understanding is she's pretty fresh," Webb said. "But we'll know more in a minute."

Several white-clad CSU techs were walking to and fro, scanning the ground for evidence. A pair of uniformed officers stood guard outside the tent. Webb held up his gold shield.

"How about the rest of them?" one of the uniforms asked.

"They're my squad," Webb said.

"Copy that," the Patrolman said. "Can't be too careful. We've had press all over the place, trying to sneak in. Our Lieutenant made them move a ways off. They're over there."

He pointed to the clump of people which appeared to include several representatives of the media.

"Any Feds here?" Webb asked.

"I haven't seen any," the Patrolman said. "But the ME's inside. She arrived about fifteen minutes ago."

"We're late to the party," Vic said, lifting the tent flap.

Erin was braced for something awful. She was accustomed to the sights and smells of violent death. But it wasn't as bad as she'd feared. There wasn't as much of a stench as she'd been expecting. The grass had been cut the day before, so the overpowering odor was of fresh-mown clippings; not a bad smell at all. She let out the breath she'd been holding and followed the other detectives to the body and the lab-coated woman kneeling next to it.

"Dr. Levine," Webb said to the Medical Examiner. "What've we got here?"

"Caucasian female," Sarah Levine said without looking up. "Late adolescence, approximately eighteen. Blonde hair, height one hundred sixty-seven centimeters, weight approximately fifty-six kilograms to judge from build."

"Five-foot six," Piekarski translated. "Weight around one twenty-five." She'd mastered metric to English conversions, something Erin had never quite been able to manage.

"Based on body temperature, time of death was approximately nine and one-half hours ago," Levine continued.

"Midnight," Vic said. "Spooky."

"Cause of death?" Webb asked.

"Preliminary COD is strangulation," Levine said. "Ligature marks indicate a scarf or other narrow strip of material. I speculate silk, but will need to examine the marks more closely to make a final determination."

"There's blood on her face," Vic observed.

Erin made herself look. "Jesus," she said. "She's cut to ribbons."

"The facial lacerations are superficial, but appear to have been inflicted by a bladed implement," Levine said. "Though some are deep enough to score the cheekbones, they are not life-threatening."

"I don't see any defensive wounds," Erin said. She was looking at Laurel Peterson's hands, mostly so she didn't have to look at her face.

"Your observation is accurate," Levine said. "There appear to be no lacerations or contusions on the hands or forearms. Note the victim's fingernails, which are an impractical length and painted with blue lacquer. There is no unusual chipping or breakage of the nails."

"Were the cuts made while she was alive?" Webb asked quietly.

"Judging from blood flow, I believe they were inflicted postmortem," Levine said.

"Thank God for that," Piekarski said. "But it's a little weird, isn't it?"

"Define 'weird,'" Levine said.

"Don't bother," Vic said. "Some maniac grabbed a homecoming queen, held her almost a week, strangled her, carved up her face, and dumped her in the park. Nothing about this screams 'normal' to me. And you all know what we're thinking, but I'm not gonna say it."

Webb nodded. "True," he said. "This has all the marks of a sex crime. Do you see any signs of sexual assault?"

"The victim is fully clad," Levine said. "I won't be able to make that determination until the postmortem examination. But I see no bloodstains or other fluids on her pants."

"Other fluids?" Piekarski echoed. She looked suddenly ill.

"If you need to vomit, do it outside," Webb said automatically.

Piekarski turned and lurched out of the tent. Vic cursed under his breath and went after her.

"You all right, O'Reilly?" Webb asked.

"I'm fine, sir," Erin said. "I've seen plenty worse. Our girl's wearing pretty tight jeans."

"She is," Webb said.

"It seems unlikely the perp would go to the trouble of dressing her after killing her," Erin said. "I think she was wearing them when she died."

"Not necessarily," Webb said. "I've heard of cases where a rapist-murderer covers up his victim after he's done with her. It's usually a sign of shame or remorse."

"Sir," Erin said in a very low undertone. "This really looks like the start of..."

"Yes," he said unhappily. "It looks like it to me, too. And that's how it's going to look to everyone else. I can already see it. They're going to call him the Central Park Slasher."

"We'll get him, sir," she said.

"I don't doubt it," Webb said. "Eventually. Guys like this almost always get caught sooner or later. But how many more bodies are going to drop before we catch him? Because perps who do this never stop at one."

He took a deep breath.

"That's why we call them serial killers," he added.

Ready for more?

Join the Clickworks Press email list
for the latest on new releases, upcoming books and
series, behind-the-scenes details, events, and more.

Be the first to know about new releases in the Erin
O'Reilly Mysteries by signing up at
clickworkspress.com/join/erin

About the Author

Steven Henry learned how to read almost before he learned how to walk. Ever since he began reading stories, he wanted to put his own on the page. He lives a very quiet and ordinary life in Minnesota with his wife and dog.

Also by Steven Henry

Fathers

A Modern Christmas Story

When you strip away everything else, what's left is the truth

Life taught Joe Davidson not to believe in miracles. A blue-collar wood-worker, Joe is trying to build a future. His father drank himself to death and his mother succumbed to cancer, leaving a broken, struggling family. He and his brother and sisters are faced with failed marriages, growing pains, and lingering trauma.

Then a chance meeting at his local diner brings Mary Elizabeth Reynolds  into his life. Suddenly, Joe finds himself reaching for something more, a dream of happiness. The wood-worker and the poor girl from a trailer park connect and fall in love, and for a little while, everything is right with their world.

But suddenly Joe is confronted with a situation he never imagined. What do you do if your fiancée is expecting a child you know isn't yours? Torn between betrayal and love, trying to do the right thing when nothing seems right anymore, Joe has to strip life down to its truth and learn that, in spite of the pain, love can be the greatest miracle of all.

Learn more at clickworkspress.com/fathers.

Ember of Dreams

The Clarion Chronicles, Book One

When magic awakens a long-forgotten folk, a noble lady, a young apprentice, and a solitary blacksmith band together to prevent war and seek understanding between humans and elves.

Lady Kristyn Tremayne – An otherwise unremarkable young lady's open heart and inquisitive mind reveal a hidden world of magic.

Robert Blackford – A humble harp maker's apprentice dreams of being a hero.

Master Gabriel Zane – A master blacksmith's pursuit of perfection leads him to craft an enchanted sword, drawing him out of his isolation and far from his cozy home.

Lord Luthor Carnarvon – A lonely nobleman with a dark past has won the heart of Kristyn's mother, but at what cost?

Readers love *Ember of Dreams*

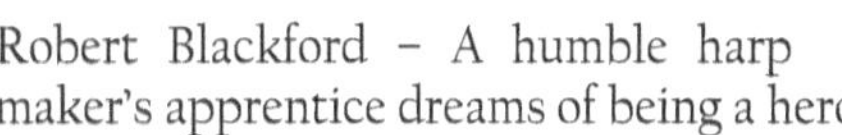

"The more I got to know the characters, the more I liked them. The female lead in particular is a treat to accompany on her journey from ordinary to extraordinary."

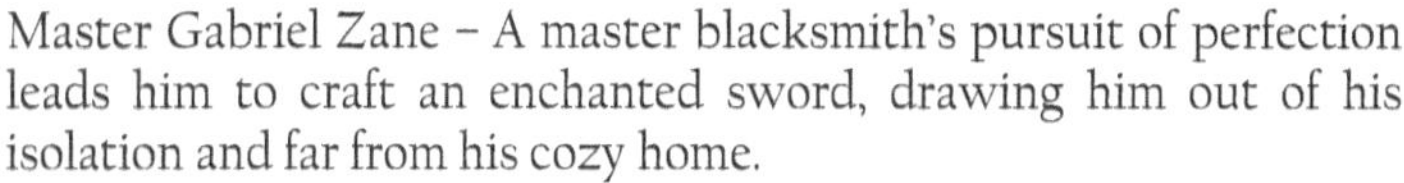

"The author's deep understanding of his protagonists' motivations and keen eye for psychological detail make Robert and his companions a likable and memorable cast."

Learn more at tinyurl.com/emberofdreams.

More great titles from Clickworks Press

www.clickworkspress.com

The Altered Wake
Megan Morgan

Amid growing unrest, a family secret and an ancient laboratory unleash long-hidden superhuman abilities. Now newly-promoted Sentinel Cameron Kardell must chase down a rogue superhuman who holds the key to the powers' origin: the greatest threat Cotarion has seen in centuries – and Cam's best friend.

"Incredible. Starts out gripping and keeps getting better."

Learn more at clickworkspress.com/sentinel1.

Hubris Towers: The Complete First Season
Ben Y. Faroe & Bill Hoard

Comedy of manners meets comedy of errors in a new series for fans of Fawlty Towers and P. G. Wodehouse.

"So funny and endearing"

"Had me laughing so hard that I had to put it down to catch my breath"

"Astoundingly, outrageously funny!"

Learn more at clickworkspress.com/hts01.

Death's Dream Kingdom
Gabriel Blanchard

A young woman of Victorian London has been transformed into a vampire. Can she survive the world of the immortal dead— or perhaps, escape it?

"The wit and humor are as Victorian as the setting... a winsomely vulnerable and tremendously crafted work of art."

"A dramatic, engaging novel which explores themes of death, love, damnation, and redemption."

Learn more at clickworkspress.com/ddk.

Share the love!

Join our microlending team at
kiva.org/team/clickworkspress.

Keep in touch!

Join the Clickworks Press email list
and get freebies, production updates, special deals,
behind-the-scenes sneak peeks, and more.

Sign up today at clickworkspress.com/join.